Advance Praise for THE DRAGON'S C.L.A.W.

"This book is a masterful collection of spies, intrigue, and the ever present government bureaucracy churning too slowly and at cross-purposes with both offensive weapons and efforts at peace. Yes, it is a work of fiction (especially the "science") but, as in reality, the spy hunters find spies, real and imagined: the bean counters care only about the numbers; and, the scientists either see their weapons as protecting against the "Other" or maintaining peace. Read this book to find out how it all plays out. You won't put it down until the final page."

Nancy Hollander, internationally recognized criminal defense lawyer. She has represented scientists accused of spying and peaceniks accused of getting in the way.

"Gerry Yonas introduces current day science concepts in a realistic manner into his plot along with characters who are credible based on my experience working in the national laboratories. The book is fast paced and easily readable by all audiences. While this is science fiction, the science involved in the plot makes one ponder what other ideas are out there for development into either good or evil applications, like the Manhattan Project quandary in WWII over nuclear energy for weapons or electricity. I thoroughly enjoyed reading this book and highly recommend it to sci fi aficionados and the general public alike."

Dr. John C Browne, Los Alamos National Laboratory Director 1997-2003

"A sexy, intelligent thriller. Dragons C.L.A.W. is a compelling melange of science, national security intrigue, mystery, politics and a dash of the supernatural. It's a rare novel that so expertly depicts the role government scientists play in foreign policy, particularly when it comes to big power rivalries between the United States and China.

If you're a fan of James Bond, this is the book for you. And like all good novels, or meals, it leaves you hungry for the next course."

Sidney Balman Jr., Pulitzer-nominated war correspondent and author of the Seventh Flag Trilogy

THE DRAGON'S C.L.A.W.

A Project Z Novel

Dr. Gerold Yonas

Artemesia
Publishing

ISBN: 978-1-951122-58-4 (paperback)
ISBN: 978-1-951122-59-1 (ebook)
LCCN: 2022949301
Copyright © 2023 by Dr. Gerold Yonas
Cover Illustration and Design © 2023 Derek Weathersbee
https://derekweathersbee.com/

Artemesia Publishing
9 Mockingbird Hill Rd
Tijeras, New Mexico 87059
www.apbooks.net
info@artemesiapublishing.com

PROLOGUE

AS A HINT OF PINK streaked across the horizon, lighting the indigo sky with the promise of dawn, Alek pulled his dirty white Ford Focus to a stop and sat behind the wheel, the engine still running. From his position on the empty road at the top of a hill, he gazed down at the nondescript stucco house standing alone on the edge of a cul-de-sac in the shallow valley below.

Alek shivered. Why had he driven here in the middle of the night, in the darkness, without telling anyone, without making a plan?

His stomach clenched as he thought about the two men who he believed lived inside the two-story, tan house on the dusty street. *What am I doing here?* Alek thought. *I'm a scientist, not an action hero.* But being a scientist also meant being a problem solver. Alek worked as a physicist at Los Alamos National Laboratory, the United States Department of Energy lab that gave birth to the Manhattan Project and was now one of the largest science and technology institutions in the world. For most of his adult life, scientific research had occupied the majority of his time. Since the accident, however, work had become Alek's obsession, driving him to seek answers in a relentless effort to overcome his guilt and grief. Alek's work had also driven him to this spot on a hill looking down at the house where the stolen components of his research and experiments might be concealed. He had to find the answers. *None of this makes sense.*

Alek knew that the two physicists, his employees, had rented a house on the outskirts of Altavaca, New Mexico

1

about a year ago. A suburb of Albuquerque, Altavaca consisted largely of abandoned real estate sold to unsuspecting East Coast buyers who came to New Mexico dreaming of the Land of Enchantment, and who left when they couldn't find jobs. The house below looked desolate, half abandoned. Wind-swept tumbleweeds lingered on the street. If this were the land of enchantment, the spell cast was a curse.

Alek reflected on how less than 24 hours ago he had discovered that two of his employees had vanished. The men... their research... their knowledge... all had disappeared. *I must find out why*.

Alek shifted the car into park and flipped on the radio, hoping to distract himself with some meaningless background noise. On the early morning radio newscast on New Mexico's News Leader 77KOB, the anchor rattled off headlines. Alek sat in the car, trying to work up the courage to move forward. Should he knock on the door and risk a confrontation? Should he try to find a way to sneak a look through a window to see if anyone was home?

Alek's mind drifted back to a time when he had lived in a similar stucco house not far from here. Back then, life had made sense. Before the accident, before his marriage ended, he had felt anchored. Now he felt alone and adrift. Alek shook his head, trying to focus on the present. He had to move on.

Something in the distance caught Alek's eye. Leaving the car running, he opened the door and got out, craning his neck in an attempt to identify the flash of red.

That's when it happened.

A blinding sheet of light shattered the darkness. The house below exploded, painting the sky with a blast of intense white light. Slammed back against the car by a wave of pressure, Alek found himself breathless in the brilliance of the blast, baffled by the eerily soundless explosion. He realized that his car had joined in the silence. The engine had stalled, the radio had quit playing, the car's headlights and dashboard indicator lights had gone out.

Giving himself a shake to clear his head, Alek slowly lowered himself into the driver's seat. He turned the key, trying the ignition, but nothing happened. The dark grey dawn reclaimed the New Mexico desert as the unexpected brightness began to fade.

Alek squinted, trying to see the stucco house, his destination. It was... it was no longer there. Nothing remained but swirling dust. Where the house once stood sat a shiny footprint. It looked as if the desert sand beneath where the house's concrete slab foundation had once been somehow had turned to glass. Overwhelmed and dazed by the implications, Alek wondered if he had just watched years of research vanish in an explosive burst of light.

PART ONE

Chapter 1
Death Rays and Delusions

THE SUN ROSE OVER THE sprawling complex known as Los Alamos National Laboratory, painting a glow of orange and pink across the undersides of the lacy network of clouds spanning the vast sky. Dr. Alek Spray pulled his car into a parking spot. Exiting the car, he took a deep breath of the crisp mountain air before hustling to his building and swiping his security badge to enter the restricted area. Alek hoped he'd have time to grab a cup of coffee before his first morning meeting. Caffeine was a necessity since he anticipated a fight.

"Nothing good ever comes of violence." Embracing teachable moments, Alek's overprotective Jewish mother would often repeat this quote by Martin Luther King Jr. when he was growing up. She'd say it after Alek had lost yet another fight with a class bully. Scrawny and bookish, Alek wouldn't have won even if he had fought back, and his mother probably knew that. Perhaps that's why she always encouraged peaceful approaches to solving problems. Nothing good ever comes of violence after all.

But violence was exactly what Alek's colleague, Dr. Sunli Hidalgo, supported. In fact, she regularly spoke out in favor of embracing violence as quickly as possible. She was waiting for him in the breakroom.

"I know you don't like the idea of pursuing weapons development," the dark-haired scientist said, leaning forward and commanding Alek's attention with a penetrating stare. "But after all, this is a nuclear weapons lab.

Here's the issue," she continued. "We need the funding, and we know D.C. is far more likely to invest big bucks in weapons technology than in energy research. So why not pursue the defense applications, while exploring ways to use the same technology to create a limitless clean energy source?"

Alek smiled. "Well, I like to think of myself as a pacifist. No pun intended, but the thought of using this research for weapons development kinda makes my head explode."

"No wonder people call you Smart Alek," Sunli said. "Always ready with a corny joke."

Alek bustled about fixing his coffee, keeping his back turned to hide the embarrassment that her comments had caused. *Why does she make me feel so uncomfortable?* he wondered. He was actually her supervisor, but somehow, he always felt as if she were the one in charge.

Like Alek, Sunli had relocated to Los Alamos to pursue research at the lab. The highly driven 30-year-old mathematician had only recently become a U.S. citizen. She had been raised in Mexico, her father a Mexican citizen, but her mother was Chinese. Alek's theory was that Sunli's unapproachable demeanor stemmed from growing up as a child of two different backgrounds; perhaps she didn't feel as if she belonged to either the Mexican or the Chinese culture. Surely it must have been difficult if she felt she never quite fit in. At least that's what he told himself as he struggled to get to know his colleague. Some of his other coworkers just described Sunli as aloof and overly ambitious. In other words, they called her "a cold, pushy bitch." Even in 2023, sexist attitudes prevailed in the male-dominated workplace of the national lab. Alek found himself making excuses for Sunli's distant behavior, even as he admitted that her brilliance and beauty were intimidating. It seemed that she would stop at nothing to achieve her goals.

"How can you be against weapons development?" Sunli asked. "Weapons development is why this lab was founded. This is Los Alamos. The lab is famous for the development and creation of the atomic bomb."

"Actually, the name 'Los Alamos' came from the Spanish word for the cottonwood trees that line the Rio Grande River east of the town," he mumbled, turning around to discover that Sunli had already left the breakroom. Regardless of where the name came from, most people believed that Los Alamos represented secrecy, weapons, and nuclear war.

Despite these public perceptions, the city was a peaceful place to live. Situated on the Pajarito Plateau on the eastern flank of the Jemez Mountains, the area offered spectacular scenery ranging from forested peaks to waterfalls and even a dormant volcano. He enjoyed the small-town feel and the outdoor activities. He loved living on the edge of the national forest and knowing he could immerse himself in nature every day. He felt comfortable with his coworkers at the lab and found his work both intriguing and fulfilling. The only thing that really bothered him about living and working in Los Alamos was... well, it was Los Alamos, the birthplace of the Manhattan Project and a city that nuclear weapons research and development both created and sustained.

Alek was stirring powdered creamer into his coffee when the lab director, Dr. Harold Percy, suddenly swept into the room. "You're late for the special meeting in my conference room," he muttered, popping a K-cup into the Keurig machine. Percy, a tall, African American man in his early sixties, always dressed elegantly. Most of the other men who worked at the lab chose worn-out khakis and wrinkled button-down shirts for their work-day uniforms. Percy's highly polished shoes and ever-present cufflinks distinguished him as the leader of the lab. He had spent his entire life working hard for his achievements. He expected the same level of commitment from his staff.

"We have to prepare for the hearing. Lateness is not tolerated," added Percy, prompting Alek to wonder why he was tardy, but the lab director, who was still fixing his coffee, was on time. *Don't question authority*, Alek told himself. He grabbed his notes and his rumpled sport coat and scurried toward the meeting room, running a hand over his head in an attempt to tame his unruly brown hair. Sunli was already waiting in the conference room, well-prepared and completely composed, while Alek scrambled awkwardly to his seat next to her.

Several men and women were seated around the long table, with laptops and file folders close at hand. The group was made up of scientific division directors, associate laboratory directors, and senior lab management. They assembled periodically to examine initiatives and make recommendations. Percy viewed the meeting as a formality. He fully expected the team to follow his lead and rubber stamp his proposals.

The lab director entered the conference room briskly, indicating the time had come to start the meeting. "As you all should know, I've called this proposal review panel together today to go over our progress on the Low Energy Nuclear Reaction project. The congressional appropriations hearing is next week, and we need to fine-tune our approach." The lab director gestured to Alek. "Dr. Spray, is the lead scientist for this project. He's helped the lab win national recognition since coming to Los Alamos, and he's been named as a Fellow of the American Physical Society, recognizing the significance of his contributions to the field. Alek, please introduce your team and provide us with an update on your group's accomplishments."

Percy sat down, kicked back in his chair and began checking his emails on his laptop. Alek was accustomed to the lab director's tendency to pay attention only to matters that related directly to him. Alek rose, cleared his throat awkwardly, and shuffled his notes.

"For those of you who don't know me, I'm Alek Spray. My background is in pulsed power energy and fusion research, and for the past five years, I have headed up our work on Low Energy Nuclear Reaction or LENR. Our team is small, but we have big goals when it comes to revolutionizing energy production, and we've been making slow but steady progress."

Alek gestured to Sunli, suddenly conscious of the contrast between his disheveled and her professional appearance. He cleared his throat awkwardly and continued his presentation. "Dr. Sunli Hidalgo holds PhDs in mathematics and chemical engineering. She's been developing the theoretical models behind the LENR process and recently has solved several complex equations describing the theory of collective enhancement. Dr. Hidalgo has been my right hand on this project." Alek smiled at Sunli, who looked away, disinterested, picking an invisible bit of lint off her grey skirt.

"About three years ago, we hired Will and Joe Ramos, who both have their PhDs in nuclear engineering from the University of New Mexico. They are working on executing some of these theoretical concepts in the lab." Across the table from Alek, Will and his identical twin brother Joe both looked ill at ease. Since coming to Los Alamos, the two had spent most of their time in their small out-of-the-way lab facility working in relative secrecy because, as Alek described it, some of their research was highly experimental. Percy had told Alek he thought the Ramos brothers' work bordered on outlandish, but the lab director was so excited about any hire that helped him meet the lab's diversity target that he supported the venture and even provided the Ramoses with some discretionary funds.

"Will and Joe are working on developing schematics to build the Low Energy Nuclear Reaction device based on Sunli's theoretical model. Their primary focus has been researching methods to trigger the reaction that will provide the energy source." Will gave the committee a smug grimace, while Joe looked down at the table uncomfortably. Alek wondered if he had made a mistake asking the twin scientists to attend this meeting. They were much better suited to working alone in their lab.

"So, we have a way to go, but I am confident that we'll soon find the breakthrough we need to create a transformative new energy source and I'm hopeful that we will be able to secure sufficient funding to continue our research." Relieved that his presentation was over, Alek resumed his seat, wondering if he had said too much or left out anything important. Regardless of what the committee members thought, Alek knew that Percy would have the final say about their strategy for the congressional funding request.

Alek trusted Percy. The lab director had good connections, not just with the scientific community, but also within the halls of Congress and the White House. Percy prided himself on being in touch with the endless political manipulations of science investments and having his hands on the congressional purse strings for his lab. At the latest count, there were 42 separate federally-funded research and development centers under his control, and more were added every few years with ever increasing budgets. Convincing Washington to invest in advanced technology required a nuanced approach, and no one understood the politics of scientific research better than Harold Percy did.

Percy closed his laptop, taking back control of the meeting. Several of the attendees perked up at the signal that it was time to pay attention again.

"So, the hearing is next week," Percy noted. "The President is aware of speculative applications of the LENR technology, not to energy research, but to a beam weapons development concept," he continued. "As Alek mentioned, this project could lead to the creation of a new form of clean, affordable energy, but key legislators have suggested that their interest lies in the weapons research. The creation of a compact power source using the LENR concept would be an ideal way to drive a directed beam of energy that could be used as a space weapon. In fact, the Defense Intelligence Agency recently uncovered rumors that the Chinese government is getting close to building a successful collective laser accelerator weapon."

"That seems unlikely," Alek interrupted. "Scientists have tried for decades to make the collective laser accelerator concept work."

"True," agreed Percy. "But if, or rather when, we master the LENR technology, a small amount of fuel will produce a tremendous amount of energy. All we have to do is figure out how to trigger the reaction. If we can use a high-power laser to modulate the electron beam to trap ions, we'll able to build and deploy a powerful weapon that could target our adversaries from space."

Alek opened his mouth in protest, but Percy held up one finger to silence him. "So," continued the lab director, "the question is whether weapons research is an angle we want to emphasize in our proposal."

Percy turned to Will and Joe Ramos. "Gentlemen, the outcome of this hearing could provide funds to expand and move your research and experiments to the forefront. What are your thoughts about making a significant departure from energy applications to weapons research?"

The two exchanged panicked looks and Joe muttered something under his breath in Spanish.

"Honestly, we have never intended to explore weapons development," Will said.

"*Nunca en la vida.* Never," reiterated Joe emphatically.

"But this concept could be the key to a compact energy source for a space weapon," Sunli pointed out. "The application would have to be based on entirely new physics, but, with the proper theoretical framework, we could build a directed-energy, speed-of-light weapon unlike anything ever created... an unprecedentedly powerful weapon that could allow the U.S. to dominate space."

Nervously running his hand through his hair, Alek felt his frustration level building. He couldn't support Sunli's advocacy of weapons research. He had to speak up. "Uh, if you don't mind... I mean, I think I have to say something," Alek sputtered, his voice rising. "The point of this project is finding the right reaction trigger to use the emerging theories of LENR to create a clean, inexhaustible energy source. Many of you are well aware of this initiative— the program I call Project Z. How is it that we are talking about weapons?"

Percy raised an eyebrow. "Yes, Alek, we are well aware of your Project Z initiative," the lab director replied calmly. "But we all know that energy research is just a benefit of the work we are doing to develop weapons technology to ensure national security. You have to remember that technology is just a knife."

"A knife?" asked Alek. "What do you mean by that?"

"A knife can butter your toast for breakfast, but a knife can also slit someone's throat. Whether this technology is used for weapons applications or alternative energy sources isn't the issue. Our job as scientists is to build the knife, not to determine how it's used."

Percy stood up, signaling that the issue wasn't open for further debate.

"Our goal... what I care about... is getting the funding to pay for this research and development," he said. "Congress will fund weapons technology. Weapons prevent wars. Weapons fund our lab. Weapons pay your salary. The technology we develop is just a knife. How our government decides to use that knife... well, that's out of our hands."

The lab director glanced at Alek. His lead scientist looked down at the table, fists clenched, scowling. Percy walked over and placed a hand on Alek's shoulder. Alek squirmed. He hadn't meant to disappoint Percy. The younger man looked up to his supervisor who, in many ways, he saw as a father figure, since his own dad had died when he was a toddler.

"Alek, the last thing I want to do is discourage you. You are a gifted researcher and a creative thinker." *Creative? Alek wondered. Is that a euphemism for 'way off base?'*

The lab director turned to the review committee. "Is anyone opposed to postponing our pursuit of the weapons angle, at least initially? We can start by asking for funds strictly for energy research. Maybe with the current emphasis on ecological preservation and clean energy sources, we'll have a chance this time. Anyhow, most congressional staffers can be won over with entertaining stories about complex technical issues," Percy added with a wink at Alek who had helped him prepare many government funding requests based on the philosophical approach of baffling with bullshit.

The committee members murmured their approval. All were anxious to get back to work.

"Great," said Percy. "Alek, you, Sunli and I will need to meet to put the finishing touches on our congressional presentation. In the meantime, Joe and Will, please continue your research. Meeting adjourned."

"Congratulations, Smart Alek," said Sunli, not even trying to hide her displeasure. "In any case, the sooner we can get funding, the sooner we can find a way to build the LENR trigger, so let's get back to work."

Will and Joe Ramos exchanged glances and left the room hurriedly. "I can't figure those guys out," Alek said to Percy as he watched the pair exit. "They rent a house in Altavaca, own a condo in Mexico, and share an Italian sports car. They take expensive vacations that seem unusually luxurious on a typical lab employee's budget."

"That is concerning," Percy replied. "Of course, they have passed extensive security screenings and they seem to spend all their time on the LENR project. Maybe, they're just odd."

"I guess," said Alek, continuing to wonder about his mysterious employees. The two rarely made casual conversation with their coworkers, and, when they did, they tended to talk about their exercise routines. Alek had always disliked people who bragged about working out, and so he hadn't really tried to get to know them. *Maybe I am just intimidated by their well-defined muscles and classic Latino good looks*, thought Alek, who was thin and wiry, perhaps due to his devotion to jogging daily on the nearby mountain trails. In any case, while the Ramoses didn't seem particularly friendly, they were committed to the research and Percy was right, that's what mattered the most.

"Let's grab a beer and a burger after work at the Friggin Bar," Percy told Alek. He wasn't using the word 'friggin' as a substitute for swearing—that was actually the name of the nondescript establishment located next to the lab. It was named after the first owner of the dive bar, Joe Friggin, who'd opened it in the 1950s—it had been a Los Alamos icon ever since. The Friggin Bar was a favorite lunch spot for lab employees craving a greasy cheeseburger and a good place to unwind after a long day of research. It was also the place where many of the lab's staff members had some of their best conversations about science and life.

"Uh, we're going to get a drink after work. Would you like to join us?" Alek asked Sunli awkwardly, wiping his sweaty palms on his khakis.

"No, I've got some things I have to finish up here tonight," she said. With an elegant flip of her hair, she left the room.

* * *

The piercing New Mexico sun struggled to penetrate the small, dusty windows on the west side of the lab that Alek had assigned to Will and Joe Ramos for their Low Energy Nuclear Reaction research. Joe studied the narrow beams of sunlight stretching across the dirty floor. The only advantage of their small, rundown lab was its isolation on the edge of the Los Alamos National Lab campus. Although Alek occasionally dropped in to check on them, the number of visitors was few and far between.

Joe walked to the window and scrubbed some dirt off the glass with the heel of his hand so he could see the mountains in the distance. The heavily forested peaks jutted skyward as if reaching to touch the clouds floating above. Joe sighed, wishing he were out hiking among the ponderosa pine and aspen trees instead of trapped in this lab arguing with his brother about the experiment. Soon the sun would be setting, and they would have spent another entire day indoors. Although Joe had joined Will in graduate school and had completed his doctorate in nuclear engineering, he had never shared his brother's love of science nor his determination to make this project work.

Old equipment littered the corners of the room, discarded bits and pieces of years of failed experiments. This was not a shiny, high-tech laboratory where scientists gathered to make important discoveries. The dimly lit room smelled of sweat and desperation, long hours spent conducting research with nothing to show for all the hard work.

"*Nos estamos acerando...* We're getting closer," muttered Will as he bent over the contraption he had built on the counter on the far side of the room. The device consisted of a series of high voltage capacitors attached to a vacuum chamber with a target at the top. The machine was designed to focus an electron beam on a target in order to create a low energy nuclear reaction. If they could just find a way to make it work.

"But what are we doing?" Joe asked. "Shooting holes in targets... randomly trying things with no theory and no plan?" Joe had long ago lost interest in his brother's experiments. His only focus was the money. Other than that, he was just along for the ride.

"*Para atrás.*" Will gestured to his brother to stand back as he flipped the switch feeding current into his device. The men waited expectantly, watching the device in anticipation.

Nothing happened.

Joe put his hand on his brother's shoulder. "Uh, I think maybe it's time to try something else."

Flicking Joe's hand away, Will bent over the machine he had constructed. "Maybe if I just adjust the current," he mumbled to himself. He flipped the switch again. Still, there was no result.

Joe picked up the target, a round piece of copper, and began tossing it from hand to hand. "Tell me again. How exactly does this dense plasma focus thing work?" Joe asked.

"Sometimes I think you're dense. We've been working on this project for three years," scoffed Will. "Don't you remember anything from grad school? I never should have agreed to complete your projects and write your dissertation for you."

Joe sighed. "It's not like I had much of a choice about going to school. Once El Verdugo figured out how smart you were, our future was set."

Will shrugged. "Did you want to stay in Mexico, living in a shack and running errands for the cartel? We were lucky that our powerful friends decided to sponsor our education."

"Yeah, I guess," said Joe. "I don't mind the money, but I didn't expect we'd end up here."

Will sat on the end of the counter, facing his younger-by-three-minutes brother. "Look, working here at Los Alamos is just a means to an end. The cartel wants a weapon and by getting hired here, we have access to the technology. Now, pay attention. A dense plasma focus is a remarkable gadget that converts a low voltage slow energy source into a very fast, focused high voltage beam of electrons and ions. It's based on the idea of slowly building up energy in a magnetic field that compresses the superheated ionized gas carrying the current."

"Oh, I remember. An extremely high electric field suddenly extracts ions and electron beams in opposite directions. It's like a whip with the handle moving slowly and the tiny tip moving faster than the speed of sound."

"Yeah, we're trying to crack the whip," Will replied.

Joe looked at the copper target he was holding. "Why do you use copper as a target?"

"Everyone uses copper." Will shook his head in frustration. "Haven't you read any of the literature? The cold fusion experiments? Anything? We're trying to create electron beam transmutation, so it makes sense that we build on other scientists' experiments. What do you suggest we use?" he sneered.

Joe was accustomed to his brother discrediting his ideas. It didn't bother him. He just wanted to wrap up their work for the day so he could get outside before the sun went down.

"Let's make a bet," Joe said, pulling a handful of change out of his pocket. He laid a nickel on the counter. "Flip this. If it comes up heads, we try a different target. If it comes up tails, you keep on doing what you're doing, and I'll just sit here and watch your experiments fail."

Angrily, Will grabbed the nickel and flipped it. The nickel landed on the ground, spun on its side, and finally came to a rest. Heads.

"Okay *sabelotodo*, what do you suggest we use for a target?" he growled at Joe.

"Don't call me a smart ass," Joe said sulkily. He picked up the nickel from the floor and handed it to Will. "Here, use this."

"Sure, *pendejo*, we'll try this nickel as a target. You know a nickel is partly made of copper. It's a copper/nickel alloy."

"We flipped," replied Joe, crossing his arms.

"What the hell. It's just five cents." Will placed the nickel in the device and hit the switch. The nickel exploded in a spray of tiny molten particles, as a jagged bolt of lightning exploded from the instantaneous, high-current electron beam. Joe jumped back in shock, a smile splitting his face as he watched the threads of brilliant light flash out from the target in the dusky room. Glimmering trails of electricity flickered, illuminating the lab with a short-lived, eerie glow.

"*Bueno*," Joe exclaimed. "You see! I was right. We just needed a different target. We are so close! We just have to figure out how to control the beam and the energy output. Then we'll have the ultimate weapon in our hands."

Will shook his head. "*Desafortunadamente*, it's not that easy, *mi hermanito*. We need to figure out how to use the dense plasma focus device as a miniature pulsed power trigger for the LENR weapon."

Will studied the melted bits of metal left of the nickel. "Do you have another nickel?" Joe sorted through his pocket change and handed his brother a second nickel. "I'm going to increase the current to 50 kiloamperes," Will said.

Once again, Will flipped the switch feeding the electrical current into the piece of machinery on the lab counter. A flash of light streaked across the room toward the ceiling, punching a large hole in the steel beam running overhead.

The brothers ducked as molten metal rained down on them, their ears ringing from the blast.

"*¡Dios mío!*" Joe exclaimed, using his jacket to extinguish a small fire that the falling metal had sparked in a pile of papers on the desk.

"Now we're getting closer," he said gleefully. "We figured it out."

Will grabbed his laptop. "Maybe. I need to make some calculations. We have to refine the trigger, so we have more control."

Will tapped on the laptop keys and muttered, "*¡Que mierda!* My computer is dead. It won't even turn on."

"Here, use my phone," Joe said, handing his brother his iPhone.

"You brought a phone in the lab? You know that's against regulations. Are you trying to get us fired?" Will looked at the iPhone and flung it back at Joe. "Your phone is dead too. That beam must have put off a hell of an electromagnetic pulse that fried our electronics. I'm going to try rebooting the computer. I sure hope the hard drive is alright."

After a few tense moments, the laptop rebooted. Joe watched his brother type some figures into the computer. Energized by the success, he was no longer consumed with the desire to end the work day and go hiking. The excitement of scientific discovery gleamed in Joe's eyes. "What if we use 100 percent nickel and turn up the juice? Let's do some more experiments right now."

"I'm not sure that's a good idea," Will replied. "With Percy starting to discuss weapons applications, we need to move this work to our house. Plus, we can't keep blasting holes in the ceiling without someone noticing. What if we had gotten hurt? What if that fire had spread? What if a lab safety inspector had caught us? We'd lose our jobs and our security clearances in an instant. Of course, you could get us in trouble just by bringing your phone in here. How many times do I have to tell you to follow the rules?"

"Come on, Will. ¡No seas gallina!"

"Look, I'm not being a chicken. This is seriously dangerous. I knew a guy who was experimenting with this kind of stuff in his garage and his whole house blew up. Most importantly, we can't have Alek catching on to what we've really been up to here. My contacts have made it clear that we can't let the Los Alamos scientists find out about our progress. And Alek especially can never know we've been doing weapons research. If the lab discovers what we've been doing, we'll get fired and maybe go to jail. We'll also never get paid by our sponsors, and they might come after us too."

Will turned on the overhead lights and started cleaning up the work area. "Plus, there's that part about going to prison for espionage," he added. "I don't want to become the next Wen Ho Lee."

"Who?" asked Joe.

"That scientist accused of stealing secrets about the U.S. nuclear arsenal for China back in the 90s. He spent nearly a year in prison although in the end, the U.S. government dropped the espionage charges and he was freed. Lab security is always on the lookout for spies. If they find out about our connections, we could face years in federal prison."

"I don't want to go to prison, Will," said Joe. "I just thought we were making some easy money helping our old friends."

"We are... we are. Honestly, I'm more worried about our 'friends' than about lab security. But I'm kinda worried that others are watching us."

"Others?" Joe asked with a laugh.

Will looked around, even though they were alone in the lab. He lowered his voice. "Others. The Russians, or the Chinese. There might be a sleeper cell of Chinese agents and they could be watching us." Will drew a finger across his throat ominously. "Trust me, Joe, if we piss the wrong people off... that's it."

Joe began pacing back and forth across the lab. "Will, you're scaring me. What are we going to do?"

Will placed a hand on his brother's shoulder reassuringly. "We just have to dismantle this device and copy all of our notes and research onto thumb drives. Then we can destroy the computer hard drives so Alek and Sunli won't be able to duplicate our work."

"Ummm, okay," replied Joe. "When are we going to do this?"

"Right now. Tonight," Will said. "Let's get to work."

Chapter 2
Just Build the Knife

DEEP RED LIGHT PAINTED THE peaks of the Jemez Mountains as shadows crept across the dark green forest below. The work day had ended and the sun sank below the horizon, casting streaks of pink, orange, and purple across the lenticular clouds hanging low in the sky.

Alek Spray and Harold Percy sat across from each other in a red, cracked Naugahyde booth in the Friggin Bar. Alek noticed that the table was slightly sticky, and the waitress was nowhere to be seen.

"The service in this place is awful," Alek grumbled. "Last time I was here that blonde waitress spilled my Dos Equis and then brought me a Corona Extra to replace it. Who drinks Corona? And how can you get Corona and Dos Equis confused?"

"Well, she's not just a waitress," said Percy, defending the woman as he watched her sneaking a French fry off a customer's plate while she delivered the food. "Plus, she does have great legs," murmured Percy. "I hear she ran track at Española High School."

Just then, the object of Percy's admiration approached the table. "Hi y'all. I'm Gabi. What will it be?" the waitress asked, tucking her long, curly blonde hair behind one ear and gracing the two with a friendly smile. Alek tried not to notice the short skirt or the tight, low-cut sweater. Gabi leaned forward to take their order, making Alek's struggle that much more difficult. Embarrassed, he took off his glasses and started cleaning them energetically with the hem of his untucked shirt. *Sometimes it is helpful not to be able to see*, Alek thought.

The men both ordered bottles of Dos Equis and green chile cheeseburgers. Ever since Alek's divorce, he either grabbed something greasy on the way home or skipped dinner. Percy was married, but his wife traveled a lot and she never seemed to care if he made it home for dinner.

After the orders were placed with the kitchen and the beers delivered, Percy got serious. "Look, I know you want us to steer clear of the weapons research, but we can't ignore the rumblings that the Chinese are looking at LENR technology as a component of advanced space weapons. We need to make sure we stay ahead of the enemy," he said.

"Are the Chinese really the enemy?" Alek asked.

"Of course," Percy replied. "The Chinese are the dominant threat to U.S. military performance, and intelligence sources say that they are making progress developing advanced space weapons. If the Chinese develop space attack capabilities, they will gain immense power." Percy took a drink of his beer and settled back in the booth. He was now in his element, pontificating about the intersection between science and politics—his favorite topic.

"China possesses the largest economy, the greatest industrial base, the most powerful military, and the leading centers of technological and scientific innovation," Percy continued. "Just due to its sheer size, China is a geopolitical threat. Plus, the Chinese see our country as ideologically opposed to their way of life. Protecting the Communist regime is paramount to them, and they see America as a hostile force that threatens the stability of the Chinese party state."

Percy paused when Gabi arrived with their food, dropping a few fries and knocking over the ketchup bottle as she set the plates on the table. "Uh, I ordered mine with no onions," Alek said as she leaned over Percy to pick up the bottle of ketchup. Percy, meanwhile, had forgotten about China and was focused on the waitress' low-cut sweater.

"The, uh, onions." Alek tried again to get the woman's attention. "Never mind. I'll just pick them off."

"Nice girl," Percy said, admiring the view as Gabi headed off to the next table. Alek pushed up his glasses, which had slid down on his nose, and tried not to look.

"Now, as I was saying," Percy continued, "China is America's primary threat. President Thornton has talks scheduled next month in Beijing to try to hammer out a new arms control agreement with a joint space weapons ban, but an agreement doesn't seem likely. There are some rogue military groups in China that are outspoken about their opposition to any kind of arms ban. And we have our fair share of hawks in D.C. too."

"I'm just hoping we can find a way to collaborate with the Chinese on energy research," interjected Alek. "Maybe the scientists can get along even if the politicians can't. Energy research is all I'm interested in." He spit out an onion lurking on his cheeseburger. "Imagine if Project Z succeeded. A limitless supply of clean energy could dramatically transform every aspect of the world."

For the past few years, Alek's work at Los Alamos had focused on Low Energy Nuclear Reactions, which built on his longtime obsession with fusion as an energy source. "Do you remember when I first started at the lab, when we first began discussing the LENR concept?" Alek asked.

"Yeah, I remember how nervous you were," Percy said with a chuckle. "Now that was an ambitious sales pitch."

"Well, I'd spent most of my career chasing after the impossible dream of using hot fusion to provide the ultimate clean, cheap source of energy. I was ready to try a different approach."

Percy snorted. "You actually explained to me the concept of fusion, of bringing together charged particles within ionized plasma gas to combine with each other at the right temperature. By heating the plasma, the particles move rapidly and collide, releasing energy, but only if the plasma can be contained long enough to react."

Percy took a swig of beer and looked Alek in the eye. "Remember what I said then?"

"Of course," replied Alek. "You said, 'Fusion doesn't work.'"

"And what did you say, Smart Alek?" asked Percy, finishing the last of his French fries and reaching for Alek's.

"Umm, I said, 'Technically it does. Check out the sun.'"

The two laughed, enjoying yet another discussion of the frustrations of fusion—Alek's favorite topic. His obsession was evident in every word.

"I remember how I pointed out to you that untold thousands of scientists have sought this goal and many billions of dollars have been invested in major laboratories around the world to deal with the containment problem. But the contained plasma always behaved like a fistful of Jell-O oozing out between someone's fingers. The search for the fusion power reactor began in the 1940s and many of the most talented technical experts in the world have invested their lives in this research—all in the interest of lighting the ephemeral spark to start and then release the energy from the fusion reaction. The problem is that even if that works, the energy output will destroy nearby materials, and even if the material problems are solved, converting the energy output to a useful form of electric power is problematic."

Percy sighed. "Every few years, the quest for a fusion power reactor grabs the attention of the press. Remember how I told you I'm not going to let you waste your time and my lab's money on a wild goose chase."

Alek chuckled. "And remember how I said, 'What if we're chasing the right goose, but just headed in the wrong direction?'"

"Yeah, you started talking about how in graduate school, you did research on cold fusion and were thinking that if the energy output could be contained without material damage, it could be efficiently converted to a useful source of electricity."

"And then you said cold fusion is just bullshit."

"Cold fusion is bullshit. Well, it's kind of bullshit," said the lab director. "The phenomenon scientists called cold fusion was a nuclear reaction that produced more energy output than input at room temperature. It allegedly was discovered in 1989 by two physicists, which led to an international avalanche of experiments to confirm early claims. The possibility of developing the ultimate source of clean, cheap, unlimited energy attracted world attention and resulted in early excitement, but it was followed by almost immediate frustration when scientists couldn't duplicate the claims.

"Several experiments created excess heat generation, but the reaction couldn't be carried out in a predictable manner. There were reports of mysterious explosions that occurred from cold fusion experiments, but nothing was ever confirmed. At best, some small-scale lab experiments generated energy but only in an unpredictable process with no defined trigger. No one really understood what caused this reaction to take place."

"I know," Alek said. "Cold fusion is like making wet wood burn. It just won't work; you can't get it to light. But then it occurred to me, what if you had an intense electron beam that could overcome the dampness and cause the wet wood to ignite? What if a nuclear core of ordinary materials could be made to react energetically at room temperatures?" asked Alek. "What if we could actually make this work?"

Percy swallowed the last bite of his cheeseburger and Alek continued reminiscing, his own food forgotten. "That's when I realized that what scientists have mistakenly been calling cold fusion is actually a type of Low Energy Nuclear Reaction," said Alek. "It isn't really cold fusion. In fact, it's not fusion at all. It's actually a catalyzed LENR. Something has to trigger the process for the particles to combine. I really believe that these emerging theories will make sense if the right reaction trigger can be found."

Percy shook his head. "Alek, you are definitely a

dreamer. I remember when I was more like you—young, driven, idealistic... Of course, that was before all the government red tape wore me down."

"But you gave me your blessing to do the research," said Alek. "Even though you told me that you wanted me to know, on the record, that you didn't think it was going to work."

"It still hasn't," said Percy. "But you have made huge strides in the LENR research, and have worked around the clock to alleviate my doubts."

Alek nodded, remembering how he had named the initiative Project Z in honor of nuclear weapons research and development history. Project Y had been the code name given to Los Alamos, the primary site of the Manhattan Project, the top-secret laboratory responsible for the building of the first atomic bomb. Project Y had resulted in the threat of mutually assured destruction, but Project Z would usher in peace and prosperity as unlimited clean energy could resolve problems worldwide. Alek also thought the "Z" was fitting since it was the last letter in the alphabet and Project Z would be the last source of energy mankind would ever need. Plus, earlier fusion research had relied on a pulsed power device called the Z machine. The Z machine used high magnetic fields associated with strong electrical currents to produce high temperatures, extreme pressures, and powerful X-rays, but it had not yet achieved the goal of producing commercially available fusion and creating an unlimited energy source. Project Z would be the answer that scientists had sought for decades. Alek was certain. Successfully harnessing the Low Energy Nuclear Reaction could produce an enormous energy output that would solve the world's need for an unlimited source of clean energy. Someday, Project Z would be a reality. He would keep pushing forward until he met that goal.

Sometimes Alek wondered if he would be this driven, this obsessed, if it weren't for the accident. Regardless, he knew he had to make this research work. The problem was that in order to continue Project Z, Alek needed money. But was he ready to compromise his nonviolent principles and embrace weapons research just to get funds? He had put in too much time on this research to give up now. They were so close.

"Maybe you're right," he told Percy. "Maybe technology is just a knife, but I do think as physicists we have an ethical obligation to help people use that knife properly."

"That could be true," Percy replied. "But for now... just build the knife."

Percy's cellphone buzzed. He glanced down at a text. "Shit, the wife's back from her business trip. I'd better get going." He took a final swig of beer as Alek reached for his wallet.

"Go ahead, I'll get this. You get the next one." Percy clapped Alek on the shoulder and headed out the door as Alek opened his wallet. A tattered photograph fell out onto the table with the cash he pulled out. Alek froze, paralyzed, looking at the photo of a younger version of himself standing beside an attractive woman and holding a curly-headed toddler in his arms. The perfect happy family. Alek had deleted all of the photos stored on his iPhone and social media accounts, but he still carried this one dog-eared photo. He grimaced and shoved the photograph back into his wallet. Leaving the money on the table, he muttered to himself, "Just build the knife."

* * *

The sky had taken on a periwinkle hue with twinkling stars already emerging as Alek headed to the place he now called home.

While the city of Los Alamos offered all the charms of Northern New Mexico, from authentic Mexican food, to excellent ski runs, to vast unbroken vistas of the state's legendary turquoise skies, apartments in Los Alamos were far from luxurious. Unlike Santa Fe, only 40 minutes away and home to wealthy art connoisseurs seeking elegance and ambiance, Los Alamos catered to scientists. Alek drove down the winding streets of the small town, past buildings that remained stuck in the past. Los Alamos began as a hastily-built military installation constructed during World War II, and much of town had not been updated since the 50s and 60s.

It's a wonder some of these places are still even standing, he thought.

Alek's one bedroom at the Arroyo Vista apartment complex was new—by Los Alamos standards, built in the 70s. It could be described as utilitarian at best. Arroyo Vista translated to "ditch view," so his expectations weren't very high. From the dingy once-white paint to the shallow, scratched aluminum kitchen sink, to the chipped linoleum and single bulb overhead light... the entire place (all 560 square feet of it) gave off a scent of musty desperation. Alek figured it was what he deserved, after all.

One thing Alek felt certain he didn't deserve was a position running high profile experiments as a senior scientist at one of the nation's three nuclear weapons labs. The job was a gift... a lifeline. Percy had reached out with the job offer when Alek had hit his lowest point.

Alek let himself into the dark apartment and switched on the floor lamp. Moving a pile of laundry from the couch to the coffee table, Alek sat down and reached for the TV remote, but didn't push the button. His thoughts tugged him back into the past.

When Percy had first contacted him, nearly a year had passed since that unspeakable July afternoon when Alek's life had changed. He was still struggling. He had tried counseling, medication, extra leave from work. Then he tried drinking too much, excessive exercise, and even a visit to a Native American sweat lodge. With nothing helping him to heal from the trauma of the accident, that phone call from Percy and the thought of joining Los Alamos National Laboratory captured his interest. His then wife Julie, now his ex-wife, announced he would have to choose between her and the new job.

"I have no intention of moving to that backwater town

in the middle of nowhere New Mexico," Julie had decreed, pointing out that, as an attorney, she could support them with the salary she earned at her law practice. If he wanted to, he could even quit his job at Sandia Laboratories in Albuquerque. "Anyhow, you have a perfectly good job as at Sandia. You can't fix things by running away."

Ironically, it was Julie who had pushed him to take a job at Albuquerque's Sandia National Laboratories, because the position "paid highly, was well-respected, and made good use of his physics degree." Because Alek balked at the idea of working on weapons research, he had spent much of his time at Sandia trying to find a way to apply his findings to developing new forms of energy rather than nuclear weapons technology. That's why the offer from Los Alamos appealed to him. He would finally be able to pursue the kind of research he had been interested in all along.

"I don't understand why you'd want to take a chance with a speculative subject," snapped Julie. "Sometimes I feel like I don't even understand you anymore."

Had she ever understood him? Alek wondered. *What did they have left in common since... since the accident? Or even before then?* he thought.

"Stop being such a dreamer," Julie had frequently told Alek. Somehow, she couldn't accept that he had spent the year after his college graduation volunteering in Africa, trying to help the people there meet basic human needs. Julie never seemed to understand that ever since then, Alek had been haunted by the desperate poverty that plagued so many. He clung to the hope that science held the answer. He looked to a future when children didn't die of hunger and water flowed, making the desert green.

Rising from the couch, Alek walked to the vertical blinds to close them, lost in memories of his ex-wife. *Had he simply chosen to marry her just to balance out his impractical tendencies?* Julie was organized and extremely disciplined. Her career in tax law suited her personality perfectly, and she didn't tolerate any disruption of her carefully ordered life. Alek remembered how Julie had mastered the art of compartmentalizing, which served her well in her choice to shut out the past and move forward. "I know how to control my emotions," she told Alek. "You should learn to do the same."

If Alek were to be honest with himself, even before the accident he was finding his relationship with Julie to be a lot like his job at Sandia Labs—boring, unsatisfying, and frustrating. During those awful months after the accident, the gap between them had grown—a chasm filled with unspoken words, accusations never uttered but deeply felt.

Instead, they quarreled over inconsequential issues and discovered new ways to get on each other's nerves. "You take the absent-minded scientist thing too far." Julie would scold Alek when, on many occasions, she found him staring into space, lost in his thoughts. Julie grew even angrier on the days Alek would become distracted by a new idea or project and would forget to eat or shower. "You have to either get some help or get out," she admonished. Alek knew she was right.

He did need help, but he didn't know how to ask for it. The issue ate away at his self-confidence and then turned on his marriage. The unspoken problem was that, no matter how hard either of them tried, they simply could not find a way to move past the accident. Julie blamed Alek. Alek blamed himself. Once they had been a family, but now their life had disintegrated into reminders of their loss played out against a background loop of petty arguments about minor crises that really didn't matter and would never be resolved.

Alek had tried to throw his energy into his work, but Sandia Labs wasn't focused on the areas he wanted to investigate. With Percy's call, he had found the answer, just two hours north—a lead research scientist position at Los Alamos Labs.

So, Alek had packed his belongings and headed to Los Alamos, leaving all the trappings of his former life behind.

He had kept only the one photo, tucked inside his billfold. Sometimes, when he felt frustrated or overwhelmed by his work, or was searching for breakthroughs, he would pull out the photo and remember what happened. He would think about his failures and then he would push even harder on his research. Over time, the snapshot had become weathered and frayed. As the months at Los Alamos became years, Alek looked at the photo less often. He redirected his thoughts toward his research and threw every ounce of his energy into the struggle to make the Low Energy Nuclear Reaction succeed.

All in all, the move to Los Alamos suited Alek. While Julie disliked the small town feel of the city, Alek liked the community and enjoyed living closer to the mountains. He made time to go for a run on the trails of the nearby Pajarito Mountain Ski Area almost every evening after work. The high elevation and clear mountain air helped Alek focus and he felt he did some of his best thinking alone beneath the vast New Mexico sky.

Yes, there were lonely days and even lonelier nights, but the work was all-encompassing and lab management allowed Alek to let his imagination soar. Alek knew he had to create technology that would help people. He owed that to the world. He needed to find a way to atone for his mistakes, even if Julie wouldn't forgive him and even if he couldn't forgive himself.

Over the past few years, Alek had developed a good relationship with Harold Percy, his most senior boss. The lab director encouraged his lead scientist's wandering and curious mind. The two often exchanged new ideas when they traveled to technical conferences or entertained distinguished guests from Washington. Percy had a knack for marketing technology and research. He could always deliver the convincing sales pitch about the potential payoff, and he soon discovered that Alek's passion and limitless imagination provided the ammunition he needed to gain funding and support.

Percy had even found the funding to hire the Ramos

brothers to conduct off-site experiments that could fast track their research on the Low Energy Nuclear Reaction project. Though the two hadn't made much progress, they showed initiative and enthusiasm about the concept. Alek was grateful that Percy had secured the funds to allow them to focus on their research without distractions from the rest of the lab.

Percy's support meant a lot to him. True, the lab director always put funding first, but his willingness to focus on energy applications in the upcoming congressional hearing instead of pushing the weapons angle—that represented a significant sacrifice. *I may not have any real friends or social life at the lab*, mused Alek, *but at least I have a supportive boss.*

In any case, he thought, settling in on the lumpy beige couch that came standard with his furnished apartment, *Los Alamos isn't so bad.* Though difficult, the divorce had been the right choice. Julie deserved the chance to be happy. Her life was better off without him. Now he could work on the kind of projects he had only dreamed about when he was completing his PhD in physics and engineering at Princeton.

Despite this, Percy's desire to push the weapons angle disturbed him. Yes, there was plenty of funding for weapons technology, but that didn't make it right. He didn't want to be responsible for giving the world a new weapon. The goal was unlimited, clean energy—an achievement that could truly change lives.

If we could only find the trigger and get the LENR to work, thought Alek. Project Z had to become a reality.

He had to build the knife.

Chapter 3
Middle of the Night Mysteries

LOS ALAMOS AFTER DARK HAD no nightlife. In fact, the city only had a few street lights. When darkness fell, the residents went home, and the stars took over the indigo sky.

When the ringing cellphone woke Alek, it took him a minute to realize where he was. He had fallen asleep on the couch, watching TV. Based on the pain in his neck, that was not a smart choice.

"What time is it," he mumbled, fumbling for his iPhone. It seemed like the middle of the night, but the clock on his phone said it was only 11:30 p.m. He tapped the answer button.

"Alek, it's Percy. I need you to get over to my house. Right away."

Still bleary with sleep, Alek grabbed a University of New Mexico Lobos sweatshirt and headed out the door. *Percy never calls this late*, mused Alek. *Whatever is happening, it must be big.* Alek stepped into the cool night air and looked up at the carpet of stars overhead. Living at high altitude meant the stars seemed brighter and closer in the dark sky. Alek admired the spectacular display of diamonds on black velvet as he walked across the apartment complex parking lot to his car.

Pulling up at Percy's, Alek noticed two cars in the drive. He recognized one car as Sunli's. *What on earth was going on?*

Percy answered the doorbell almost immediately and

ushered Alek down the stairs into the basement. Sunli was sitting on the couch waiting. Not a hair on her head was out of place, her makeup was flawless, and she was dressed in tailored black pants and an emerald green blouse that perfectly suited her olive complexion. Alek ran a hand over his stained sweatshirt and wondered why he hadn't taken the time to comb his hair.

Percy offered Alek a drink, which he declined, and ushered him toward an armchair. A blonde woman in jeans and sneakers came down the hall from the bathroom. Alek was perplexed. The woman looked oddly familiar, but he just couldn't place her. Who did he know who wore her hair pulled into a ponytail and had tortoiseshell glasses? Why did he feel like he had seen her somewhere? And what was she doing in Percy's basement late at night?

"Hi, y'all," said the newcomer.

"Oh my God," said Alek. "It's you, with the beer and the ketchup and the onions."

Percy immediately took control of the situation. "Alek, I believe you have met Gabriella Stebbens at the Friggin Bar. Gabriella is an agent with the FBI and is joining us tonight in an official capacity related to an ongoing investigation."

"Please, call me Gabi," the woman said.

Alek tried to reconcile the modestly dressed, nondescript woman with the flamboyant waitress he had seen earlier that evening. "But you... I... you... look different," spluttered Alek.

"Well, I've been working undercover," she replied.

"See, I told you she wasn't just a waitress," said Percy. "Now, let's get down to business."

"I apologize for the late-night meeting, but I just received an important call on my encrypted phone line suggesting that this simply can't wait," Percy said. "What we have to tell you tonight is extremely sensitive. This is a complex and rapidly developing situation, and we can't afford for any of this information to leak."

Percy gestured to Gabi to continue the debrief.

"For several months in my role as an FBI investigator, I have been working with Director Percy to monitor your fellow employees, Joe and Will Ramos," Gabi said. "Our investigation picked up a chain of messages between the Ramoses and scientists and ex-military officials in China."

"The two often stopped for a drink at the Friggin Bar after work, and my assignment was to listen to their conversations to see if I could obtain more information about their Chinese connections," she said. "They had a tendency to tip unusually generously for physicists, and they frequently spoke to each other in Spanish, but they never revealed anything about connections to China. Meanwhile, I had to keep pretending to be a waitress, which, frankly, I'm not very good at."

You certainly aren't, Alek thought to himself, then said aloud, "So what changed? Why are we here tonight? Lots of physicists have contacts in China. In fact, those connections have become routine ever since the Chinese increased their science investments and expanded the number of college students and high-tech employees in the U.S."

"True," noted Percy. "But the Ramoses behaved very oddly during the management meeting this morning. They seemed unnaturally reserved and hesitant, almost nervous, about the prospect of transitioning to weapons research."

"Now that you mention it, they were acting strangely," said Sunli. "Their behavior was disturbing. Extremely odd."

"I had the same reaction," agreed Percy. "And, as you know, I have a vested interest in this particular project and have been keeping the President posted on our progress. This could be very meaningful research for our national defense."

Alek cleared his throat in protest, but Percy ignored him, continuing with the story. "So, after Alek and I met at the bar for dinner, I decided to give Will and Joe a call.

Neither answered his cellphone and I just had this nagging feeling something was wrong."

"A lot of times they work late in the evenings conducting experiments at the lab," Alek noted.

"Absolutely," said Percy. "That's why I asked our security team to pay a visit to their lab. But they called tonight to inform me that they didn't find Will or Joe there. Instead, the secure safes were unlocked, the laptops were missing, and the computer hard drives were gone."

"What? Gone?" Alek reeled with shock. "The hard drives? The laptops? All their findings and records of results?"

"Everything," replied Percy. "There was also evidence that some sort of explosion had taken place in the lab. The ceiling was damaged as if there had been some kind of significant energy release. Naturally, I contacted Gabi since this could mean we have lost track of vital information, not to mention losing track of two key scientists researching concepts tied to advanced weapons development. My guess is that our conversation earlier today about pursuing weapons research spooked them and they decided it was time to bug out and hand their discoveries over to the Chinese."

"Do you think they discovered the secret of the LENR... that they figured out how to trigger the reaction?" Sunli asked, leaning forward.

"Their abrupt disappearance certainly suggests that," replied Gabi. "The FBI has been trying to track them. Our sources suggest they are either at the house they rent in Altavaca, just north of Albuquerque, or they have headed to their condo in Mexico."

"If they've found the answer, we have to find them," said Sunli. "We can't let them leave the country with that information."

"No, but we also don't want to alert them to the fact that we know what they're up to," noted Percy. "That's why I called you all in tonight."

"Alek and Sunli, I want you to go out to their lab in

the morning and see if they left any files or information behind that the security team may have missed," Percy ordered. "I'm going to head to D.C. in the morning. President Thornton wants me to brief him in person about the possible weapons applications of the LENR project."

Sunli turned to Gabi. "And what's the FBI going to do?" she asked. "Seeing as they haven't done a thing to prevent this from happening."

"I'll check in with the team of FBI agents stationed in Mexico who are scoping out the Ramoses' condo," Gabi responded coolly. "We are doing everything in our power to keep this situation under control."

"Should we contact the local authorities?" Alek asked.

"We can't risk raising any suspicions," Percy replied. "There are rumors that the Chinese Ministry of State Security has operatives here in Los Alamos. We have to fly under the radar as much as possible and not let on that anything has changed. Plus, there's no reason to draw any attention to this matter. The last thing the lab needs is bad press."

Alek knew how hard Percy had worked over the years to improve the lab's reputation and overcome past scandals. Still, he wasn't convinced that this plan made sense.

"Let's all check back with each other tomorrow night, well, technically tonight, when I get back from D.C. and compare notes," said Percy.

Alek glanced at his watch. It was past midnight, and he was still trying to shake the sense that this was all a dream brought on by falling asleep right after eating a green chile cheeseburger. He rubbed his eyes. Sunli Hidalgo, Harold Percy, and the mysterious Gabriella Stebbens were all still sitting in Percy's basement.

"Uh, I'll let myself out."

"I'd better head out too," Gabi said.

Alek walked up the stairs, glancing back to see Percy and Sunli huddled together, speaking in hushed tones. He wondered what they were discussing.

As they walked out the front door together, Gabi grabbed Alek's elbow. "Can I ask you a question? A scientific question?"

Alek turned. Without the heavy makeup and low-cut sweater, Gabi had an earthy, outdoorsy look, like someone who knew how to build a campfire and shopped at L.L.Bean.

Alek shook his head. Where were these ridiculous thoughts coming from? "Yes, of course. What's your question?"

Even in the dim porch lights, Alek could see a sheepish look on Gabi's face. "I don't really want Director Percy to know this, but my scientific knowledge is kind of limited. There isn't any actual lab equipment missing. What exactly did the Ramos brothers take?"

"That's actually a valid question," replied Alek, comfortable and in his element discussing his area of expertise. "The issue is that Will and Joe have disappeared with their knowledge and the digital records of all their calculations. They have high-level information about LENR technology that could be used to develop nuclear weapons. If we don't recover the hard drives, the laptops, and, most importantly, Will and Joe, this could be one of the most serious cases of espionage that has ever taken place at the lab."

"That makes sense," Gabi said, nodding. "It explains why Percy is so concerned about spooking them. I wanted to call in an FBI team, but he refused."

"I wish he hadn't," said Alek. "I'm not very comfortable with this approach."

"I know... let me give you my phone number. I already have yours."

Alek handed Gabi his iPhone so she could enter her contact information. In some ways, he didn't like knowing that the FBI already had his number and could track him, but, on the other hand, it was somewhat reassuring. He felt a little less alone.

"Call or text anytime you need me," Gabi said, smiling.

"And I'll see you tomorrow night, I mean tonight."

Alek waved goodbye and got in his car, his thoughts swirling. His employees, his research, his life's work were all missing... and an intriguing woman had given him her phone number. He couldn't decide which of these things was more shocking. This certainly had been an unexpected night.

* * *

Alek couldn't sleep. After tossing and turning for a couple of hours, wrestling with his need to do something, anything, he decided to pay his former employees a visit. He headed for the Ramos brothers' rented home in Altavaca. He wasn't sure what he would do when he got there, but he couldn't just sit in his apartment and wait. He kept hoping this was all just a mistake. At the same time, Alek couldn't stop feeling excitement over the idea that the Ramoses might have solved the mystery of the LENR trigger. He had spent so long dreaming about the possibility of creating an endless source of energy. Perhaps the elusive goal was finally in his grasp.

Altavaca was south of Los Alamos and just north of Albuquerque, so Alek figured it would take him about an hour to get there—a straight shot down I-25, first taking the cut off to avoid going through Santa Fe. He stepped on the gas as he headed down the winding mountain road from Los Alamos to Santa Fe. While fun to drive, the curvy road also served as a speed-trap where New Mexico State Police frequently issued tickets. Los Alamos scientists had been known to flash their lab badges and mutter something about important Department of Defense business when stopped. Alek hoped he would not have to resort to that tonight. He wondered why the two scientists had chosen to rent a place so far away from Los Alamos. There wasn't much to choose from near the lab, but it still seemed like an unusually long commute. Lost in thought, Alek made it to Altavaca in under an hour. He checked the GPS for directions to the Ramoses' house.

Altavaca wasn't even a town—it was a census designated place peppered with a handful of shoddily-built, stucco houses rapidly erected to accommodate East Coast transplants who came from out-of-state seeking something affordable and pseudo-Southwest. Most of the homeowners had long ago transitioned from being captivated by desert sunsets to becoming frustrated by living in a place where the humidity was less than five percent. This left a number of relatively new, but already crumbling, homes largely unoccupied in the area. The Ramos brothers' rental house sat alone in a cul-de-sac in a small valley.

Dawn was nearing when Alek rounded a hill, spotted his destination, and felt his excitement rising. The pinkish orange glow from the west lit the edges of the dark mesa. Alek wondered what he should do next.

He checked his watch. Nearly 5 a.m. Hardly an appropriate time for a casual visit. He should have brought doughnuts. After all, you can't just knock on someone's door and say, "Hello, we suspect you are spies, thieves, or maybe both."

Alek braked his car to a stop at the top of the hill and shifted into park. Gazing down at the house, he flipped on the radio. The house lights glimmered in the clear desert night. Lost in thought, Alek caught a glimpse of something moving out of the corner of his eye.

Leaving the car running, Alek jumped out to see another car speeding away in the darkness. It looked like the Ramos brothers' distinctive red Alfa Romeo heading up the hill in the opposite direction. Where were they going in such a rush? Before he could decide whether to get back in his car and try to follow them or check the house, a flash filled the indigo sky. Alek winced in the blinding white light.

The blast was silent. Alek felt a wave of pressure knock him back against his car. The air crackled with electricity as if lightning had struck. With a sputter of static, the electrical systems in the Ford Focus stopped working. The engine died. The radio stopped playing. The dash lights and headlights went dark. Alek squinted, feeling disoriented, struggling to make sense of what was happening. He had never seen this kind of energy release. It was a blast, but more of a burst than an explosion. It could not have come from any sort of chemical reaction. The air seemed to quiver as Alek stood next to his still and silent car watching swirls of smoke rising from the valley below.

Alek tried to stay calm and understand what was happening. The brilliant blast of light and the intense radio frequency pulse could only mean some sort of nuclear detonation—an explosion that not only released accelerated electrons and ions but generated an electromagnetic pulse. Although he knew that theoretically such a burst of electromagnetic radiation could be created by a high-altitude nuclear explosion, Alek couldn't believe that an explosion could spark such a pulse in the atmosphere. Did this mean the Ramos brothers had successfully developed the LENR trigger? Why would they detonate it? Could it have been a mistake?

Unable to fully comprehend the implications of what he had seen, Alek surveyed what was once the Ramos brothers' home. Swirling ash and dust were all that remained. It was as if the energy release had disintegrated the very structure of the nearby materials, reducing them to their molecular constituents. If anyone had been in the house when the explosion took place, surely they were vaporized instantly—along with any equipment or lab notes. If the solution he was seeking had been in that house, it certainly was gone now. And had it been the Ramoses driving off in that sports car right before the blast?

Alek heard sirens in the distance. *Now what?* If he stuck around to talk to the authorities, he would face hours of questioning. He had to get to a secure location as soon as possible to contact Percy and report what had happened. Alek got back in his car and turned the key in the ignition. On the fifth try, the car's electrical systems mysteriously resumed working and the engine turned over. Spinning the steering wheel, Alek made a U-turn and headed through the clouds of dust back to Los Alamos.

Chapter 4
D. C. or Bust

THE EVENING SUNSET TRANSFORMED THE sky from pastel pinks and blues to an explosion of reds and oranges, lighting up towering cumulus clouds that held just the slightest hint of rain.

The group met as planned in Harold Percy's basement the minute he returned from his whirlwind trip to D.C.

Percy's suit was rumpled after a long day of committee meetings and travel. He looked worn out. In contrast, dressed in a magenta silk blouse and charcoal slacks, Sunli looked professional and composed, as if she had come directly from the office. Excitement shone in her eyes. It seemed to Alek that Sunli only showed emotion when discussing the LENR project. *The woman barely has human feelings*, thought Alek. The only way to impress her would be to solve the mystery of the trigger, and so far, that was still out of reach.

Alek had ironed a semi-new, button down shirt and then, asking himself who he was trying to impress, discarded it in favor of a Grateful Dead T-shirt that could have used a wash. He had spent the long day updating Percy and Gabi over the phone about the explosion in Altavaca, examining the Ramoses lab with Sunli, and trying to piece together everything that had happened in the past 24 hours. He kept wondering if the whole thing could be a dream. Gabi's most recent transformation only contributed to the dreamlike feeling. She was dressed in a sleek black pantsuit with her blonde curls contained in a ponytail. Any remaining vestiges of the dive bar waitress in the low-cut sweater were gone.

Everyone was eager to discuss what had happened in Altavaca along with the other discoveries of the day. Alek took center stage as his colleagues peppered him with a barrage of questions about the explosion he had witnessed.

"So, the house just... vaporized?"

"Was there a sound or a blast of pressure?"

"You said your car stopped running?"

"You think you saw Will and Joe driving away?"

"Hang on, hang on!" Alek shouted. "Everyone is talking at once."

Alek filled them in as best he could, despite their continued interruptions. The scientists quickly grasped the magnitude of the situation, but Gabi was still confused.

"Guys, just for a sec, pretend I'm not a physicist. 'Cause guess what? I'm not. I've taken a few engineering classes at the university and I always thought I was a decent student, but I'm still confused. Could you explain this electromagnetic pulse thing so maybe someone without a PhD can understand it?"

"An electromagnetic pulse or EMP is a short burst of electromagnetic radiation," Alek explained. "I believe this EMP was caused by a nuclear detonation originating from the Ramoses' house. It created an enormous stream of electrons that somehow interacted to form the pulse. A larger EMP could cause power grids to fail, airplanes to fall out of the sky, computer systems to go haywire. A high-altitude detonation of a megaton nuclear explosion above an American city would wipe out all electrical components, all communications. No phone, no internet, no power. It would be a disaster."

Gabi nodded. "So, this... this detonation was caused by something new... an... unprecedented... explosion?"

"You got it," said Alek. "We know a nuclear detonation at high altitude can create an EMP, but this originated from the Ramoses' house. It has to be entirely new physics... it has to be the LENR."

"In the wrong hands, this technology could be devastating," Percy mused. "A rogue state could cause massive destruction by launching a ballistic missile and sparking an EMP."

"A high-power microwave weapon driven by a giant capacitor bank could also cause such destruction, but in a very limited area," Alek continued. "In fact, many compact but enormously powerful microwave devices deployed in critical U.S. cities could be used as terrorist weapons. With enough of these gadgets delivered in the back of pickup trucks and parked near strategic power control stations throughout the country, you could bring down the entire grid."

Percy looked solemn. "Rather than the unlikely prospect of attack by a nation state, the existence of such a compact electromagnetic pulse weapon in the hands of terrorists is truly frightening," he mused.

"I think you both are missing the point," said Sunli. "This detonation means the Ramos brothers have discovered how to enable the trigger and make the LENR work. They have uncovered the solution we've been seeking. Why do you guys look so worried? We should be celebrating. This is a breakthrough."

"I think we need to address the seriousness of this situation," said Gabi. "The FBI has secured the site of the explosion, but we recovered nothing. Everything down to the building's foundation is gone. So far local law enforcement and the media are accepting our cover story that the destruction was the result of an accidental explosion in a hidden meth lab. Authorities believe the Ramos brothers died in the blast."

"But they didn't. I saw them drive away," Alek interjected. "Or someone drove away in what looked like their car."

"Right," Gabi agreed, "but they have vanished, and it sounds like all their work was vaporized. If they are alive, they clearly are no longer working for you. On top of that, our surveillance suggests that they have been passing their research along to someone in China, which means the very scenario you painted could be happening. It's possible that this technology is already in our adversaries' hands."

"Also, this could impact America's ongoing weapons negotiations with the Chinese leaders who are playing games with us," Percy pointed out. "If they have the upper hand in developing a new weapon, they are bound to take advantage. Beating the Chinese in the race to develop this weapon just became even more important. That's why Congress has been funneling money indirectly into our research all along."

"So indirectly, all along, we've actually been doing weapons research?" asked Alek sadly.

"Basically, yes," replied Percy. "And now President Thornton wants to kick it into high gear. I also met with several congressional committees. President Thornton and the Senate Select Committee on Intelligence are implementing a crash program to accelerate our ability to develop the trigger and catch up with the technology the Ramos brothers may have transferred to the Chinese. This project is highly classified. Only a handful of us can actually know what's going on. I'm putting together a team of my best people and all of you need to plan to head to D.C."

Percy turned to Sunli and Alek. "Did you find anything left in the Ramoses' lab?"

"The ceiling was damaged from some sort of high energy discharge. Other than that, the only thing we found was an old notebook, but I'm not entirely sure I understand the calculations scribbled in it," Sunli said. "It seems like most of their real research was taking place at that house in Altavaca. No wonder they lived so far away. No chance anyone from the lab would just drop by."

Percy nodded. "That makes sense," he said. "Gabi, any report from your team in Mexico?"

"No," Gabi replied. "I haven't heard back from them,

but if there is anything suspicious happening at the Ramos brothers' place in Mexico, we should know soon."

"Good." Percy leaned forward, giving his full attention to the odd trio assembled in his basement. "Alek and Sunli, you should gather up your stuff and plan for several weeks in Washington," said Percy, his forehead creased with worry and exhaustion. "President Thornton has asked me to lead a team to develop a full report on the LENR technology and the strategic political issues this technology represents. We'll need to work with other experts and coordinate with Congress and the Pentagon to develop a funding proposal and forecast of how the release of the LENR technology could contribute to the arms race. The LENR is now at the top of the President's agenda and he wants every piece of information he can get. Everyone start thinking about who else we need to add to our team. While we work on this report, we also need to figure out how to create the LENR trigger. Unlocking this mystery will be the key to the President's success in the arms negotiations with the Chinese."

The lab director turned to Alek. "We need to prepare to testify before the Senate Select Committee on Intelligence. The questions will be brutal, and we must be prepared with answers that guarantee support and funding but also reflect the truth."

Alek's head was reeling. Sunli looked solemn and lost in thought. Only Gabi was smiling.

"Thank God," she said. "I never have to go back to work at that friggin' bar."

* * *

Two days later, Sunli, Alek, and Percy arrived at the Hart Senate Office Building in Washington, D.C. In the building's expansive atrium, a giant black steel piece of artwork designed by Alexander Calder rose five stories high. "Looks evil," Alek said, examining the colossal work of art.

"It's called Mountains and Clouds," replied Percy. "But

they removed the cloud part of the sculpture."

"So much for our silver lining," quipped Alek as they headed for the elevator that would take them to the most tightly secured area on Capitol Hill. The electromagnetically shielded room, the Sensitive Compartmented Information Facility known as the SCIF, was on the second floor. An armed guard sat outside the door, screening everyone seeking to enter the chamber. After the facial recognition imager scanned and verified each of them, the guard inspected their credentials, checked them into the security computer, confiscated their phones, and directed them to sign a form promising not to reveal anything. The three walked through the heavy door into a fairly small room furnished with a table and chairs for the witnesses and a circle of seats surrounding them for the senators of the Senate Select Committee on Intelligence. Sunli, Alek, and Percy took their seats at the witness table, while the full array of committee members filled the circle.

Sitting in a straight-backed chair slightly apart from the senators was Dale Croft, the President's science adviser. Croft was new to his job, and the bow-tie clad, former Stanford professor looked uncomfortable and out of place.

Senator Larry Plumkin, the head of the committee, called the meeting to order. The Republican from Mississippi spoke with a relaxed drawl that contrasted with the serious issues they were gathered to address.

"Director Percy," began Plumkin, "I understand you have reason to suspect the recent explosion in New Mexico revealed breakthroughs in the development of this new Low Energy Nuclear Reaction technology. Please explain to this committee the applications of this technology."

"Senator, we have been researching the LENR technology for several years and we do believe this incident indicates significant progress," Percy replied smoothly. "With the appropriate funding, we feel confident that we will be able to duplicate construction of the triggering process used in this unfortunate event."

"I have been briefed on the connection between your missing employees and China," noted the senator. "Does this mysterious explosion suggest the Chinese now have the ability to create a powerful space weapon? With all the money we send to your lab each year, we shouldn't be worrying about espionage or playing catch up with the Chinese."

Alek cleared his throat. "With all due respect, senators, our research has focused on applying this technology to energy generation. My goal as a scientist is to create a source of clean, affordable power."

Plumkin snorted. "Peace doesn't win elections. What are you doing to protect America from its adversaries?"

"Dr. Spray hasn't captured the full picture of our work," interjected Sunli, shooting a hostile glance at Alek. "We believe that this explosion demonstrates that we can harness this technology for multiple uses—especially national defense."

"Can you duplicate what happened at Altavaca, New Mexico?" asked Plumkin. "I mean," he corrected himself, "we don't want you to duplicate the explosion. We want you to duplicate the research. Can you pull together a team of scientists who can accelerate the process and provide us with the same technology and information that we believe the Chinese now have? Can you prepare an in-depth report and funding proposal to duplicate those results?"

"What are the political implications of building this weapon?" asked another senator. "If the Chinese already have this technology, will our efforts plunge the world into another arms race?"

"That's why this technology is essential for deterrence," Percy noted. "We need to keep pace with our adversaries."

"But as I understand it, you still haven't figured out how the LENR trigger mechanism works," Plumkin said accusingly.

"We're getting close," said Alek, wincing as he heard a defensive tone slip into his voice. "By pulling together the experts, we can thoroughly examine the different paths we can pursue to launch the Low Energy Nuclear Reaction that we're seeking."

"And then create a space weapon?" asked a senator in the corner of the room.

"Well, my goal is energy research..." began Alek, trailing off when he noticed Percy's pointed look.

"The President has already authorized the study," interrupted Plumkin. "We need to know all the possible paths to creating this weapon and the funding that will be needed to make this happen. Secrecy is essential. We have many concerns about Chinese operatives accessing classified information. Every precaution must be in place. Locate the experts you'll need. We'll provide you space at the Pentagon. Figure out what secrets may have been sent to China and how America can develop the same technology to protect the country. We expect the report in no more than three weeks, so be prepared to brief the President and this committee."

"Respectfully, sir, that's hardly enough time," said Alek, ignoring the look Percy shot at him. "We need to pull together a robust committee of experts and review numerous proposals regarding what strategy to take."

"Three weeks," said Plumkin. "You'll report back to this committee then."

Plumkin and the other committee members rose, almost simultaneously, and began filing out of the room. Alek, Percy, and Sunli were left behind with Dale Croft, science adviser to the President.

"This is a waste of time and money," Croft spluttered. "I told the President not to bother with this amateur hour. For all we know, that explosion could have been a gas leak. I still can't understand why President Thornton gives any credence to the work going on at that obsolete nuclear weapons lab."

Croft fixed his beady eyes on Percy. "By the way," he

said, "we're calling this the Percy Study. That way, when the press gets ahold of it, it's clear who wasted the government's money and the President's time."

Croft skulked from the room. Percy was the first to break the nervous silence.

"The Percy Study," he said. "I like the sound of that. Let's get to work."

Chapter 5
The Percy Study

THE NEW MEXICO SKIES WERE one of the reasons Alek preferred Los Alamos to the East Coast, and he was reminded of that as he walked through the bland corridors of the Pentagon under the dreary fluorescent lights. He felt claustrophobic and trapped working in the small offices and conference room the team had been assigned to in the bowels of the Pentagon. Everything looked the same, and he never seemed to be able to locate his new office without getting lost.

Percy and Alek sat at the conference room table, with their open laptops nestled amongst papers and reports covering the table. "So, where do we stand?" asked Percy. "Let's hear your recommendations for members of this team."

Pulling up a document on his computer, Alek leaned forward. "The first is Ron Digali from Sandia. We worked together on several projects when I was there, though Digali always had a convincing explanation for why none of my ideas would work."

"Well, it's good to have checks and balances," said Percy. "He's the ideal technical expert, always ready to debunk a wild idea. If anyone can make something real out of a speculative new idea though, it will be him."

"I agree," replied Alek. "One area that seems to be his strongest suit is pulsed power. He developed compact electrical pulse generators and everyone in the field recognizes him as the 3M guy, the creator of the world's leading source of millions of volts and millions of amperes in one-millionth of a second."

"Yep, he's a great choice. Who's next?"

Alek nodded, looking down at the computer screen. "Tom Lowe from our sister lab, Lawrence Livermore. Tom can outthink anyone I've ever met. More importantly, he has a creative and optimistic attitude about even the most unlikely outcome."

"True," agreed Percy. "Digali can always converge to a narrow solution, while Lowe is able to diverge into alternate explanations. You and Lowe are two-of-a-kind—always going off on creative tangents, but that does open up new paths to problem solving."

Alek laughed. "Well, we were both labeled as hyperactive as children due to our tendency to get distracted easily. Tom's a good friend."

Lowe had worked at Los Alamos when Alek first started there and the two quickly formed a strong friendship. Although Alek understood why his friend and colleague chose to leave Los Alamos for a better offer at Lawrence Livermore, Alek had missed Lowe's company and was excited to be able to work with him again.

Percy rose and looked over Alek's shoulder at the laptop screen. "Ah, Candale Gregory. Now, that's an interesting character."

"Candale can defeat even a fast computer with his back-of-the-envelope calculations," said Alek. "Although he sure isn't what I would call personable."

Percy chuckled. "True. Like many Los Alamos scientists, he's pretty bad at making eye contact. Most of the time I find him looking at his shoes."

"He never speaks up in group conversations and always seems to be off in a cloud solving equations in his mind," noted Alek. "But Candale has the rare combination of both Digali's convergence and Lowe's divergence. It's hard to get him to contribute, but when he does, it's worth the wait."

Alek sighed. "And then there's Sunli. I wish she

weren't the only female scientist in the group. You'd think by now we'd have more diversity in the field."

"I'm done with all this pressure to achieve diversity," Percy scoffed. "Whatever happened to finding the best person for the job? Yes, I'm Black, but I didn't land my job as lab director because of diversity quotas. I earned this. I prefer to avoid adding team members who don't belong here just to meet an agenda. Plus, Sunli is used to working with all men. She doesn't pay attention to anything but the research."

"Actually, she has a tendency to intimidate her co-workers," said Alek. "And me, to be honest. But I admire her dedication to solving any problem that stands in her way. Does anyone know anything about her personal life? Does she have a personal life?"

"Hmm, I doubt it," Percy said. "She graduated from the *Instituto Technologic de Estudios Superiories de Monterrey*, also known as Monterrey Tech, in Mexico, with a double chemical engineering and mathematics PhD. I think she lives in Santa Fe and I've seen her driving an old Porsche 911, but I have no idea what she does in her spare time."

"Well, she doesn't date, I know that," said Alek. "The few guys I know who have asked her out have gotten brutal rejections. Not that it matters. If anybody at the lab stands a chance of winning the Nobel Prize, it will be Sunli."

"You've lined up a good group," Percy said. "How soon will everyone be here?"

"They've all agreed to the assignment, gotten permission from their supervisors, and are making travel arrangements. We should be ready to go by the end of the week."

"I'm counting on you, Alek. You don't have much time to pull this together and you'll have to meet with Congress along the way. Be sure to pad the funding proposals. Don't skimp on any recommendations."

Alek snorted quietly, closing his laptop. *Of course the lab director was focused on money, not life-changing sci-*

ence. Nothing new there.

* * *

Later that week, the full team was assembled. They quickly got to work discussing theories, making calculations, and preparing simulations of the LENR trigger process. Their computers were safeguarded, and any notes they wrote went into a burn bag each night. All of their completed work was encrypted and backed up in secure computer storage that could only be accessed by a limited number of people. They collected as much information as they could find on existing LENR research and often worked late into the night inventing, arguing, and imagining.

Alek was pleased with the other scientists' commitment to the project, but Digali seemed distracted, spending too much of his time staring at Sunli. The object of this attraction didn't appear to recognize that her small size, delicate features, and long dark hair had captivated his interest. Sunli made it clear that her only interest was science, but she did spend a great deal of time talking to Digali. *What was she trying to learn?* Alek wondered.

Alek eavesdropped as Sunli cornered Digali in the conference room one afternoon. "Tell me about that invention you developed a few years ago called the plasma focus," she said.

Digali smiled, pleased by the attention. "This device produces a high voltage discharge from a compact pulsed power device without using any high voltage components," he said. "Instead, it uses high current to magnetically sweep up plasma into a small, dense, high voltage particle-accelerating region. It's probably the only plasma phenomenon that takes advantage of an instability to create a useful output."

"I understand the basic idea, but I think we need a computer simulation to perfect the theoretical formulation of the compact device so we can use it to spark the reaction using an intense electron beam. Can you do that?" asked Sunli. "To transform the work we have already done on energy research into a weapons application, we won't be able to use a giant electron beam accelerator. We have to miniaturize everything. Can you do *that*?" she asked pointedly.

"Ummm no," said the lovelorn physicist, soaking up the attention. Sunli threw up her hands in frustration and stalked out of the room.

The team fell into a routine, and their first week at the Pentagon passed quickly. On the rare evenings they wrapped up work before 9 p.m., Alek would go for a jog around the National Mall, dodging tourists and admiring the monuments. He also cursed the humidity and longed for the arid New Mexico mountains. One night, as he ran, Alek watched the image of the Washington Monument rippling in the reflecting pool and wondered how he had even ended up there, working on weapons research of all things.

His frustration finally erupted the next day at their morning meeting in the Pentagon conference room. They had spent several hours in the stuffy, windowless room writing up a complex funding proposal. Alek sighed heavily and put his head in his hands.

Percy put a hand on his shoulder. "I think we're making great progress. What's the problem?"

"I'm tired of bending over backwards to help Congress justify spending more money on another weapons system," Alek exclaimed. He turned to Tom Lowe. "I know you've been working on space weapons research at Lawrence Livermore, but I'm still struggling to see how the LENR technology fits into national defense. Please tell me it's not just about money."

Percy smiled. "Of course, it isn't just about money. It's also about politicians who need votes. Not to mention the fact that scientists need sports cars too."

Alek groaned. "It isn't funny. Someone explain what we are doing before I lose my precarious grip."

Lowe walked over to the coffee pot on the counter

behind the conference table, poured some stale coffee into a Styrofoam cup and handed it to Alek.

"Look, many groups have been funded to develop space control weapons. In fact, it once was a stated U.S. Air Force strategy to achieve what they called 'space dominance,'" he said, returning to his seat at the table beside Alek.

"The notion is that one country could dominate the ultimate high ground. The idea only really attracted the unrealistic fancy of some Air Force Space Command enthusiasts, but the concept has to be pursued even if the only reason behind the research is to show it isn't possible. Plus, there's a long history of investing in space weapons research." Lowe raked a hand through his sandy blonde hair, making it stand up. Looking like the epitome of the mad scientist, he continued to explain.

"Space weapons research has included everything from thousands of ground-launched interceptor missiles, to the vast waste of money championed by Edward Teller to create the nuclear weapon pumped X-ray laser, while other scientists wasted money researching giant electromagnetic sling shots, basically railguns, that could hurl hypersonic projectiles thousands of kilometers through space. Untold billions have been spent chasing wild ideas, but so far, no practical and affordable space weapon has emerged."

"Recently, however, we've been working on a concept we call the Collective Laser Accelerator Weapon or the CLAW," Lowe continued. "The CLAW was inspired by a particle beam weapon called Teleforce created by Nicola Tesla. It's a close-to-the-speed of light ion beam that could be used in space."

"That's where LENR comes in," Percy interrupted. "A compact high energy source is critical to creating an energy-beam space weapon. We need the LENR trigger in order to deploy the CLAW."

"And why is this suddenly so important?" Alek asked.

Candale looked up. The pale, chubby scientist spoke

for the first time that week. "The Chinese," he muttered, immediately returning his gaze to his feet.

"That's right," said Percy. "Intelligence information has indicated that China is basing its advanced warfighting concepts on space capabilities. The side that can successfully attack space capabilities will have a tremendous advantage. That's why the Pentagon has been so concerned about the nation's security reliance on precise space-based surveillance, reconnaissance, communication, and decision making," he said. "If the Chinese can knock out our systems, they have the ultimate bargaining chip."

Sunli looked lost in thought. Alek wondered if hearing them discuss China as the enemy disturbed her. While Sunli hadn't been raised in China, her half-Chinese heritage and the fact that her mother lived in China, could skew her allegiance. Alek studied Sunli. Her dark eyes, shaded by long eyelashes, gave no hint of her feelings.

"So," Alek said, coming to his senses, "I understand the urgency. If we can figure out how to build the LENR trigger, we can use it for both energy creation and weapons applications. Based on what happened to the Ramos brothers, we know it has been built—we just have to recreate their work."

"Okay, what are we waiting for?" asked Percy excitedly. "Let's buckle down and figure this out."

Chapter 6
In Search of Answers

AS THE SUMMER HUMIDITY WRAPPED the nation's capital in its suffocating grip and area residents retreated on vacation, the members of the Percy Study remained trapped in the conference room in the Pentagon basement.

Every morning they met to share their plans for the day and every evening they reconvened to share their frustrations. At the end of one long day, as the team gathered to discuss their latest findings, Dale Croft showed up, saying he was there to "check on their progress." He barged into the conference room just as Tom Lowe was in the middle of describing one possible design.

Lowe wasn't eager to entertain the President's science adviser, but knowing Croft would report back to his boss, he continued their discussion, hoping to baffle their visitor with high-tech terms. "We know that if an electrified, lithium-doped, palladium wire is surrounded by a cloud of charged deuterium, it will make tritium and then start a fusion reaction, but I can't find any trigger mechanism that will consistently create an energy-producing reaction."

"What about super-heated nickel and hydrogen?" asked Alek.

"No, the numerical results of rates of nuclear reactions are off," Digali said with a sigh. "We looked at using a deuterium-tritium neutron generator to produce an alpha particle, but the energy transfer is way off."

"What do you think?" Alek asked Sunli. She glanced up from her laptop.

"Oh, I'm not sure. We know an LENR using a small shot glass filled with the readily available materials could produce as much energy as a ton of TNT, but we still don't know how they triggered it. Also, there was the intense pulse you experienced when the Ramos brothers' house blew up."

Croft sniffed. "I still say it could have been a gas leak."

"No," said Digali with a condescending tone that suggested the 'science adviser' needed a stronger background in science. "The explosion in New Mexico was definitely an EMP—an electromagnetic pulse. EMPs are rapid, invisible bursts of electromagnetic energy caused by gamma rays slamming into the upper atmosphere following a nuclear explosion. EMPs can disrupt or destroy nearby electronics."

Croft looked annoyed at being talked down to and was about to say something when Percy stood up and started pacing around the windowless basement room. "Here's what we know," he said. "Somehow the Ramos brothers triggered a powerful LENR. That means the goal we've been working toward can be—and has been—achieved. The problem is, we don't know how they sparked the reaction, but we do know they had the materials and equipment to create it. Did they get lucky, or did they figure something out?"

"It sounds like you haven't figured out a damn thing," Croft scoffed, trying to regain some measure of power.

The lab director exhaled a deep sigh of exasperation. "No, Croft, we've figured out quite a bit. Instead of being completely in the dark on the LENR process we only have to answer three questions. Where did they get the materials and equipment to build their device? How could they afford them? And finally, how do we replicate their results?"

"Yet you don't seem to be any closer to answering those questions. I'm sure President Thornton will be happy to hear how little progress you have made." Croft stood up and hastily headed out of the conference room, narrowly avoiding slamming into Gabi as she entered the room.

Gabi watched Croft stalk away then turned to face her colleagues. "Well, I may have the answer to two of those questions," she said.

* * *

Alek made an executive decision that they needed a change of scenery before they heard what Gabi had discovered. You could only spend so much time in a windowless basement conference room. So, a half hour later they had relocated to McNamara's Bar, a dark, crowded dive minutes from the Pentagon. They grabbed a booth in the back where no one was likely to hear them and ordered a round of Guinness Dark. Digali tried to squeeze in next to Sunli, but she excused herself to use the restroom and sat on the opposite side of the table when she returned.

When everyone was settled, Gabi looked around. "You guys comfortable having this conversation here? I'm not really accustomed to conducting briefings over drinks."

Percy laughed. "We do some of our best work over a beer or two," he said. "Some people say Los Alamos is a drinking town with a science problem."

"Okay," Gabi replied with a smile. "I need to explain what the FBI team has learned about the Ramos brothers' connections in Mexico." She lowered her voice and leaned forward as if that could defeat any electronic listening device. "We uncovered a paper trail that leads from Will and Joe straight to the Cincoleta Cartel, one of the most powerful drug trafficking organizations in Mexico."

"What would a drug cartel have to do with this?" Percy asked. "It makes no sense. Drug lords aren't interested in nuclear energy."

"No, but they might be interested in nuclear weapons," Alek said.

Gabi nodded. "It seems the cartel was paying the Ramos brothers to conduct their extracurricular research and providing them with the funds they needed to buy equipment and materials. Surveillance shows Will Ramos met with the cartel kingpin several times during the past six months. This guy is known as El Verdugo, The Executioner. He has a fierce reputation for violence."

"Isn't the Cincoleta Cartel one of the main suppliers of illegal drugs to the U.S.?" Lowe asked.

"Yes," Gabi said. "The Cincoleta dominates northwest Mexico and has grown more powerful over the past few years. It is one of the most aggressive cartels and has been known to attack security forces and public officials. This group has downed a Mexican army helicopter with a rocket-propelled grenade, killed dozens of state officials, and has been known to hang the bodies of its victims from bridges to intimidate its rivals. It seems to me that El Verdugo would be happy to add a nuclear weapon to his arsenal of tools."

Percy mopped his forehead with a napkin and turned his gaze to Sunli. "Didn't you grow up in Mexico? You studied with that well-known Mexican physicist at Monterrey Tech?"

Sunli began peeling the label off her beer bottle. She seemed visibly nervous. "Yes, I was a double chemical engineering and mathematics student. My principal professor was Roberto Rodriguez."

"I remember him," Lowe interrupted. "He was the runner-up to Mario Molina who shared the Nobel Prize for chemistry in 1995. Rodriguez is one of the world leaders in LENR theory. In fact, he's the only theorist who has discussed combining modeling of low energy chemical reactions with high current electron interactions.

"Honestly, Dr. Rodriguez's theories never made sense to me," said Sunli evasively. "I've lost touch with pretty much everyone I used to know in Mexico since my father passed away and I moved to the U.S. I haven't talked to Dr. Rodriguez in years." Sunli shifted in her seat awkwardly.

Alek wondered if sharing personal information was making her uncomfortable. She certainly didn't act like she wanted to talk about her former life.

"Nevertheless," said Percy, "Rodriguez could have some valuable insight for us on the LENR process. We really need to try to talk to him. Sunli, maybe your connection can get us an appointment?"

Sunli shrugged. Clearly, she wasn't enjoying the direction the conversation was taking. "I guess. I'll try to get in touch with him," she said. "Just because I grew up in Mexico, doesn't mean I know anything about cartels," she added. "That's a rather racist assumption to make."

Ignoring Sunli's comment, Percy focused his attention back on Gabi. "So, you honestly think this cartel kingpin had something to do with the Ramos brothers?

"That's what our surveillance suggests," answered Gabi. "We have records of encrypted correspondence between El Verdugo and Will Ramos. My team is working on trying to decipher the conversations. So far all we know is that the Ramoses were talking to the cartel and money changed hands."

Gabi leaned forward. "There's one more thing... a strange thing. The FBI received an anonymous call today. The caller just said, 'Tell them to stay away from Rodriguez and out of Mexico.'"

"That's ridiculous," exclaimed Percy. "Between Dr. Rodriguez and the cartel connection, it looks like it's time for a little road trip. We're going to Mexico."

After another round, the team members made plans to reconvene in the conference room in the morning and make arrangements to travel to Mexico. Alek and Gabi found themselves sitting together at the table in the bar, the last remaining members of the group.

"Did Sunli seem to be acting strange tonight?" Gabi asked, tucking a stray strand of hair behind her ear. Alek still couldn't reconcile Gabi's many different looks. There was Gabi the FBI agent and Gabi the waitress. Today, instead of the short skirt and red lipstick or the professional pantsuit and slicked back hair, Gabi wore glasses and no makeup and was dressed in cargo pants, a T-shirt, and Doc Martens. She seemed like an entirely different woman—again.

"Sunli? Umm... maybe. I don't think she likes talking about herself very much. I don't know."

Gabi smiled. "Oh, Alek, you're blushing. You're sweet on her. Of course, that's it. The beautiful and brilliant physicist with the air of mystery and the long dark hair. How did I miss that?"

"No, that's not it," Alek lied rather unconvincingly. "I just really respect her. I think she's shy."

"I'm not so sure," replied Gabi, twisting her napkin. "There's something strange about that woman. It seems like she's hiding something. I don't trust her. How much has she contributed to the project so far?"

"Not much," Alek found himself forced to admit. "She's been really quiet. Spends most of her time listening and taking notes. She did seem interested in Digali's research on the plasma focus invention, but that's where her interest in him ended and where his interest in her began."

"Yeah, he definitely has the hots for Sunli," Gabi agreed. "And it's clear it will never be reciprocated. Did you see how she moved when he tried to sit next to her tonight?"

"Digali's not one to pick up on that sort of signal," said Alek. "You'd better watch out. When he gives up on Sunli, he may move on to you."

"I doubt I'm his type," Gabi laughed. "And I'm not looking to hook up with anyone right now."

"I feel that," said Alek. "It's been almost a year since my divorce was finalized, and I'm enjoying being alone and concentrating on my work."

"Sure you are." Gabi raised an eyebrow. "Unless pretty little Sunli changes her mind."

"I'm not interested in Sunli." Alek was getting annoyed.

"Relax," said Gabi. "I was joking. I heard your nickname is Smart Alek. I thought that might mean you'd have a decent sense of humor."

Alek laughed awkwardly, pushing up his glasses as they slipped down on his nose. He couldn't remember the last time he'd had a casual conversation with a woman.

"How about you?" he asked, trying to change the subject. "Are you leaving anyone at home when you run off to D.C. and Mexico for work?"

"Just my pit bull mix. His name is Max," said Gabi.

"Max? Not Maxwell? So, he's a casual dog?"

"Yeah, Max. He's the only guy for me."

Gabi launched into a description of her dog and Alek relaxed, enjoying the opportunity to have a pleasant conversation about something other than work. He couldn't quite figure Gabi out. At first, when he had met her working as a waitress in the Friggin Bar, he thought she lacked both class and brains. Then in Percy's basement, she was all business, tough and unexpressive. Tonight, she was... different. The sharp edges were missing, but so were the frills.

They chatted about pets and childhood and college, pretty much everything except work. Alek was enjoying the conversation in spite of himself, even though he occasionally remembered that, after the accident, he had no right to be happy. Nevertheless, he found Gabi easy to talk to. He couldn't remember the last time he had connected with someone like this.

Suddenly, Alek noticed how late it was getting. Although he wanted to keep chatting, it was time to call it a night.

"Okay then, I'll see you in the morning," said Alek. For the first time in what felt like years, he had a reason other than his research to look forward to the next day.

Chapter 7
Off to Mexico

AS IT TURNED OUT, GETTING an appointment to meet with Dr. Rodriguez required more than one phone call. Percy informed Alek that the team needed to avoid any actions that could possibly offend Mexican authorities. Professor Rodriguez was highly esteemed in Mexico and bypassing proper protocol could lead to backlash. The State Department liked to stay abreast of international science issues and encouraged the team to call the U.S. ambassador to Mexico first. From there they were told to contact the governor of the state of Nuevo Leon, Enrique Cardoza.

Alek arranged a Zoom call with Cardoza, who joined by video from his office. Alek noticed the bronze statue of Don Quixote displayed in the bookshelf behind his desk.

"Ah, I see you are admiring the statue," Cardoza, an overweight, balding man in his sixties, said in heavily accented English. "I consider myself *un estudiante de* Cervantes and I sponsor an annual statewide high school essay writing contest based on Don Quixote. The annual prize is a statue produced by a local artist." He gestured to the bronze figurine behind him.

"Sounds like you are very supportive of education," Alek said, wondering when they could dispense with the awkward small talk and get to the issue of Rodriguez.

"Yes," Cardoza replied, leaning forward. "The future of Mexico will depend on the quality of its educational system and that's why we consider Professor Rodriguez and his colleagues at *la universidad* so important. The professor is a national treasure, and we must guard him against harassment from the cartels."

"Cartels? The cartels are a danger to a physicist?" asked Alek.

"Ah, yes. Dr. Rodriguez was recently approached by the leader of a powerful cartel from Guadalajara. The professor sought my help to end the harassment. Apparently, it had to do with a technical issue. So, before I give my approval to this meeting between your team and the professor, I need to know for certain that you have no connection to the cartel."

Alek was surprised Cardoza would suggest this. "No, of course not. We are American physicists seeking guidance about scientific matters."

"*Muy bien*," Cardoza replied. "In that case, I will be happy to give you Professor Rodriguez's phone number. But be careful when you are here. While it's unusual for cartel representatives to approach foreign travelers, there have been some recent problems, particularly for scientists. Naturally though, the police have everything under control."

The entire situation was making Alek feel uncomfortable. Cardoza looked extremely serious and almost worried. Would going to talk to Dr. Rodriguez put team members in danger? It hardly seemed likely, but the Mexican official seemed oddly concerned.

They wrapped up the conversation with typical pleasantries, but Cardoza had the final word with an ominous warning. "*Señor* Spray, I hope you enjoy your upcoming visit to Mexico. Be very careful who you trust."

* * *

Percy needed to return to Los Alamos to check on some things at the lab. Lowe, Candale, and Digali felt they were nearing a breakthrough on the trigger, so Alek and Sunli were given the task of going to Mexico. Gabi decided to join them to touch base with her FBI colleagues working in Mexico.

Alek had called the professor, making it clear that in exchange for his help with the LENR project, they might be able to arrange for some much-needed research funding from Los Alamos. Rodriguez seemed pleased at the thought of seeing his former student and the possibility of financial support, but he said he would only speak to them in person and encouraged them to come as soon as they could.

The three flew from Dulles International Airport to Monterrey on Aeromexico. Alek had hoped the flight might give him a chance to spend more time getting to know Gabi, but, citing an important deadline, she pulled out a laptop and buried herself in her work.

Sunli had arrived at the gate just before boarding time and seemed distracted. During the flight, Alek tried to get her to reveal more about the research she had done with Rodriguez as a student. Professor Rodriguez was one of the leading experts in LENR theory and Sunli had been his research assistant for several years, but she continued to claim not to know much about his work.

"I saw Dr. Rodriguez present at a conference a few years ago about how he had discovered that the repulsive forces preventing the collision and reaction of low energy particles could be overcome using the collective field of a very highly focused electron beam. The barrier to the reaction could be overcome when the material is transformed into an incredibly energetic nuclear reaction by the super pinched electron beam. Isn't that right?" Alek asked.

"Hmm, maybe. I don't entirely recall Rodriguez's work," Sunli replied dismissively, glancing at the clouds outside the plane's window.

"Really?" Alek suspected his colleague was concealing the extent of her knowledge. Dr. Sunli Hidalgo was one of the most competitive people he had ever worked with, so he wouldn't put it past her to hide her findings in order to triumph over her coworkers with a breakthrough that saved the day. Alek felt certain that Sunli's ability to develop theoretical models and provide new ideas would be the key to the Percy Study team's success in building the trigger, but so far, she hadn't been much of a team player. He hoped he could win her over and forge a better working relationship during this trip. Sunli closed her eyes and Alek decided to drop the conversation about Rodriguez, at least for now.

They landed at Monterrey International Airport without incident, although Alek had an odd feeling that someone was watching them as they walked through the airport. After collecting his suitcase from the luggage carousel, he turned quickly and saw a man in a dark suit and sunglasses walking away.

The three checked into the Holiday Inn at *Parque Fundidora*, which was closer to the university. Sunli and Alek were scheduled to meet with Professor Rodriguez the next morning. Claiming a headache, Sunli announced she wanted to lie down before dinner. Gabi turned to Alek. "How 'bout we grab a cup of coffee? I know a coffee shop in the area called the *Barrio Antiguo*, or Spanish Old Quarter."

Alek smiled. "Let's go."

They took a taxi and in 10 minutes the two were sipping their lattes at the *Tierra Libre* coffee shop. They sat at a quiet outdoor table with a good view of the cobblestone streets and 19th century buildings contrasting with modern bistros and boutiques.

"You know, it doesn't seem dangerous here," said Alek. "Everyone acts so terrified of the cartel activity in Mexico, but this is a charming area."

"It was a hot spot for nightlife for many years," said Gabi. "But the violence and the drug traffic closed down many of the clubs and bars. In 2013, the government started a restoration project to preserve the historic heritage and create a space for cultural recreation. Even so, organized crime is always an issue in Mexico. Between the corrupt government officials and the criminal groups,

I'd never come here unarmed."

Alek gulped nervously. "You have a gun?"

"Of course I have a gun. Don't be so naïve. I'm an FBI agent," laughed Gabi.

"When I met you, you were a waitress," said Alek.

"I was never much of a waitress."

"That's true." Alek marveled at the woman beside him. She seemed like an average businesswoman in her mid-thirties, but somehow, she was secretly a badass.

"Well, I feel much safer now," said Alek.

The pair left a tip on the table and strolled down the street along the banks of the Santa Lucia Canal. The clear skies and gorgeous 70-degree weather seemed out of touch with the anxiousness Alek felt. He struggled not to think about the many questions swirling through his brain.

"Honestly, I don't think I know the first thing about protecting myself. I've never even held a gun."

"I'll take you to the shooting range sometime and teach you," she said. "If you're going to get involved in this kind of intrigue with crazy scientists and drug cartels, you're going to have to learn a little about self-defense."

"I've always been, well, basically, a pacifist," said Alek. "I just don't believe in any kind of violence."

"Yet, you're involved with building a key component for a nuclear weapon?" Gabi asked arching an eyebrow. "It doesn't quite fit."

"The LENR has weapons applications, but it also could prove to be an unprecedented source of cheap, clean energy. I call it Project Z." Now Alek was talking about his favorite subject. "Imagine how having an endless energy source, with no pollution, no danger, no high costs... imagine how that could transform the world."

"This science stuff really turns you on, huh," said Gabi.

"I mean, think about it," Alek replied, his eyes shining. "Physics touches every aspect of our lives. Scientific advancements have given so much to mankind, and we can do so much more. An affordable energy source could bring power to slums and could break down so much inequity in the world. I guess you could say science is my religion." He shrugged.

Alek reflected on how his devotion to his research had only increased since the accident. Somehow, he felt that if he could make a significant scientific breakthrough, he could redeem himself from his past mistakes. Not that he was about to share any of these thoughts with Gabi. It was best not to think about the past. Instead, he focused on enjoying the company of his beautiful companion as they strolled down the quaint cobblestone streets. Unfortunately, the moment was brief.

"We should head back to the hotel. I'm meeting some of my FBI colleagues for dinner," said Gabi. "Then tomorrow morning, we're meeting with the Mexican authorities to compare notes. I'll catch up with you and Sunli tomorrow after your appointment with the professor. Hope you guys find out something that will put us on the right path."

Alek was glad to see Sunli in the hotel lobby looking better after her rest. He asked her to recommend a restaurant for dinner. Soon they were headed to Sunli's favorite spot in Monterrey: *La Quintonilla*.

"Order the specialties," said Alek. "I want to try the real stuff."

In rapid Spanish, Sunli ordered *escamoles* and *chapulines* as appetizers, followed by *cabrito con mole* as the main dish.

"It sounds delicious," said Alek, not knowing that Sunli had just ordered ant larvae and grasshoppers with an entrée of baby goat in chocolate chili sauce.

Over the meal—which Alek actually did find to be delicious—he tried to get Sunli to open up a little. "So, are you originally from this area?" he asked.

"I grew up in a small town near here," Sunli admitted. "My family was well-off in comparison with our neighbors because my father owned the local pharmacy. He groomed my much younger brother to take over the business and I was expected to marry. Unfortunately, I let my father down by choosing to go to pursue my education instead of marrying and raising kids."

"Let him down?" scoffed Alek. "You are a successful physicist working on projects of national importance. How can that be considered letting him down?"

"My father was a Mexican man, with all of the typical machismo. He and my mother met in college, and she gave up her career and her homeland to marry and live with him in Nuevo Leon."

"So, when did she return to China?" Alek asked.

"She went home to Beijing when my father passed away. There was nothing to keep her here. My brother and I lost touch. I believe he still runs *la farmacia*," Sunli said sadly. "As for me, I successfully escaped through academics. I did well in school and all of my teachers said I would be the first Mexican woman to win the Nobel Prize. When I received a fellowship to study with Dr. Rodriguez at Monterrey Tech, I was ecstatic. I knew that science was my ticket to a new life."

Sunli pushed her food around on her plate, lacking Alek's enthusiastic appetite. Talking about the past seemed to be upsetting her, so Alek tried to change the topic to Professor Rodriguez.

"So, you did work on Low Energy Nuclear Reactions when you studied with Dr. Rodriguez?" he asked, pushing his empty plate back and downing the last of his margarita.

"We never actually discussed LENR or any kind of fusion research," replied Sunli. "I was working on chemistry-related projects in his lab."

"Did he ever talk about his theories?"

"No, he really didn't," Sunli replied, twisting a strand of silky black hair around her finger. "I once asked him... no... no... he didn't," she said evasively. "We should get going. We have an early start tomorrow."

Sunli excused herself to use the restroom and Alek paid the bill, pondering her strange behavior. It still seemed like she was hiding something, or perhaps there was something she wanted to share but just couldn't bring herself to talk about it. In any case, she remained secretive and complicated. Alek had to admit to himself that the aura of tragic mystery made Sunli even more appealing. Not that she appeared even slightly interested in him. Why would she be? She was beautiful, intelligent, and composed, and he was just another nerdy Los Alamos physicist. Frustrated, Alek stayed silent during the drive back to the hotel, and Sunli had nothing to say until they made plans to meet for breakfast the next morning and said their goodnights.

Chapter 9
Absence Makes the Heart Grow Fonder

WHEN ALEK'S ALARM SOUNDED ON his iPhone, it took him a moment to remember he was in Mexico. Light streamed through the hotel curtains, suggesting a beautiful day for sightseeing, but they weren't there on vacation and wouldn't have time for being tourists. He sighed, rolled over, and turned off the alarm. Work first.

A half hour later, despite the smell of rich coffee wafting through the hotel dining room, Alek still felt groggy. He and Sunli had planned to meet for breakfast before heading to the university. Gabi wasn't going to join them until later that afternoon.

Sunli should have been down by now, but instead, he sat sipping his coffee and orange juice alone, watching a family with three young boys dominate the waffle maker. So far, they hadn't made any waffles, but they were making a huge mess.

He sent Sunli a text, then another.

"Where are you?" There was no answer.

"Skipping breakfast?" No reply.

"Remember we have to be at the professor's office by nine." Silence.

"Did you oversleep?" Ditto.

He called her cellphone, then her room, but got no answer. Finally, giving up in frustration, he took the elevator to her room and knocked on the door. Nothing. He knocked again.

"Sunli? Uh... Sunli, it's Alek. It's time to go." He waited a few minutes and knocked one more time. "Sunli, I'm getting worried."

Still no answer. Feeling rising panic in his chest, Alek ran down the hotel stairs to the lobby and stood in front of the desk clerk. "My colleague isn't answering her phone and she didn't respond when I knocked on the door. *Mi colega no respondió cuando... I... uh...* could you help me check on her? *¿Podrias ayudarme?*"

Alek and the clerk rode the elevator back to the third floor, where they knocked on Sunli's door again. When there was still no answer, the desk clerk used his master key to open the door. No one was there. The bed was neatly made and none of Sunli's belongings were visible. No suitcase, no clothing, nothing to indicate she had ever been in the room.

"*No está aquí, señor,*" said the clerk, shaking his head at having been bothered.

"I can see she's not here," replied Alek. He was already late for the meeting with the professor. He couldn't keep looking for Sunli. He had to go. Alek punched Gabi's number into his phone and then realized he didn't have a signal. He'd call her after the meeting.

Alek grabbed a cab to the professor's office at the university. Dr. Roberto Rodriguez was a small man with gray hair, a heavy accent, and lots of nervous energy. He also seemed concerned about Sunli's absence.

"*No estó bien.* This is not good, not good at all," the professor said, pacing back and forth in his cluttered office. Stepping over a pile of books and papers, he returned to his desk to look at his cellphone. "She said she would be here. Where would she go? I hope... I hope everything is okay."

"Me too," said Alek. "But since I'm here, could we take a little time to discuss your research? I'm familiar with the work you have done with LENR."

Rodriguez rose and scrambled across the books to pull his office door closed. "Did you notice if anyone followed you here this morning?" he asked in a hushed tone.

"I have to be careful. The cartel has certain interests in my work."

"The cartel? The governor mentioned that, but why would they be interested in energy research? Certainly I realize the cartels are an ever-present issue in Mexico, but don't they focus on illegal drugs?"

"LENR has multiple applications," explained Rodriguez. "As you know. The cartel sent a... uh representative to inquire about some of the uh... more lethal uses of the technology."

"The cartel? That's..." Alek couldn't come up with the right word. *Did the professor have information about the cartel connection? It seemed more like something out of a movie than real life*, thought Alek. He decided to skip to the point.

"Despite all that we know about LENR technology, the problem is we haven't found a way to create a reliable trigger for the LENR reaction. This stands in the way of using the technology to create a new source of energy. It also keeps us from pursuing the weapons applications you alluded to."

"Yes, I have been working on this matter and I've developed some theories, but it's going to require funding to test them. Perhaps we could collaborate?"

Rodriguez looked eager, no doubt inspired by the thought of American money funding his research. "With the help of Los Alamos National Laboratory, I could conduct the necessary experiments. It is a complex and expensive process, but think of the end goal—a clean, unlimited, inexpensive source of energy for the entire world." Rodriguez leaned forward and spoke barely above a whisper. "This technology could be revolutionary—just imagine the implications. But be careful. Too much of a good thing is not necessarily good."

Alek wasn't sure what to make of the professor's ominous tone and strange behavior. "So, could you join us in D.C. next week if we arrange to push through some grants for both you and the university?" Alek knew that the promise of funding was an irresistible lure for most professors. In fact, seeking funds might as well be part of most academic job descriptions.

Rodriguez seemed to be cautious but excited. "Yes, that will be good, and I will get to see Sunli in D.C. I look forward to working with her again. She was always one of my most impressive students," he added in a slightly suggestive way that Alek found disturbing. "Make sure you find Sunli," said the professor. "There must be a good reason she didn't join us this morning, but I look forward to reuniting with her. *Hasta la vista, mi amigo.*"

Alek and Rodriguez shook hands and agreed to get in touch later that day to finalize their plans. Alek felt pleased to have added such a knowledgeable LENR researcher to the team.

Now, he had to figure out where Sunli had gone.

* * *

The first call Alek made was to Gabi. She picked up immediately.

"I've been trying to contact you," Gabi said breathlessly.

"Sorry, I had my ringer off while I was meeting with Rodriguez. I've got to talk to you about something important," Alek said.

"Me too," she replied.

Alek quickly caught Gabi up on what had happened that morning.

"You mean she was just... gone?" Gabi asked.

"Like she'd never even been there," Alek replied. "The bed was unslept in. None of her things were in the room. It's as if she has completely vanished."

"Yeah, that's going around lately," said Gabi. "First Will and Joe Ramos and now Sunli. Who's next?"

"I've tried again to reach her on her phone, but it just rings and rings. The voicemail isn't even working now. Anyhow, you said you had news too. What did you find out?"

"Well, have you heard of the *Policia Federal Ministerial* or Federal Ministerial Police? It's basically the Mexican FBI. They go by PFM."

"What about them?"

"We've been following up on the drug connection, so my team contacted the PFM and the DEA to check on any suspicious cartel activity near Monterrey. PFM officials have been watching a building in the hills nearby that has had frequent Asian visitors and they suspect Dr. Rodriguez has also been there. I have an appointment at 1 p.m. to review the surveillance video recordings of the facility. Want to come?"

"Of course," replied Alek. "There doesn't seem to be anything else I can do, and our flight doesn't leave until tomorrow. Maybe they know something that will help us find Sunli. I don't even know if she has friends or family here in town. She mentioned a brother but said they had lost touch, and her mother is in China now."

"She may be a brilliant scientist, but there's something awfully guarded about her," said Gabi. "I just don't know about her. I'll meet you back at the hotel and then we can head over to the PFM headquarters. Pray to your gods of science we learn something that helps us find Sunli or the Ramos brothers or the secret to that trigger... or all of the above."

Chapter 9
Into the Woods

THE POLICIA FEDERAL MINISTERIAL HEADQUAR- TERS were located on a narrow street in a nondescript building that only stood out because of the officer armed with an assault rifle standing at the door. Gabi handed her credentials to the officer and they waited until the lead PFM investigator came lumbering around the corner and introduced himself as Chief Marquez. He smiled broadly and shook hands with each of them enthusiastically. Alek wondered about the rumors of corrupt and uncooperative Mexican police officers. Marquez seemed eager to help as he maneuvered his considerable bulk down the hall to escort Gabi and Alek into a small, dark room to view the surveillance videos. Alek noticed that Marquez and his fellow officers all wore guns openly displayed in their holsters. Alek felt as though he had arrived at a party underdressed.

Marquez squeezed into a chair in front of a battered desk holding a computer and cued up the video recordings they were there to see. The monitor displayed a grainy black and white image of a large warehouse-like facility surrounded by barbed wire. The building appeared to be deep in the forest.

"*¿Dónde está ese lugar? ¿Cómo llegaste allí?*" Gabi asked Marquez.

Alek knew enough Spanish to know that Gabi was asking where the building was located and how they could get there.

"*Son veinte...*" Marquez stopped himself. "I'm sorry. I forget that not everyone speaks Spanish. It's 20 miles from here through thick vegetation. We set up our video equipment on a cliff across from the building where no one could see our post."

"Wait," said Alek, staring at the screen. "I think that's Dr. Rodriguez. Can you rewind it?"

The officer rewound the video and replayed the segment that had caught Alek's attention. It appeared to show several heavily armed men escorting Roberto Rodriguez into the building. In the video, the small, wiry scientist stumbled, and one of the men escorting him grabbed him roughly by the arm.

"That's definitely the professor," said Alek. "I can't tell if he is going with them voluntarily or if he's being forced."

The officer fast forwarded the video a few minutes. "*Mira...* look," he said. "Some of the men coming in and out of the building look like they are Asian."

Gabi peered at the screen. "What's going on here? What are these people doing in a warehouse in the woods?"

"*Mas probable* it's drugs," Marquez said. "A facility like that in such a remote location with barbed wire and armed guards—it must be the cartel."

"Could the Chinese government be working with the cartel?" Gabi asked.

"*Es posible,*" Marquez replied. "If not the government, it could be a rogue group. I've heard rumors that the Chinese are shipping the chemicals used to make fentanyl into Mexico for production. It's a powerful synthetic opiate, 100 times more powerful than morphine and a very profitable venture for the cartel." He stopped the recording. "See that man? The one with the armed bodyguards? That's *El Verdugo*, The Executioner. He is the leader of the Cincoleta Cartel—a powerful man. If he is there, this facility clearly has something to do with illegal drugs."

"Stop the video. Rewind it," shouted Alek. "There! Hit the pause button. Do you see that?" Frozen on the left side of the screen were two men walking into the facility: Will and Joe Ramos.

* * *

From there, things started moving quickly. Gabi assembled her FBI team, and a contingent from the DEA arrived. Marquez and his federal ministerial police officers rounded out the group. "We always work closely with the American government to address cartel activity," Marquez assured Gabi and Alek unconvincingly. Alek glanced at Gabi and raised an eyebrow. She shrugged.

As the various law enforcement personnel arrived, boots were laced, weapons strapped on, and bullet-proof vests buckled. Then Gabi realized Alek was still there.

"Uh, do you want to go back to the hotel? This might get kinda crazy."

Alek shook his head. "Honestly, I'd really like to see what's going on. If they've been conducting experiments at this facility... I need to see it. If they're working on LENR technology, I'm the only one here who can identify that."

"It's your call. Just stay out of the way." Gabi threw a bullet-proof vest to Alek, saying, "Here, put this on."

"I don't really think..." Alek stammered.

"Don't think. Just put it on. Put this on too." She handed him a pistol and a holster.

"I don't actually know..."

Gabi grabbed the weapon and held it up. "This is a Glock 17." She removed the magazine, "It normally holds 17 bullets, thus the name, but this one," she showed Alek it didn't contain any cartridges, "is empty." She pulled the slide back so he could see the chamber was empty as well. She closed the slide and inserted the magazine and handed the Glock to Alek. "Humor me. I'd just feel better if you didn't look like the only one of us walking in there unarmed. It's all about perception and deterrence. Working at Los Alamos, you should understand that concept."

The team loaded into several jeeps that had pulled up

in front of the building. Alek noticed that Gabi was the only woman in the group. Soon they hit the outskirts of town and the highway gave way to dirt roads. Conversation was difficult over the road noise.

"What are we going to do when we get there?" shouted Alek.

"*¿Qué?*" shouted Marquez.

"When we get to the facility... what are we going to do?" Alek repeated.

"We have to take them by surprise," bellowed Marquez as they jostled over the rough, dirt road. "We are staging at the cliff to launch the raid of the facility. The cartel will not be prepared if we arrive from that side."

"But how will we get there if there's a cliff?" shouted Alek.

"What?" shouted Gabi.

"How are we going to get there?" he repeated.

"By zip line," Marquez said. "There's an old zip line stretching across the canyon behind the warehouse. We think the cartel may have used it for deliveries. It doesn't look like it has been used in a while though, so we don't think the guards are monitoring that area. Before they realize we are coming, we'll be in the facility and will have them disarmed."

Alek decided now wasn't the right time to mention his fear of heights. He could do this. After all, the Ramos brothers were in that warehouse and with them, possibly, the secret of the LENR trigger. Gabi was right, now was a good time to pray to the gods of science. He felt he was finally closing in on the goal.

The rest of the drive went by in teeth-chattering silence. Gabi, Alek, Marquez, and four jeeps filled with armed men were all alone with their thoughts.

Finally, after winding through heavy forest for what seemed like hours, they arrived at the edge of a steep drop off in front of a canyon. Crossing the rocky chasm carved into the forest on foot would have taken hours, perhaps even days, but the zip line spanning the canyon would whisk them across in minutes. On the other side of the canyon, Alek could see a large warehouse surrounded by a high, barbed-wire fence. Alek glanced at the stainless-steel cable that would transport them over the canyon and deposit them at the warehouse's back door. Alek looked over the edge and wondered what it would feel like to fall from the zip line onto the jagged rocks on the canyon floor. Was it too late to change his mind?

Alek put off the zip line as long as possible. Finally, he and Gabi were the only ones left with two *Policía Federal Ministerial* officers who would remain behind to operate the rigging. Alek buckled on his helmet and strapped himself into the harness. Gabi and the officers finished lashing him in. Alek heard the cicadas chirping in the clear mountain air. He could feel the sweat dripping beneath the heavy bullet-proof vest. He wondered again if it were possible to change his mind and catch up with the team after the raid was finished. Maybe if he just told Gabi how he felt...

"Don't be nervous," said Gabi. "Remember, it's for science." She gave him a kiss on the cheek and then, with no warning, pushed him over the edge.

Alek felt his stomach drop and then he was rocketing along the line, treetops zooming past beneath him. The wind whipped through his hair... and he was gliding like a bird. Alek wondered why he had been so frightened. The rush of adrenaline was so exhilarating, the view was incredible, and he didn't want the ride to end. Far too soon, he felt the automatic braking engage on the trolley supporting him and he saw the ground approaching. The intense rush, the feeling of his heart pounding, the sense of freedom... Alek suddenly wondered why he didn't take more chances. As he set his feet on the ground and unbuckled with the help of the waiting officer, Alek decided that this was a sign he should take more risks, should do more to challenge himself, should stop playing life so safely. He looked back up to the cliff and saw Gabi gliding down toward him, her blonde hair flying in the breeze. He reached out and steadied her as she landed and then, impetuously, gave her a kiss on the mouth.

That's when the shooting started.

Chapter 10
Time to Take a Risk

AS THE UNMISTAKABLE RATTLE OF automatic gunfire shattered the stillness of the forest, Gabi quickly unbuckled her harness and slammed Alek to the ground.

"Get down and stay down," she shouted, drawing her Glock, dropping to a crouch, then sprinting toward the building.

Alek lay on the ground where Gabi had pushed him. His face was pressed against the dark, rocky soil. He heard a burst of gunfire and then people shouting. Unintelligible men's voices screaming in Spanish and Chinese. More gunfire.

Perhaps now wasn't the best time to start taking more risks.

The air filled with the crackling of weapons once again, and then a voice shouted in English, "Take cover!" A loud pop, a blast of air, some orange plumes of flame, and then silence.

Alek waited a moment. The shooting appeared to be over. Alek lifted his head from the ground. He slowly rose to his feet and brushed the dirt off. Alek could hear birds chirping, insects buzzing, and somewhere, far off in the forest, a squirrel chattering. He began creeping slowly toward the warehouse. Smoke hung in the air.

Just inside the door, an Asian man was lying on the ground in a pool of blood. He seemed to be trying to say something. Alek crept forward.

"I can't hear you," Alek said.

The man reached for something beneath him. Could it be a gun? Alek wasn't taking any chances. He drew his Glock and pointed it at the man on the warehouse floor, hoping he had his finger on the trigger correctly.

"Don't move or I'll shoot. I mean it," Alek shouted, trying to sound as if he knew what he was doing. "Keep your hands at your sides."

The man looked like he was in bad shape, but Alek didn't want to take chances. He hoped the man wouldn't notice how badly his hands were shaking or how tightly he was gripping the gun.

"Alek!" Gabi and Marquez rounded the corner, followed by several of the team members. Marquez grabbed a pair of handcuffs from his belt and secured the injured man's hands behind him. Alek was still holding the gun, his hands still trembling.

"It's okay. You can let go of the gun now," she said gently. "Everything is fine."

"What about the others?" asked Alek.

"All dead," Gabi replied. "There were only six of them, plus this guy. I thought he was dead."

"There's no sign of the Ramos brothers or El Verdugo," she added.

Marquez bent down and checked the injured man's pulse. "He's not here for long," said the officer. "I'll call for *una ambulancia, pero* I don't think he'll make it."

Marquez stepped down the hall to contact headquarters. The other PFM, FBI, and DEA officers swept into the large room.

"Gabi, we've found no signs they're manufacturing, storing, or transporting drugs here," said one of the American officers. "There are lab benches with beakers, some strange chemicals, electric cables, and high voltage equipment. I don't know what any of it is for."

"Don't touch it," shouted Alek. "They could be working on the LENR trigger." Alek hurried toward the main room of the warehouse, shouting over his shoulder, "I need to get the rest of my team down here to check it out."

Suddenly, he stopped and turned back to Gabi. "Do you think we should call Dr. Rodriguez? Is someone from the FBI or the PFM going to question him about his appearance on that video recording?"

"Oh," said Gabi. "No one told you. We sent an officer out to talk to the professor. Rodriguez was dead in his office. Apparently, he hung himself."

* * *

The rest of the Percy Study team, minus Percy himself and Sunli, who was still missing, arrived the next morning and loaded into jeeps with a handful of PFM and FBI officers to make the drive to the warehouse. This time they approached the facility from the other side, skipping the zip line and entering through the front door.

Alek was eager to show his colleagues what he had found in the warehouse the previous day. Digali and Lowe were giddy with excitement. Candale was quiet, staring at the bloodstains left behind on the concrete floor. After examining the equipment set up in the warehouse, Digali concluded that the key to the operation was the high voltage capacitors and switches. It seemed that the scientists at the warehouse had been using the capacitors to produce a spark discharge in a small, liquid-filled chamber.

"Look at this," Digali said, grabbing Candale by the arm. "I'm sure these capacitors and switches could have been used as an LENR trigger."

Candale pulled out his cellphone and did some circuit calculations. "This equipment would most likely produce a multimillion volt, very short pulse duration output," he said. "Clearly they were exploring the trigger mechanism for the LENR energy source to determine how fast and small the trigger could be."

Digali picked up a dusty box from a lab bench in the warehouse. "These are 100-gram slugs of nickel metal. They must have been using nickel as the target."

Alek grabbed one of the slugs and put it in his pocket. "Interesting. All the previous experiments have used copper targets. That's what Will and Joe were using too. Well, at least as far as I know."

"So, we know they were working on the LENR here," Digali said. "The next step will be to find any evidence they developed a trigger that actually worked," he mused.

Lowe was listening. "If they've been experimenting with the LENR trigger, there must be a test range nearby," Lowe said.

"The forest is too dense for drone surveillance," remarked Alek. "We need to do this on foot. Let's spread out and see if we can find any evidence of their testing."

The group broke into pairs, enlisting the help of the PFM and FBI officers who had joined them, and headed into the Monterrey hills. Gabi and Alek teamed up and hiked north from the warehouse. They soon fell into a companionable silence as they wove their way through the mountainous terrain.

Alek wondered if now were the time to bring up some of the things that had happened between the two of them yesterday... the zip line, the kiss, the... feelings. "About yesterday," he stammered.

"Don't worry about it," replied Gabi.

"Don't worry about it? What do you mean, 'don't worry about it?'" asked Alek.

"Lots of people are uncomfortable handling weapons. I can set you up with some lessons."

"Oh yeah... that would be good. The thing is... I uh meant..." Alek suddenly realized Gabi probably didn't even remember the kiss at the end of the zip line. The shooting had started almost immediately, and, with the adrenaline rush and the danger, her focus had been elsewhere. There was nothing to talk about, because in Gabi's mind, nothing had happened. Nothing except proving he had no idea what to do with a gun.

"I mean, absolutely. I need lessons, for sure."

Alek hung back, letting Gabi walk ahead of him. Sunlight flickered through the leaves overhead as Alek forged his way through the brush, losing sight of Gabi.

Suddenly, the forest sounds, the buzz of insects, and the chirp of birds fell silent. Alek froze. *Was that shadow behind the trees a person? Was someone following them?*

A shout from Gabi broke the silence. "Alek, come quick," she cried and then began rattling off coordinates over her radio. The suspicious shadow forgotten, Alek raced toward her voice, pushing branches out of the way in his hurry. As he burst out of the trees, he realized why Gabi had called out.

They were standing in a small clearing that was completely bare, as if everything had been vaporized down to the ground. The trees surrounding the area appeared burned and blackened on the side facing the clearing, but were still standing, otherwise untouched.

Alek gasped as Candale and Lowe came crashing through the bushes.

"It had to be a real LENR," Candale cried triumphantly.

Candale and Lowe began collecting soil samples to compare with the samples from the house in Altavaca. Digali paced around the clearing, muttering to himself. Gabi chatted with a fellow FBI officer, while the Federales carried on a spirited discussion in Spanish about where they thought El Verdugo might have gone. Alek continued to stare at the barren area.

"Hey guys," Alek shouted. "If this damage is really from an LENR, wouldn't there have been an accompanying electromagnetic pulse, like the way the blast at the Ramos brothers' house disrupted my car's ignition system?" Alek turned to Marquez. "Did you notice anything weird recently with electrical systems, like a pulse or a surge?"

"Oh yes," Marquez replied. "Just last week, as a matter of fact. It really messed up our computers."

"See!" Digali shouted triumphantly. "An LENR can produce an electromagnetic pulse that works on the ground and has the same effect on communications and computers as a high-altitude nuclear weapon explosion. Remember how North Korea was threatening to detonate a weapon like that over American cities to wipe out the electronic equipment controlling the energy grid?"

"Hang on a minute," Gabi interrupted. "I'm still trying to understand this technology. Is the LENR the same thing as cold fusion?"

"Just forget about cold fusion," Alek responded. "It is totally irrelevant for any reactions at room temperature. The best theory, which Professor Rodriguez developed, was based on the concept that the electrons in ordinary materials in normal low energy chemical reactions could be forced to collectively interact to combine strongly with positively charged protons to produce neutral particles. These neutrons could then, through nuclear reactions, create heat and other reaction products including huge bursts of electrons and ions."

Gabi nodded. "That makes sense, but why does the reaction generate an electromagnetic pulse?"

Alek smiled. He loved talking about his work. "It seems that the high currents of electrons and ions are the source of the electromagnetic pulse output. The key to this really strange process is the trigger to generate the initial collective electron interaction."

"And if you have that trigger, you have the ability to create a really powerful weapon?" asked Gabi.

"Powerful is an understatement," said Digali. "Imagine using a source of energy as powerful as LENR in space."

Candale interrupted, which was unusual since he rarely spoke at all. "With a source of energy as powerful as LENR, a combined ion and electron cloud could be simultaneously generated so that streams of clumps of energetic matter would be focused, self-contained, directed over great distances in space, and would not be deflected by the magnetic field of the earth. The energetic beam moving at close to the speed of light through the vacuum of outer space could literally destroy any object it targeted."

"Nothing could defeat it," Lowe chimed in. "No simple

counter measure like a shiny surface that could defeat a laser beam or a thick shield to block particles... nothing would work."

Digali's eyes shone as he thought about the possibilities of their discovery. "This could mean the production of a true space weapon is nearing reality or already being created," he said.

"Okay, stop the Star Wars geek out session for just a second," Gabi interrupted. "What you are saying is the people who detonated this... this thing... here in the forest... they are probably creating an invincible space weapon?"

"Yeah, that's pretty much it," Alek said.

"So, here's my concern," said Gabi. "Who has this amazing weapon?"

Digali, Lowe, and Candale all looked at each other, their minds racing.

"That's what I thought," said Gabi. "Who has the weapon? And why were Chinese citizens, cartel members, and missing Los Alamos scientists testing it in the middle of the forest?"

"On top of that," Alek interrupted, "where is Sunli and what does she have to do with this whole thing?"

Chapter 11
On the Move

WHERE IS SUNLI AND WHAT does she have to do with this whole thing? Sunli had wondered that herself a few times lately. Things certainly hadn't gone according to plan. The train went off the rails the minute she'd said goodnight to Alek in the hotel lobby in Monterrey after dinner. Sunli took the elevator to her floor, opened the door to her hotel room, and then everything fell apart.

Standing in her room were two large men armed with assault rifles. They appeared to be Mexican and were dressed all in black.

"*Vienes con nosotros,*" barked one of the men, grabbing her by the arm.

"You don't have to tell me to come with you if you're not giving me any choice in the matter," Sunli muttered to herself. "Who are you? What do you want from me?" she asked, first in English then in Spanish.

"*Te llevamos con el jefe,*" was the reply.

The men held Sunli roughly by the arms and hustled her out of the hotel where a jeep waited at the curb with an armed driver behind the wheel. They blindfolded her and shoved her into the jeep.

They drove a long time. The sound of city traffic faded, and the jeep wound around steep turns, bumping across rocky roads. Finally, they came to a stop. The men grabbed Sunli and dragged her out of the jeep. Her guides pushed her through a doorway and removed her blindfold. As her eyes adjusted to the dimly-lit room, Sunli came face to face with Will and Joe Ramos.

"What are you doing here?" Sunli gasped, looking around the warehouse. "What is this place? Are you manufacturing drugs here?" she asked.

Will laughed. "In a manner of speaking we are," he said. "We are manufacturing your drug... the LENR. We made it work."

Sunli's eyes lit up. She forgot about everything except the LENR. "You figured out the trigger? Tell me about it. Show me," she exclaimed.

"Well, we still have to refine it," Will replied. "We consulted with your professor, Dr. Rodriguez, but he was not very helpful. I think he knows more than he will say."

"We warned him," said Joe. "We told him not to cross the cartel, but he doesn't seem to want to listen. I certainly hope he isn't going to share the secrets of the LENR trigger with Alek Spray."

"This makes no sense," Sunli interrupted. "Who are you working for? What are you doing here? What happened at the house in Altavaca?"

"Ah, Altavaca. We made a bit of a miscalculation. Honestly, I expected a much smaller, explosion, something less likely to catch the authorities' attention. Still, it turned out to be an excellent way to destroy the evidence of our experiments, and it brought you to Mexico, which is certainly serendipitous." Will curled his lips back in a semblance of a smile. "The real work was going on here. As for who we are working for..."

"They call me El Verdugo, The Executioner," a man said, emerging from the darkness of the vast warehouse. Short, stocky, and heavily armed, the man radiated a sense of power. Sunli found herself oddly transfixed.

"The ultimate weapon," mused the cartel leader. "Think of the power it will give us."

Will stepped forward. "A stream of high velocity particles from a defensive weapon that can create an EMP and can be detonated from a compact trigger... think about the possibilities. It's something we've been seeking and something both the cartel and the Chinese People's Consortium want."

"The Chinese People's Consortium?" Sunli asked.

"They are a group of former Chinese generals who don't support their country's current desire to sign a treaty with the United States agreeing to a ban on nuclear weapons," said the drug lord. "The CPC believes in power, just like the Cincoleta, which is why we work together so well.

"Together we will develop this collective laser accelerator weapon," El Verdugo continued. "We call it the Dragon's CLAW."

"But we need your help," Will interrupted. "You understand the science. We got lucky, but we need your expertise to duplicate our results."

Sunli hesitated. The appeal of working with people who were close to solving the secret of the LENR trigger was drawing her in... but to align herself with a Mexican cartel leader and a rogue group of Chinese dissidents? After all, she was an American citizen. Why would she help two groups of people who were developing this technology simply to gain power? On the other hand, the Ramos brothers were so much closer to success than she had ever gotten. This might be the only way for her to make it work. Yes, it was tempting but... Sunli wanted to achieve this breakthrough on her own.

"I'm sorry," said Sunli. "I just can't help you."

"*M'ija*," El Verdugo said, walking toward Sunli and caressing her cheek with one finger. "I think I can convince you to change your mind."

She jerked away, eyes blazing, when the drug lord whispered something in her ear.

A few hours later, Sunli was on a plane to Beijing.

* * *

The Percy Study team along with the PFM and DEA officers photographed the set up in the warehouse and packed up all the equipment there to ship to their offices at the Pentagon. Every scrap of equipment, from tables to trashcans was collected. They left the building spotless, as if locusts had descended on the place.

Alek rode back to the city with Marquez, taking advantage of the drive to ask some questions about the cartel.

"It's not unusual that we find facilities like this in the forest," Marquez said. "*Pero* this is the first time I've seen a warehouse that's not actually a drug lab or distribution center. *Es muy extraño, pero* it kind of makes sense with Professor Rodriguez working nearby."

"You think they were trying to get the professor to help them?"

"From what you've said, he was an expert in this area. His student, Sunli, the one who is missing, didn't she study this technology too?"

"Yes," Alek replied thoughtfully. "That's why Sunli and I went to talk to Rodriguez. I was hoping he would share his expertise with his former student, but she disappeared, and he didn't really give me any useful information. And now he's gone too." Alek sighed. The whole situation seemed hopeless.

"The cartel leaders don't take any chances," Marquez said. "Perhaps Dr. Rodriguez's so-called suicide was designed to send a message that anyone else with insight into this technology should cooperate."

"But none of us have any insight," Alek practically shouted in frustration. "Maybe the Ramos brothers or Sunli knew more than the rest of us, but now all of them have disappeared."

"There's something I must tell you," Marquez said, focusing his eyes on the winding highway. "I received an alert about an hour ago that a woman matching Sunli Hidalgo's description was seen at the Monterrey airport. The plane reservations showed her destination as Beijing."

"That doesn't make sense," Alek exclaimed. "Although... Sunli is half Chinese," he mused. "Her mother lives in China, but it's not like her to decide suddenly it's time for a family visit. She also has relatives in Monterrey, and she expressed no interest in seeing them."

"This Sunli, she sounds complicated... and suspicious," Marquez said. "With ties to both China and Mexico and her mysterious disappearance... how do you know she's not working with the people running the lab? After all, the cartel can be very persuasive, and El Verdugo is known for compensating those who help him extremely well."

Alek was shocked at the implication. "The Sunli I know would never do anything like that. She's a brilliant scientist who stays focused on her research."

"Hmm, you seem rather fond of this woman," Marquez said. "From my experience, I must advise you not to let affection and admiration stand in the way of good sense."

"I just can't believe that Sunli would work with the cartel," Alek said, shaking his head.

"As we say here in Mexico, *cada chango a su mecate*."

"What does that mean?" asked Alek.

"The literal translation is, 'every monkey to his rope,'" Marquez replied. "In English, I think you'd say, 'to each his own.' From what I can tell, this Sunli is trouble, but I can see I won't convince you. I hope that I'm mistaken and there's a logical reason for her disappearance, but, in any case, it seems that finding her is your next step."

Finding her and figuring out how to use the information we gathered today to finalize the LENR trigger will be our next steps, Alek mused to himself. *We have our work cut out for us.*

Marquez continued talking, oblivious to the fact that Alek was lost in thought. "You scientists go back to your labs and we'll keep investigating how the cartel is involved with this whole thing. We have enough trouble with drug trafficking as it is. The last thing we need is El Verdugo getting a hold of the ultimate weapon."

Marquez pulled the jeep to a stop in front of the hotel. Just two days ago, Alek had thought his visit to Mexico

would involve doing some research, enjoying the pictur-
esque city of Monterrey, and getting to know Sunli better.
Now, nothing made sense.

Candale, Lowe, and Digali were already there un-
loading equipment. Gabi was talking to the DEA and
FBI agents. She smiled when she saw Alek and Marquez
arrive.

"How are you holding up, Spray? This has to be a lot
of excitement for someone who spends most of his time
in a laboratory."

"I'm fine," replied Alek. "Probably not going to go out
to a nightclub tonight, but I'm holding up."

Alek glanced at his iPhone. "Hey guys," he hollered at
the other scientists. "Percy has lined up a C-130 to transport us and this equipment back to the states tonight.
We have to go through this stuff with a fine-tooth comb.
The Chinese may be a few steps ahead of us and unlike
me, they aren't interested in energy research. We have to
catch up."

Chapter 12
Politics as Usual

TWO DAYS EARLIER, WHILE HIS team headed to Mexico, Percy spent a morning in Los Alamos making sure everything at the lab was running smoothly. He then returned to D.C. only to find himself drawn into the complex intersection between science and politics. Senator Larry Plumkin and the Senate Select Committee on Intelligence were demanding a report on the Percy Study team's progress on the LENR.

The lab director's plane landed at Ronald Reagan Washington National Airport and Percy's reserved car and driver were ready to transport him to Capitol Hill. Over the years, he had become accustomed to the once-jarring transition from small-town New Mexico to the energy of D.C. He felt his adrenaline rising as he prepared to negotiate and dazzle the senators with science that was more speculative than factual.

Percy knew what to expect. He was used to the game and had played it many times. Yes, it was a necessary waste of time and energy, but it never failed to annoy him. *Couldn't everyone find better ways to spend their time than reenacting this political theater over and over?*

Percy despised when politicians used technological advancements and research as bargaining chips in political arguments. At the same time, he knew this could not be avoided since science had to play a strategic role in negotiations involving foreign relations and defense. Unfortunately, Percy had little progress to report to the

Senate Select Committee and even less patience for dealing with uninformed, impatient senators who had very limited understanding of the technology. He hoped Alek and Sunli would come back from Mexico with some sort of breakthrough, but he hadn't heard a word from them since they left.

Percy arrived at the Hart Office Building, handed his cellphone to the capitol police officer and was ushered into the SCIF. Plumkin, Dale Croft, and a handful of senators from the Senate Select Committee on Intelligence sat around the highly polished mahogany conference table. The seats that were intended to hold the full Select Committee sat empty—surrounding the table with a ring of unoccupied chairs.

Plumkin began the meeting by addressing Percy by his first name, which even Percy's wife rarely used. "Harold, you know it is a stated U.S. Air Force strategy to achieve space dominance and demonstrate our nation's ability to base advanced warfighting concepts on space capabilities. Your team's work is essential to this effort."

Croft interrupted. "So, what can I tell the President? Are you making any progress?" Croft rose and began pacing back and forth in back of the small room. "The American public is getting increasingly concerned about the threat of the Chinese," he muttered under his breath.

Percy ignored the President's science adviser and turned calmly to Plumkin. "Yes, we have made some significant breakthroughs in understanding the trigger mechanism for the LENR. We're extremely close to being finished with the funding proposal and recommendations for implementing this discovery." Percy wondered if he should cross his fingers beneath the table. What he had just said was more than an exaggeration. In fact, it bordered on a lie. *Well, time to double down*, he thought. "The President will be pleased with our findings. This technology combined with the collective laser accelerator could be an invincible weapon."

"The President wants to make it clear to the Chinese

that we have mastered this technology," Croft said pointedly.

"Well, I wouldn't exactly say that we've reached the stage of mastery," Percy replied with a raised eyebrow. "These things take time... and money."

Percy had always been adept at talking politicians into giving the lab more money. Although money really wasn't the issue with the LENR project, he was not about to pass up an opportunity to request additional funding.

Plumkin cleared his throat. "Perhaps we should stage a demonstration to ensure the Chinese are aware of our capabilities... some sort of secret test that gets accidentally leaked?"

"That could work," Percy replied, nodding. "We will need to run additional computer simulations first and then conduct field experiments. I do believe this is the kind of weapon that can be used to dominate space, but we can't rush the process."

"So, what do you suggest as the next step?" asked Plumkin.

Percy smiled. He knew he had a talent for discussing complex technical issues with non-technical decision makers. The key was to make the explanation complicated enough to confuse them, while managing to keep the answers vague.

"We need to ensure we understand the way neutrons through nuclear reactions can create huge bursts of electrons and ions. To generate the initial collective electron interaction, we need to develop a trigger with an advanced degree of control."

Senator Ruth Marshall, a Democrat from New Hampshire, cleared her throat loudly. "Our focus as a nation should be to improve humanity, not invent new weapons," she said.

"True," replied Percy. "For every weapon we invent, there is a counter weapon, but proving our technological superiority both offensively and defensively will create a stability that can protect us. It's not about using the weapon, Senator Marshall. It's about having it. Just as we defeated the former Soviet Union by convincing their leaders we were developing space-based weapons through the Strategic Defense Initiative, we will eliminate the threat of the Chinese in exactly the same way."

"I disagree," Marshall said, shaking her head. "The Strategic Defense Initiative didn't eliminate the threat of the Soviet Union. The Soviet Union committed suicide. Have you even considered the implications of space weapons in destabilizing worldwide economies?"

"It's too late to debate about our intent, Ruth," said Plumkin. "We are already deep into this project. The question is, what will it take to wrap it up? Harold, when will you and your team be able to show us some progress?"

"Soon, sir. Especially if we get some additional funding to carry out more complex simulations."

Percy noted several of the senators were nodding as Plumkin adjourned the meeting, walking over to shake Percy's hand. Croft left the room the room in a huff. *Well, he can get over himself*, thought Percy, no longer worried about the science adviser's attitude.

Percy was pleased with himself. He had not been looking forward to this meeting, but it had gone remarkably well. Any conversation with politicians that leads to more funding could be considered a success.

Percy left the secured room with a sense of accomplishment mixed with disbelief. So much of both science and politics were built on smoke and mirrors. Deception, delusion, disagreement... all in a day's work. He glanced down at his cell and saw Alek was calling. Good. Time to see if they were making any progress in Mexico.

* * *

"Hey, can I ask you a few questions?"

As Alek sipped his lukewarm coffee in the Pentagon cafeteria, he looked up to see Gabi standing over him. They had made it back to D.C. late the previous evening and Alek was operating on very little sleep.

"Questions? Sure. What about?"

"Well, I'm really out of my league when you guys start talking about this project. What is it going to take to make your research a reality? I guess I don't really understand what we know or what we do next," Gabi said, taking a seat next to Alek.

"We really don't know either," Alek replied with a shrug. "Digali just wants to keep building things until we find something that works, which appears to be what the Ramos brothers and their cartel buddies were doing in the forest back there. The thing is, it's not like Edison inventing a lightbulb by just trying a bunch of different materials. You have to have a theory, a mathematical model, a computer simulation, and then experimental verification. That's the only way we can get this to work."

"But someone managed to vaporize a big chunk of the Mexican forest. Doesn't that mean the trigger is working?" she asked.

"It's sort of working, but they clearly didn't have control over it. The trigger mechanism must be fast, small, and entirely controllable to be a success. It all has to start with the mathematical theory. Sunli was making a good start on that, but now she's gone," Alek said.

"Who else would have that expertise?"

"Well, the first person I would have asked would have been Rodriguez, but he's gone for good, so we have to cross our fingers that Candale can build on the work Sunli had been doing. Then we'll need to do computer simulations to monitor the many integrated relationships of the variables to understand the process. Digali and Lowe can handle the hardware, but we need to bring in someone with the computer background to run the simulations we'll need."

"Do you have anyone in mind," Gabi asked, tracing the coffee rings on the white Formica table with one finger.

"I went to grad school with someone who would be a great addition to the team."

"Who are they? I'll call the FBI headquarters and we

can get them on the team."

"Well…" Alek rubbed his head. "The thing is…"

"What?"

"He's a Chinese citizen."

Gabi frowned. "That's not going to work. China is the new evil empire."

"Yeah, maybe I can just consult with him. I don't know."

Gabi pulled the elastic band out of her hair and combed her fingers through her blonde curls. "So, the goal is to create a new kind of trigger for a collective accelerator, right? Collective accelerators aren't anything new though, are they?" she asked.

"Not at all," replied Alek. "The concept was invented by a physicist in Novosibirsk, Siberia back in the 50s. The basic notion was to make a powerful electron beam and then modulate the beam to carry along much heavier and more lethal ions. It was kind of like an ion surfer riding along on the crest of the electron wave."

"I remember reading about that," said Gabi. "I didn't really understand it. But it kinda scared me. Wasn't the concept rediscovered by the U.S. Air Force in the 80s? Didn't some Air Force general claim a single Soviet collective accelerator could destroy our entire nuclear retaliation capability? He said the beam accelerator would be powered by a nuclear explosive energy source and the particle beam would propagate over thousands of miles and destroy anything in its path."

"Yes, but there never was any proof of that," said Alek. "The Soviets did have a facility in the wilderness of Kazakhstan, but there was no evidence their fictitious collective accelerator was ever built."

"So basically, we're trying to revive the failed dream of a forgotten former superpower," Gabi said with a laugh.

"When you put it like that, it sounds totally logical." Alek chuckled, adding, "What's your next step?"

"I'm going to brief my deputy assistant director on what we found out about the cartel involvement and see if they have anything concrete to tie El Verdugo or the Cincoleta to that warehouse. It's possible, there were Chinese scientists there with guards from the cartel who were supervising and protecting them. What I can't figure out is whether the Chinese are working for the cartel, or the cartel is working for the Chinese."

"I just feel like we are running out of time," admitted Alek. "I saw on CNN this morning that President Thornton has scheduled arms talks with the Chinese government next month."

"All you can do is your best," Gabi said, reaching out as if to give Alek a hug or a pat on the shoulder, but then pulling away awkwardly as the rest of the team walked up to the table.

Candale was carrying an empty ice cream container. He scraped his spoon around the empty bowl, making Alek wince.

"We had gelato," Candale exclaimed. "It was delicious. I had half chocolate fudge and half Italian cream."

Digali shrugged. Alek smiled. Candale didn't talk much, but there were certain things he really cared about—apparently one of those was ice cream.

PART TWO

Chapter 13
Deadlines and Threats

TWO WEEKS HAD PASSED SINCE Sunli had found El Verdugo's men waiting in her hotel room. She laughed bitterly, thinking of how the drug lord had tried to blackmail her to help them develop the LENR trigger. Little did he know that she had seriously considered joining their effort even before she learned about their plans. But the Chinese and the cartel had made sure she would cooperate. They revealed their undeniable leverage when El Verdugo informed her they had captured Sunli's mother and were holding her hostage. "Make the weapon work if you want your mother to live" were the orders she received.

Sunli was worried. Her mother's fragile health weighed heavily on her mind. Not to mention her mother's short temper and critical tongue. Although Sunli was trying everything she knew to do to grant the drug lord's wishes, she wasn't making much headway and her deadline was approaching. Since arriving in Beijing, she had spent about 18 hours each day in the lab. With her sleeping and dining quarters located nearby in the facility, she had no reason to leave other than to grab something to eat and get a few hours of rest each night. The Chinese guards assured her that she was not a prisoner, but when she asked to leave for a few hours to go shopping or perhaps to a café, they always replied, "*Bù, bù kěnéng. No, not possible.*" *That certainly seems to fit the definition of a prisoner*, Sunli thought to herself, but she responded by smiling politely and returning to work.

Her instructions were clear. Take the work the Percy Study team had done, and the experiments carried out in the Mexican jungle, and find the secret of the LENR trigger. The problem was, Sunli didn't think she could do it. At least not alone.

She did have assistants—Chinese scientists who stood ready to do her bidding, but she wasn't certain how to use them or what tasks she should tell them to carry out. The problem certainly didn't stem from a lack of access to technology. The Chinese People's Consortium lab was state-of-the-art. No expense had been spared in constructing the facility. Everything she needed was provided in the lab.

The attached dining hall served a varied menu ranging from American dishes to the traditional Chinese items that most of the staff seemed to prefer. The small room she was assigned resembled a luxury hotel room with high thread count sheets and a bathroom stocked with tiny bottles of shampoo, conditioner, lotion, and soap. The suitcase filled with her belongings that she had taken to Mexico had been waiting in her room when she'd arrived in Beijing along with a few extra outfits that matched her sense of style and were just the right size. All she had to do was leave her dirty laundry outside her door each evening and it was returned the next day, cleaned and pressed.

Sunli was even allowed some limited internet access, although all her time spent using the computer was carefully monitored. There was no way to send any sort of message about her whereabouts. Everywhere she went, even in the hallway outside of her bedroom, armed guards stood watching. The atmosphere was eerie, and Sunli's only interaction with the other scientists in the facility was giving them instructions and handing them daily reports.

She frequently found herself wondering how long the Chinese had been planning this. Were there Chinese operatives planted in Los Alamos? She had heard many stories from her mother about the power and reach of the Chinese Ministry of State Security. For all she knew, any one of her colleagues at the Los Alamos lab could have been working for the MSS. Clearly, they knew everything about her life, her background, and her motivations. They had done their research before bringing her here... wherever here was.

Sunli had no idea where the facility was located. When she arrived in the Beijing airport, she was met by Chinese officials who blindfolded her and drove her to the lab. There were no windows, and she never left the building. If it weren't for her wristwatch, she probably wouldn't even know the difference between night and day.

It was thanks to that watch that she knew it was 10:27 a.m. when Will Ramos walked into the lab. Sunli wasn't sure of the day, but she did know the time.

"Ah, the brilliant mathematician Dr. Sunli Hidalgo, hard at work," Ramos said smugly. She fought the urge to lash out at him, to condemn his sloppy science and haphazard experiments that she was now struggling to understand. She thought of her personal hero, whose name resembled her own. Sun Tzu, the Chinese military strategist and philosopher, wrote *The Art of War* about the importance of forming alliances, the need to use deceit, and the willingness to submit, at least temporarily, in order to triumph over powerful foes. Channeling Sun Tzu, Sunli turned to Ramos and smiled sweetly.

"Will, I'm so glad you're here," she said. "I could really use your help."

Sunli saw immediately that her friendly greeting had defused Ramos' hostility. Relaxing, he walked over to the lab bench where Sunli had spread out various possible LENR components and leaned over her.

"What seems to be the problem, sweetheart?" he asked in a condescending tone.

Sunli had to struggle to choke down her feelings of

disgust. Will had never spoken to her like that when they worked together at Los Alamos. Now, it appeared he felt he had the upper hand and could be himself.

Just ignore him, Sunli told herself. She had to meet her captors' demands, there was too much at stake and she needed Ramos' cooperation. Sun Tzu wrote that to win a battle, one must pretend inferiority and encourage the enemy's arrogance. Will Ramos had plenty of arrogance to encourage.

"I was just wondering if you could tell me a little bit more about the people we are working for here," said Sunli. "I really don't know much about the Chinese People's Consortium, and I barely met El Verdugo."

Sunli hoped Will would welcome the chance to demonstrate his knowledge and superiority. She was right.

"El Verdugo's name is Juan Velásquez, but only those of us who know him well can call him by his name."

"And how is he connected with the Chinese?" asked Sunli. "I know that Chinese fentanyl producers have been exporting the chemical components of the opioid to Mexico. Is this about smuggling drugs?"

"Only in a manner of speaking," Will replied. "Velásquez began working with the CPC a few years ago when he met the group's leader, General Wu, at a Chinese-run *maquiladora* in Mexico."

"I'm sorry, what's a maqui... what's that?" Sunli asked even though she knew the answer. She wanted to give Will the chance to share his knowledge and prove his superiority. So what if he thought she was stupid? The more he underestimated her, the better.

"A *maquiladora* is a manufacturing operation or factory established in Mexico, usually near the border, that imports raw materials and equipment for assembly, processing, or manufacturing. Its products are then exported under a special program that grants them tax breaks and other benefits. General Wu had retired from the People's Liberation Army and built an aerospace assembly plant in

Juarez. His plan was to produce advanced weapons built on stolen U.S. technology."

"And the PLA was okay with that?" Sunli asked.

"Wu has friends in high places, plus he works closely with China's Ministry of State Security—the real power in China. The Chinese government tends to look the other way, especially when dealing with their own retired generals. It works out better that way."

"Anyhow," Will continued, "when Wu and Velásquez met, they discovered they had similar interests and desires. Wu longed to have control of an invincible weapon that would guarantee China's power. Velásquez sought a weapon that would ensure his power and control of the cartel. And Velásquez had plenty of drug money to invest in his new pet project."

"So, did General Wu already know about the work we were doing on the LENR technology?" Sunli asked.

"He did. As you know, China has its own LENR program that has been less successful than ours. That's why Wu and Velásquez wanted a way to get into Los Alamos and find out what researchers there were doing. And that's where Joe and I came into the picture. We had some... uh... connections with the cartel during our youth."

Sunli's thoughts were racing, but she managed to keep her face neutral. "So, you began researching at Los Alamos, while Wu and Velásquez set up the warehouse outside of Monterrey?"

"Yes," he replied. "We started our experiments at Los Alamos, then we moved to the house in Altavaca, and finally to Monterrey. We made some significant breakthroughs when we tried using nickel as the target, but we still need to learn how to control the beam and the energy output. They key is to create a reliable trigger, and I'm certain we could have, but Velásquez was getting impatient. He insisted we bring in Rodriguez, but we couldn't get the professor to cooperate. That's when Joe remembered that you had studied with Rodriguez. The rest was, as they say, history. El Verdugo is very persuasive and now you are here."

"Well, I'm doing my best. Thanks for giving me a little background." Sunli swallowed hard and forced herself to conclude the conversation with, "I really appreciate your help."

"Anytime, *preciosa*," he replied. "I'm just going to sit here and keep an eye on you, y'know, in case you need anything. General Wu and I are looking forward to seeing your progress on the research."

The problem was Sunli hadn't made much progress, but she wasn't about to let Ramos know that. Will leaned back in his chair as Sunli turned to her computer, praying for a breakthrough. The stakes were far too high.

Chapter 14
The Truth is Out There

"I JUST DON'T GET IT," Alek said. "It makes no sense to me."

Alek, Lowe, and Percy were in their Pentagon basement conference room discussing their recent discoveries.

"I'll be happy to explain again," Percy replied patiently. "Intelligence from the CIA suggests that Sunli was abducted by the Cincoleta drug cartel and transported to China. It is believed that she is being held near Beijing by a rogue Chinese military group called the Chinese People's Consortium, which may be secretly funded by the Chinese Ministry of State Security."

"But why?" Alek asked.

"My contact at the CIA believes the Chinese hope to use Sunli's Los Alamos expertise in the LENR technology to build a lethal space weapon. The cartel has been collaborating with the Chinese on the production of fentanyl. I suspect the cartel may be helping fund this research in exchange for the chance to get their hands on a weapon of their own."

Alek began pacing back and forth in the small room.

"It makes no sense. What about Will and Joe Ramos? Where have they gone?"

"They are also believed to be in China, collaborating willingly with this group. That's why we absolutely have to figure out what's happening in Beijing. Alek, you and Gabi have to go to Florida right away."

Alek abruptly stopped pacing. "Uh, what?"

"Boss, are you okay?" Lowe asked. "What does Florida have to do with the Chinese?"

"I'm fine," Percy said in an exasperated tone. "Here's the thing. The top expert in remote viewing lives—

"ESP!" Alek said with a derisive snort. "Remote viewing is complete hogwash!"

"I believe you're wrong," replied Percy with unusual calm. "As I was saying, the top expert in remote viewing, Benton Stuart, lives in Orlando. Maybe we can learn something about what the Chinese are up to if we consult with him. I know it's a long shot, but this guy has been helpful in the past. Think about it. What do we have to lose? It's just that you need to meet with him in person. He's a little eccentric, so the best way to work with him is face to face."

"But remote viewing is a Hollywood hoax," Alek said with a grimace.

"I believe you're wrong," repeated Percy. "Remote viewing or anomalous cognition or second sight or extrasensory perception, whatever you want to call it, has been scientifically proven to work. The CIA developed a system of coordinate remote viewing, and I want you to meet with one of the program's original trainees."

"Hey, didn't U.S. intelligence agencies use psychics to try to find the American diplomats taken hostage by revolutionary students who seized the U.S. Embassy in Iran in 1979?" Lowe asked.

"Yes, they did use psychics during the hostage crisis and many other occasions. It has been proven to work."

Lowe nodded. "I actually know a lot about remote viewing. Researching it has become kind of a hobby of mine. Remote viewing is just the psychic ability of some people to describe and experience what is happening in a distant place. I read a paper about how the U.S. had used remote viewing during the 80s to figure out what was taking place at Soviet facilities. The CIA program called Stargate studied psychic phenomena in order to answer military intelligence questions. Using the power of their minds, the remote viewers could see inside distant buildings."

"That sounds ridiculous," sniffed Alek. "Why don't we go down to Roswell and meet with some aliens while we're at it?"

Ignoring his colleague's skepticism, Lowe continued. "There was one time when a remote viewer was brought to a shielded room, given a pencil and sketch pad and the coordinates of an enigmatic and heavily guarded facility in Kazakhstan, and instructed to 'see' and report the details of what was taking place inside. The viewer sketched the facility that he had never seen, drawing a giant crane covering up the entrance to an underground facility in which people were fabricating a giant steel sphere. After the Cold War ended, the CIA verified that the crane actually existed in that very spot, and it was covering up the structure where the Soviets were building a containment vessel for a particle beam weapon. The device they had been constructing resembled a giant steel sphere."

"Sounds like a coincidence to me," Alek said.

Alek began pacing again, unable to contain his agitation. "We have important work to do and instead you want me to go on some wild goose chase to Florida? Did one of the senators suggest this?"

"Alek, sit down," Percy said. "It's important to Plumkin and the Senate Select Committee on Intelligence to know what the Chinese are doing. They also want to know that we are ahead of the Chinese. The problem is, we aren't."

"I feel if we can isolate the variable causing the transmutation reactions, we can build an acceptable trigger," Lowe interjected.

"Acceptable isn't the goal," said Percy. "It has to be perfect. If we can gain some insight into what they are doing in China, maybe we can move this project along." Percy stood, blocking the path of Alek's pacing. "Alek, I need to know what's happening in China. Who knows, this might just help."

Percy slapped Alek on the shoulder. "Expand your

horizons a little. We've barely tapped into our understanding of the capabilities of the human brain. Just because something is a little strange and unexplained, doesn't mean it's impossible. Plus, I told you to go to Orlando and I'm your boss."

"Fine, I'll go," Alek said. "But just because you're making me. I don't know anything about remote viewing except that it sounds like garbage science that someone in Hollywood made up."

Percy sighed and clapped Alek on the back. "Expand your mind and take advantage of the chance to get away for a little bit. Who knows, we just might make a believer out of you."

***

Two days later, Alek and Gabi stood at the airport Hertz counter in Florida renting a Toyota Corolla so they could drive to a trailer park near Orlando to meet with one of the original remote viewers from the 1980s. Alek had gone from cynical to slightly intrigued, but Gabi remained skeptical. As they drove north on the interstate toward Lake Shore Village Mobile Home Park, she made her feelings clear.

"So, am I Scully and you're Mulder?" she asked.

"What are you talking about?" Alek replied as he weaved through the heavy 5 p.m. traffic heading north out of Orlando.

"*The X-Files*. Didn't you watch that show? I think it came out in the 90s. It was a TV drama about two FBI agents investigating paranormal phenomena. It had David Duchovny in it. You're totally Mulder."

"Um, I think I've heard of it. I don't watch much TV."

"You should watch more TV. What about *Black Mirror*? Have you seen that?" Alek shook his head. "It's a British sci-fi series about scary new technology. Pretty freaky. You'd probably like it. My point is that remote viewing is science fiction. I mean, it makes for a good show, but it's not reality. It would be more productive for us just to go to Disney World. At least it's the happiest place on earth."

"Lowe gave me some papers to read and now I'm wondering if there could be something to this," Alek said. "Lots of well-known entrepreneurs and business people attribute their success to this ability. It's a trained skill that was developed by parapsychology researchers at the Stanford Research Institute. Law enforcement has used remote viewing to solve crimes and the army has used it to locate enemy troops."

"Hmmm. I'll try to keep an open mind, but I'm just not sold on it," replied Gabi. "I think our exit is coming up."

Following the directions from his iPhone's Google Maps app, Alek turned down North Orange Blossom Trail looking for the intersection of Silver Star Road. The street names suggested a lovely Floridian location, but the reality was trash-lined fields filled with dying vegetation. They found the entrance to the Lake Shore Village Mobile Home Park just after they crossed the railroad tracks. In spite of the name, there was no lake.

Signs posted near the entrance to the park warned of the presence of surveillance cameras and stated, "Rule-restricted community: no children allowed." The faded, single-wide trailers were short on maintenance but heavy on rickety lawn furniture and discarded beer cans. Residents sitting on their front porches or lounging on lawn chairs in their yards watched the Toyota warily.

"Rule restricted community?" Alek asked, raising an eyebrow.

"Hmm," replied Gabi. "That means Lake Shore Village is a sex-offender park."

"Sex offenders have parks? Uh, like theme parks?"

"No. All of the residents are convicted offenders. You know, they can't just live anywhere. They have to stay away from children and be monitored and stuff, so these restricted offender communities have become a thing." Gabi plugged the name of the trailer park into her iPhone. "Oh, there are several posts about this place. The owner decided to convert the park to a sex offender community about 20 years ago. She said that all the required surveillance has run out the drug dealers and prostitutes that used to live here."

"So, we're visiting a psychic sex offender?" said Alek. "It just keeps getting better and better. Now I am officially creeped out."

Alek drove slowly past a barking German Shepherd on a chain. The road was peppered with potholes.

"Working as a remote viewer must not pay very well," said Gabi. "I'm sure getting convicted as a sex offender didn't help."

"There it is. Lot 5." Alek pulled up in front of a trailer that might have been pink once. Plastic flamingos and a rusty miniature yellow windmill decorated the front yard.

"Well, let's cross our fingers," said Alek.

"Yep," replied Gabi. "Best case scenario—we don't get shot."

Stepping carefully over the trash and the tattered decorations littering the yard, they walked to the door of the trailer. Alek knocked, but no one answered. They exchanged glances and then he knocked again.

Slowly the door swung open, revealing a paunchy, elderly white man in a dirty tank top and pajama pants. The man squinted as if he hadn't been exposed to sunlight for months.

"Alek Spray," said Alek, holding out his hand for a handshake. Benton Stuart looked at the hand dubiously. "My boss Harold Percy talked to you on the about remote viewing. Uh, we're from the Pentagon. Remember, you said you'd... uh... do a viewing session for us?"

"Hmph, yes. Let's do it," replied Stuart, ushering them into his cluttered trailer. Piles of old newspapers covered nearly every surface. Gabi gingerly relocated the remains of a partially eaten TV dinner and perched on the edge of the lumpy couch.

Stuart sat down heavily in the recliner. "You know I used to be the assistant wrestling coach at Stanford. I taught civil engineering too."

"That's very impressive, sir," Gabi said politely. "I, um, like your pajamas. Very cozy looking."

He ignored her attempt at small talk. "Stanford fired me. Then there was that other trouble. But they still send people for viewing. Ever since I viewed the Kazakhstan test site, they've come to me for help."

Alek looked around for somewhere to sit. There wasn't much free space on the couch, so he awkwardly squeezed in next to Gabi.

"That's right, sir," Alek said, "we are here for help. We need you to try to see a location near Beijing, China."

"I can see it. You know I can. I've found missing people. That little girl... she was lost. I knew where to look."

"Okay then," Alek said, trying to keep Stuart focused on the task at hand. "We're also missing someone—one of my colleagues. We think she's in Beijing, but we don't know why or what she's doing. We need to know what's going on."

Stuart closed his eyes and leaned back in his recliner, making a few strange grunting sounds. Gabi and Alek waited patiently.

Alek tried not to notice the way that his thigh was touching Gabi's as they squeezed together on the small section of the couch that wasn't covered with food wrappers and newspapers.

They waited... and waited.

Gabi pointed to her iPhone. She sent Alek a text. "Do you think he's sleeping?"

"I don't know," Alek texted back. "Nothing I've read about remote viewing has discussed how long it takes."

They waited a little longer. Gabi watched a spider weaving a web between the recliner and the pile of newspapers beside it.

"Maybe he's dead," Gabi texted.

"He's not dead," Alek texted back.

They waited some more. Alek tugged at a loose thread on the couch and began unraveling a small hole.

Suddenly, Stuart sat up and grabbed a notepad and

pencil from under a pile of books and papers on the coffee table in front of him. He began drawing. After a few minutes of frantic scribbling, he handed the finished picture to Alek.

"It's a tunnel," Stuart said. "They are conducting experiments in an underground tunnel."

"That's not psychic," Gabi exclaimed with frustration. "Everyone knows the Chinese build tunnels. Haven't you heard about the 3,000-mile-long Great Underground Wall of China? They advertised it on Chinese TV as the place they hide their mobile nuclear missiles."

"This is important," Stuart said firmly. "They will solve it there in the tunnel."

Alek rose from the couch. "Uh. Okay. Thank you. Can I keep this?" he asked, gesturing at the drawing.

"Don't you see anything else," Gabi asked. "We came a long way, and we haven't learned much."

"You need to go there. To the tunnel," Stuart said. "But watch out for the small woman with the long, dark hair. She's involved with something bad," he mumbled.

Gabi pulled up a photo on her iPhone and showed it to Stuart. "Is this the woman you saw?"

"Yes, that's her," he muttered. "She's... trouble. She's in trouble. She's there."

"She's there? In the tunnel?" Alek asked, but Stuart had sat back in his chair and closed his eyes again.

"Let's get out of here," whispered Gabi. "This dude is creepy."

"We're going to go," Alek said awkwardly. "Uh, thank you, sir. We'll, uh, let ourselves out."

Chapter 15
Sunli is in Trouble

ALEK BURST INTO PERCY'S PENTAGON basement office without knocking. "Why didn't you call me back? I left several messages. I need to talk to you," he exclaimed.

Percy sat calmly behind his desk, dressed in his typical charcoal gray suit, perfectly pressed and accented with a burgundy tie.

"I've been busy. I need to talk to you too," he replied, leaning forward.

Then, both men said simultaneously, "It's about Sunli."

"She's in trouble," Alek spluttered.

"I know," said Percy. "She emailed me."

"She what?"

"She emailed me yesterday, while you were in Florida. She apologized for leaving Mexico without notice. Apparently, she had to go to China. There was a family emergency."

"But she... she disappeared. We haven't heard from her," Alek protested. "Why wouldn't she have contacted us sooner?"

"I don't know, honestly. She's always been a little odd. Said her father had fallen ill and she had to get to Beijing to care for him."

"That makes no sense," interjected Alek. "When we were in Mexico, Sunli told me her father was dead. Plus, he never lived in China. Do you think she said that to send us some kind of signal or code? After all, the remote viewer said Sunli was in trouble."

Gabi walked into the office and sat down in the only guest chair, leaving Alek standing. "The remote viewer also said Sunli *was* trouble, and we should watch out for *her* if I remember correctly. Plus, he was an 80-year-old man wearing pajama pants."

"So, the visit wasn't productive?" Percy asked.

"He described an underground tunnel near Beijing and warned us about Sunli. I didn't learn much," Gabi said with a snort.

"I think it was worth the trip," Alek countered. "We found out where Sunli is, and he confirmed our hunch that the Chinese are building something underground."

Percy sighed. "Unfortunately, we already know that the Chinese are always building something underground, and I found out yesterday where Sunli was without even leaving my office. It's too bad. I expected more from Benton Stuart. He used to be really insightful. I'm sorry I wasted your time."

"I don't think it was a waste at all," Alek said.

"I do," said Gabi, raising an eyebrow. "What's been happening here?"

"You should go talk to Digali," replied Percy. "I think he's onto something. They're all in the conference room."

Frustrated, Alek left Percy's office with Gabi following. She shared a few more critical comments about wasting taxpayer dollars on travel to see psychic sex offenders while they walked down the hall.

Digali was pacing back and forth in the conference room, stopping periodically to scribble on the white board hanging on the wall. Lowe and Candale sat at the long table that was spread with papers and laptops. Candale appeared to be making complex calculations. Lowe was scrolling through Facebook on his iPhone.

"It's really a way that collective effects of electrons can excite nuclear reactions," Digali muttered to himself. "The key is collective acceleration of particles like neutrons or ions. The collective effect energizes the heavy particles, and they can go on to create other reactions."

He stopped pacing and wrote something else on the whiteboard. "Neutrons energized by the electrons can start nuclear reactions, and then the reaction can take off producing energetic particles and an electromagnetic pulse," he exclaimed triumphantly. "Oh, hi Alek, Gabi, how was the remote viewer?"

Gabi waived her hand dismissively. Alek looked thoughtful.

"Could you use a giant accelerator to transform a slow low-power pulse into an intense ultra-high-power beam?" Alek asked Digali. "Maybe if you housed the accelerator underground?"

"Possibly," Digali replied. "You would need a huge facility, which would be hard to hide anywhere except underground, but that would never be practical as a weapon, or as an energy source."

"Why don't you call my friend, Peter Chang?" Alek suggested. ""He's an expert with computer simulations. I bet he can help you figure this out."

Lowe looked up from his cellphone. "Did you guys hear about Sunli?"

Alek decided not to bring up Benton Stuart's warnings about Sunli. "Yeah," he responded. "Percy said she went to China to care for her father who had some sort of health emergency, but I thought her mother lived in China and her father lived in Mexico. Or at least he used to live in Mexico. She told me that he had passed away."

"She talked to you about her family?" Digali asked in a jealous tone.

"A little. That's why I'm so confused about this email she sent Percy."

"I've tried to contact her, but she hasn't responded," Digali said.

"Same here," Alek said.

"That's good," Digali said.

Alek noticed Digali looked relieved to hear that Alek hadn't been in touch with Sunli. *As if I am some kind of ro-*

mantic rival and as if Digali stands a chance, Alek thought to himself.

"I mean, it's not good," Digali spluttered, correcting himself. "Do any of you know someone in China who might be able to check on her?"

"I do," said Alek. "Peter Chang."

* * *

"I think we should contact Peter Chang," Sunli said. She and both of the Ramos brothers were sharing a rare meal in the dining room of the research facility where she was basically a captive. The three were facing a deadline. They were scheduled to give a report to General Wu in one week.

"Chang works at the Chinese Advanced Energy Lab in Beijing," said Sunli. "Through my work at Los Alamos, I have met him at various technical conferences, and my colleagues and I have exchanged ideas and collaborated on research with him over the years. His expertise in creating computer simulations could be very valuable right now."

"Hmph. We never got invited to those conferences," Will sneered. "But maybe this colleague of yours is just what we need. They say that the Advanced Energy Lab is concentrating on energy research, but I bet they are working on advanced weapons. I wonder if we could bring him in."

Joe shook his head. "Bringing Chinese military officials into this secret research facility might not work well. The Chinese government is sneaky, but they work hard to create the illusion they are doing everything aboveboard."

"What if I could collaborate with the Chinese military—the People's Liberation Army—as an American scientist conducting energy research?" asked Sunli. "The technology behind the trigger should be the same regardless of whether we are using the device as a compact weapon or as an energy source."

"True," said Will. "There's an international conference

on new energy sources coming up in Beijing. Maybe that would give you the opportunity to connect with Chang and get his help. I'm sure General Wu would allow you to leave this facility to attend the conference. You could even make a presentation on your research—your energy research that is. After all, you know the consequences if you misbehave."

Sunli shoved her plate away. She had suddenly lost her appetite. "Yes, Will. I know the consequences. I am reminded every day."

The men stood up from the table, leaving their dirty dishes for someone else to clean up.

"I'll talk to General Wu," Will said. "I'm sure he can pull a few strings to arrange for you to present at the conference. Then all you will have to do is find Peter Chang and get his help with your energy research."

Sunli left the dining room and headed back to her room. *A lovely suite, but still a prison*, she thought, sitting down on the bed. Sunli grabbed her laptop and plugged in the thumb drive to play the video she watched every night. Ever since General Wu had brought her the thumb drive, this had become her ritual. Sunli's mother's face filled the screen.

"Lín dá, qǐng bāng máng... fú cóng tāmen fǒuzé tāmen huì shānghài wǒ. Tāmen huì shānghài wǒ gèng duō."

Sunli watched her mother speaking, crying at her words. *"Please help me.... obey them or they will hurt me. They will hurt me more."* She would never allow Wu and Velásquez to harm her mother. That's why their threats convinced her that she had no choice but to cooperate with the general and the drug lord. She would do anything she could to keep her mother safe.

"Don't worry, mama," she whispered to the screen, wiping away the tears. "I will do it. I will do what they want, and then both of us will be set free."

Chapter 16
Chinese Connections

PETER CHANG WAS THE SON of a farmer. Growing up in rural China after the Cultural Revolution, Chang developed a thirst for education. He excelled in school and went on to study at Princeton where he'd met his friend and colleague Alek Spray.

During college, Alek and Chang spent a lot of time talking about theoretical physics and how advances in the field could change the world. They'd been idealistic and hopeful. Looking back on those years now, Chang thought they had been naïve.

Chang's college professors admired his genius in theoretical physics and his talent for converting equations into computational physics. After graduate school, he returned to China where he honed his abilities to generate 3-D visualizations. His holographic images of simulations were sought after by engineers and physicists worldwide.

Chang had mixed feelings about working at the Chinese Advanced Energy Lab in Beijing. He knew the lab claimed to be focused on energy research, but in reality, the researchers were working on advanced weapons. Nevertheless, he accepted a position there after graduation. He'd felt obligated to return to China and serve the country of his birth.

Working at the AEL satisfied Chang's desire to tackle some of the world's most difficult scientific problems. Much of the technology he had been working on recently related to the development of the LENR.

Ever since meeting at Princeton, Chang and Alek had stayed in touch, discussing energy research and physics but being careful to avoid the fine line that could lead to sharing classified applications. Like Alek, Chang hoped to use the LENR technology to create an unlimited energy source. Neither man acknowledged that this energy source could also be used to power beam weapons, although both knew the real reason their labs received funding every year.

Over the years, the two scientists had met frequently at international conferences, sharing meals and sightseeing trips in between conference sessions. They emailed each other occasionally, always aware that their correspondence was scrutinized by both Chinese and American authorities. Most of the time, they exchanged dumb jokes and memes, but they sometimes shared theories and findings from their work.

Both would describe the other as a colleague, but not as a close friend. That's why Chang was so surprised to see Alek's name pop up on his cellphone's caller ID.

"Peter, it's Alek from Los Alamos. I need you to do me a favor."

"Alek, hi," replied Chang, feeling confused by the unexpected phone call and his friend's abrupt tone. "Let me step outside so we can talk."

"This will just take a minute. Do you remember Sunli Hidalgo? She worked with me at Los Alamos? I think you met her during that conference last June in Amsterdam?"

Chang thought for a moment. "A small woman with long black hair? Attractive and smart, a little standoffish?"

"Yes, that's her," Alek said. "She told my supervisor that she was going to Beijing to care for a sick family member, but I haven't heard from her and we are starting to get worried here at the lab. Do you think you could try to help us track her down?"

"I can try," Chang said. "I wonder why she isn't staying in touch."

"Me too. It makes me nervous. Plus, she's an integral

part of the project we are working on now."

"I'll look into it," Chang assured Alek. "Are you coming to the conference here in Beijing next week? The international symposium on new energy sources."

"I'm still debating that," Alek replied. "We are staying very busy. My colleague Ron Digali may reach out to you soon for some help with computer simulations, if you have time to work with us on that. Let me know if you find out anything about Sunli's whereabouts."

Chang hung up the phone, wondering about his old friend's abrupt behavior. What was Alek Spray's relationship to this missing woman and why did he seem so rushed and distressed?

* * *

The next day Digali barged into Alek's office without knocking. His eyes were wild, and his hair was standing on end. "You were right about Peter Chang," Digali said.

"Ron, when was the last time you slept, buddy? You're looking kinda rough."

"No time to sleep," Digali replied. "This is big—it's huge. I talked to your friend Chang yesterday and he's already finished the computer simulations. I think we're really onto something. Chang used our theories to build a 3-D model. By using the concave, multi-electrode conductor feeding the pulse into the chamber, we can change the rate of final collapse of the pinch by delaying the convergence of the multiple filaments. By changing the number of filaments, we can get ever increasing compression and particle acceleration. In other words—it makes the trigger we need to initiate transmutations."

"That's fabulous," said Alek.

"It's more than fabulous," replied Digali, practically glowing with excitement. "The key to the performance of the super plasma focus is to implode multiple current filaments. Decades ago, at Sandia Labs there was a major discovery with multiple wires instead of an imploding cylinder, and the X-ray output from the imploded wire array was enormous. This will actually work."

"Wow, that's great," said Alek. "Now we should—"

Digali interrupted Alek by grabbing his arm and dragging him out of the office. "Come on. We need to talk to Percy," said Digali. "This can't wait."

Digali repeated his no-knock barge-in entrance at Percy's office. Percy looked irritated by the unexpected disturbance, but Digali didn't appear phased by his boss' angry look.

"I should go to Beijing," Digali said forcefully. "Next week they are holding the Global Interconnection Energy and Power Conference there. If I go to the conference and somehow manage to get into the Chinese lab, I can look for evidence that they are developing the trigger. Plus, I can find Sunli and bring her back here."

"I don't know." Alek shook his head. "I don't think you can poke around in top secret labs and not get noticed. Plus, we are getting so close to a solution. This really isn't a good time for you to be gone."

"Look, if I see equipment similar to what we found in Monterrey, it will be proof that these are the same people, and they are working on the LENR trigger. I don't mean to be rude, but I don't trust that you know enough to identify it."

Percy nodded his head. "Digali has a point, Alek. He knows more than you do about the construction of the equipment. Plus, I need you here for the presentation to Congress. It's imperative that we secure the rest of the funding for this project."

Alek couldn't shake the sense that Digali was far more interested in Sunli than he was in the Chinese LENR research. He knew the lonely scientist was picturing himself as the knight riding to the rescue on his white steed. Digali had made his desire to win over Sunli clear, but she hadn't shown the slightest interest. Nevertheless, Alek was certain Digali envisioned himself as the hero, saving the damsel in distress.

Then again, thought Alek, *why does it matter*? Sunli

was even less interested in him than she was in Digali. The most important thing was to find her and bring her back to the United States. After all, she was part of his research team and he would feel better knowing she was safe.

"Yes, go, Digali, go. Find out what the Chinese are up to and why Sunli bailed on us and bring her the hell back here. Something fishy is going on and we need to get to the bottom of it."

* * *

The Global Interconnection Energy and Power Conference had brought more than 600 representatives from 60 countries to the China National Convention Center in Beijing. Exhibitions, presentations, closed-door meetings, and lots of alcohol would unite some of the most powerful scientific players during the two-day event.

Originally built for the 2008 Olympics, the China National Convention Center featured three ballrooms, six exhibition halls, and a 70,000-square foot plenary hall where several important speakers would present their work to scientists from all over the world. A last-minute surprise addition to the program had been made that morning—Dr. Sunli Hidalgo from Los Alamos National Laboratory.

General Wu Liu had jumped at the chance to show off Sunli's expertise in front of all his colleagues. China's largest state-of-the-art facility would be the ideal setting to remind the PLA of the CPC's power and control. Wu adjusted the collar of his dark green dress uniform, admiring the gold striped cuff insignia showing his many years of military service, the shoulder epaulettes for rank, and multiple service decorations on his chest. He looked forward to seeing his colleagues and demonstrating his position to the Chinese leaders. Despite the weakness his family had displayed during the Cultural Revolution, Wu had persevered and had risen to a position of great influence and power in China and, soon, the world. After all, it was only a matter of time before they completed development of the ultimate weapon. *If only the girl would work a little faster*, thought Wu. Perhaps attending this conference will spur her along.

Wu's father had been a professor in an engineering school that was swept up in the Cultural Revolution in the 1960s. Mao closed down the school, and the professor and his students were sent out into the country to learn from the peasants. Overnight, Wu watched his father go from respected academic to farmer. Seeing this, Wu had realized that the real power was retained by those with political influence, particularly those in the army. That was a turning point in his life. As a teenager, Wu vowed to gain power and influence in the military and, thanks to his charisma, good looks, and skill in dealing with foreigners, he rose rapidly. Charming and manipulative, he soon found that every system had corruption and he learned how to use that to his advantage.

After a successful army career, Wu retired from the military and created a company to develop weapons for the PLA. He hired retired military researchers and even sent his engineers to graduate schools in the United States. Wu soon learned that feeding stolen technology to his industry connections allowed him to wield great power. Using his influence in hardware buying to control technology decision making, he took over the leadership of the CPC and began expanding his empire. His breakthrough came when he purchased a computer assembly factory in Juarez, Mexico and met El Verdugo. His initial plan had been to produce advanced weapons based on stolen U.S. technology and now, with the cartel's money and the CPC's scientific ability, the ultimate weapon would soon be in his hands.

As Wu strode through the halls of the convention center greeting military officials and scientists, he thought back to that first meeting with Juan Velásquez. The drug kingpin was a small man, but he exuded a sense of power that stemmed from having an unlimited supply of money and an army of men willing to sacrifice their lives to carry out his commands. Velásquez had already visited Beijing once and would soon return to examine their progress. Wu felt confident he would have something to show El Verdugo when he arrived.

First, however, he would have to deal with Alek Spray's colleague, Ron Digali. When Wu's intelligence officers first informed him about Digali's expertise and added that the American would be attending the conference, he put his staff on high alert. Digali would have to be watched carefully. He couldn't be allowed to leave Beijing with valuable information. They were too close to success to deal with espionage.

As he walked to the plenary hall for Sunli's presentation, Wu received a notification in his earpiece that one of his security officers had located Digali. Making a detour down a nearby hallway, Wu spotted a tall, thin American studying the convention center app on his iPhone. He looked nervous and lost.

"Ah, Dr. Digali. Can I help direct you, sir?" Wu asked.

"Uh, yes," replied Digali, wondering how the Chinese official knew his name. *Were the Chinese watching him? Was he in danger?* Remembering where he was, he glanced down at the name badge he was wearing. Mystery solved. "I'm looking for where Dr. Hidalgo is speaking," Digali said.

"I'm headed there now, please accompany me," Wu responded, and together the two walked to the plenary hall.

Chapter 17
Knight in Shining Armor

RON DIGALI WAS NERVOUS AND excited. He was excited to see Sunli again and nervous because he had no idea what to say. A typical engineer, Digali tended to be awkward around women. While he could expound brilliantly on the physics of electrical pulse generators, his own pulse raced and his words became twisted whenever an attractive female walked into the room. *Sunli is different*, thought Digali. She shared Digali's scientific prowess and stubborn dedication to the research and discovery process. Although Sunli had never spoken to him about anything personal, or even about anything other than the LENR, Digali was certain that they were meant to be a match. He just couldn't understand why she would abandon the team with no communication, but he was sure that as soon as he got her alone he would find out.

As he followed the Chinese official through the sprawling convention center, Digali thought about the other reason he had flown nearly 7,000 miles to get there—the LENR trigger. He knew that if he could find his way into the Chinese laboratories, he could search for evidence that the experiments they found in the forest in Mexico were now underway here in Beijing. He just had to find a way to get into the Chinese lab.

"Are you familiar with the Advanced Energy Lab?" Digali asked the distinguished military official walking beside him. "I am an American physicist here for the conference, and I was hoping there would be a chance to tour the facility while I am in town."

"General Wu Liu," Wu said, shaking Digali's hand. "I work closely with the lab and can arrange for you to have a tour. Where are you from?"

"Sandia Labs in New Mexico. I'm Ron Digali. I was actually working on a project with Dr. Hidalgo when she had to relocate to Beijing. I'm hoping to catch up with her this week."

"Interesting," Wu responded. "I doubt Dr. Hidalgo will be available to visit right after her speech, so why don't I schedule you to join a tour of the lab this afternoon?" Wu tapped on his cellphone. "There, it's all arranged. Meet the group at the north entrance at 1400 hours. That's 2 p.m."

Digali nodded. He wanted to try to reach Sunli sooner rather than later, but he couldn't pass up this opportunity to get into the lab. Surely, he could track her down after the tour.

"Thank you, sir," Digali said. "I appreciate that more than you can know."

"Oh, I know, Dr. Digali," Wu responded mysteriously. "It all will work out just fine."

* * *

Dr. Sunli Hidalgo stood at the podium addressing about 300 scientists, engineers, investors, and politicians gathered in the plenary hall. Dressed in a gray pinstriped skirt and matching suit jacket, with her shiny black hair twisted into a sophisticated chignon, she captivated the mostly male audience in the room. Sunli was wrapping up her presentation, which, based on the polite bursts of applause when she made key points, appeared to be well received. General Wu sat in the front row, practically hypnotized by the scientist on the stage.

"Across the planet, we rely on energy to go through our daily lives. World energy demands are rising and are predicted to increase 70 percent by 2040. Clean, sustainable, and affordable energy is the key to boosting the economy, decreasing air pollution, halting climate change, and creating jobs. Our work is essential and so we are continuing our quest to create an unlimited source of clean energy and, in doing so, we will transform the world," Sunli concluded. "Thank you. *Xièxie*," Sunli said, bowing slightly and exiting the stage area. As she passed through the curtain, a hand grabbed her and dragged her down the hall. Sunli was face-to-face with Chang.

"Peter Chang! I need to talk to you," she exclaimed in a surprised whisper.

"Sunli, Alek asked me to check on you," Chang replied. "Are you okay?"

"Not really." Sunli looked over her shoulder. Surely, the armed men who'd escorted her to the plenary hall were waiting nearby to take her back to her quarters. "I'm working with a special research team here on the LENR trigger and we are desperately in need of help with some simulations. Desperately in need of help," she emphasized as she saw the guards approaching.

Sunli grabbed Chang's hand. "Have your supervisor contact General Wu with the CPC and tell him that you are interested in collaborating on the project. I can tell you more about our research when we are in the lab."

One of the guards grabbed Sunli roughly by the elbow. "*Xiànzài gāi huí dào shíyàn shìle*," he said.

"What? It's already time to return to the lab? Well, give me a minute," Sunli hissed angrily at the guard, tugging her arm from his grip, turning back to Chang, and locking eyes with him. "I look forward to working with you, Dr. Chang," she said. As the guards began ushering her down the hall, she said over her shoulder, "Tell Alek that my father says hello."

* * *

Los Alamos was footing the bill for housing Percy's team during their time at the Pentagon, which for Alek meant the economical Extended Stay America motel. However, Percy was staying at the prestigious River

Inn Hotel in Georgetown, a boutique establishment frequented by the fashionable people of Washington, D.C. That luxury meant a longer morning commute to the Pentagon, but Percy avoided rush hour by arriving at work midmorning to "give his staff time to work without the boss looking over their shoulders." Alek knew that was Percy's trick to cut down on the length of his work day, plus the River Inn apparently served an excellent breakfast featuring freshly baked croissants—and it was relatively close to the Foggy Bottom metro stop.

Alek's motel was not near a metro stop, so he had to take a bus to get to the Pentagon, but he understood that, as a representative of a national lab spending taxpayer money, he had to choose economical accommodations—even if Percy didn't. Alek joked that 'economical' was just lab speak for 'shitty,' but at the end of most of his long work days, he was too tired to care. He slept well despite the lumpy mattress, which is why he jolted out of bed disoriented when his phone rang at 2 a.m.

"Is this Alek Spray?" a heavily accented male voice asked. "The Alek Spray who works with Dr. Ron Digali?"

"Yes," Alek mumbled, trying to figure out what was going on.

"This is Wang Ye from the Ministry of Public Security in Beijing," the voice continued. "I have some news about Ron Digali. Dr. Digali has suffered an unfortunate accident. He did not survive."

"He... what? Where? How?" Alek sat up in bed, scrambling for his glasses. "What happened? Why... why are you calling me?" he asked.

"Dr. Digali's last words were, 'Call Alek Spray,'" Ye said. "It took us some time to track you down. He passed away several hours ago."

"How did he...?" Alek couldn't say the words. Digali dead? In Beijing? What about Sunli?

"He was touring the pulsed power facility at the Advanced Energy Lab here in Beijing. He took a wrong turn and got separated from the rest of the tour group.

Somehow your friend wandered into an area that is closed to the public. One of the guards tried to stop him, but it appears he did not understand and began running. He ran out of a door onto a fire escape and then tripped and fell several meters. Naturally the guards responded and attempted to provide emergency care, but his injuries were too severe."

Alek thought about Digali, the brilliant, lovelorn physicist who had unlocked so many of the secrets of the LENR technology but couldn't find the key to unlock a woman's heart. He never should have let Digali go to Beijing. He should have gone in his place. This couldn't have been an accident. Alek's thoughts were racing. He needed to contact Percy and figure out the protocol for notifying Digali's family.. Clearly, there would be no more sleeping tonight.

Chapter 19
Alien Antics

ALEK SPRAY, CANDALE GREGORY, AND Tom Lowe sat glumly around the conference table in their Pentagon basement office suite. Candale was slowly demolishing a Styrofoam coffee cup, breaking off chunks and then tearing them into smaller and smaller pieces. A mound of white fragments was building beside him.

"Explain it to me again," Lowe said to Alek. "Digali's plan was to get into the lab to look for evidence the Chinese were working on the trigger and try to find Sunli? So he just made a wrong turn and then boom he's dead?"

Alek shook his head. "I told you everything I know. It doesn't make sense to me either."

Candale looked up from the pile of Styrofoam pieces. "I miss Ron," he said.

Suddenly, Gabi burst into the room, dressed in jeans and a T-shirt, her hair secured in a high ponytail.

"Sorry, I'm late. Traffic was a bitch. What have you guys figured out?"

"Nothing," Alek shouted in exasperation. "Absolutely none of this makes the slightest bit of sense. Plus, Peter Chang, the physicist from Beijing sent me the strangest email this morning. All it said was 'Dr. Hidalgo's father sends his regards.' I asked Chang to check on Sunli, not her father. Why would I care about her father? First of all, I've never even met the man and second of all, he's dead."

"But Sunli told Percy she was going to Beijing to take care of her father, right? Because he's ill?" asked Gabi, gently sweeping up Candale's destroyed cup pieces and depositing them in the trash can. "I'll check the FBI database to get details on her family."

"Here's the thing," said Alek, rubbing his temples. "She said her father was dead. We talked about her family a little bit the night we had dinner in Monterrey, and she said her dad lived in Mexico and her mother didn't return to China until he died."

Candale looked up. "So maybe she's sending a signal."

"That's what I told Percy," Alek exclaimed. "A signal."

"Uh-huh. Maybe she's trying to find a way to let you know things aren't quite right."

Gabi nodded. "That makes sense. Maybe she can't speak freely but she wants you to know something is wrong. Like I said, I'll have my team do some research on her family. Maybe that will help us figure out what's going on. If Sunli wants you to know something is wrong but can't contact you... and Digali is dead under mysterious circumstances... this could be worse than we think."

"Oh, it is worse than you think," Percy said, striding into the room with a scowl. "Much worse."

"What's going on?" asked Alek.

"Bob Bradley, that *New York Times* science writer who thinks everything is a conspiracy, has published an article about the LENR research and the Percy Study. He claims we are basing our work on alien propulsion LENR hardware that the Air Force supposedly recovered in Roswell."

"That's ridiculous," said Alek. "No one in their right mind will believe that."

Percy slapped a copy of *The New York Times* onto the conference table in front of Alek. "It may be ridiculous, but it's already raising questions. Alek, the reporter connected the LENR work you did as a student at MIT to his crazy theories, plus he uncovered the photo of your Goddamned 'Mystery Monolith' in the Sandia lab newsletter and he's claiming it's proof you've been working with extraterrestrials for years."

Despite Percy's bad mood and the seriousness of the

situation, Alek giggled.

"Okay, what's the Mystery Monolith," Gabi asked, perching on the edge of the table. "This sounds like a good story."

"Oh, it is," Lowe interjected. "It was about five years ago. We were working on the Particle Beam Accelerator project at Sandia, and everything was running behind schedule. Alek made up a funny story to explain the delay."

Percy didn't seem to find it at all amusing. "Yes, 'Smart Alek' told everyone that the excavation had been delayed because an indestructible structure had been discovered. Then he Photoshopped a picture of the construction site with the monolith from the movie *2001: A Space Odyssey* superimposed on it and published it in the lab newsletter."

Lowe picked up the story again. "Everyone asked about the mysterious structure and Alek said he knew nothing and, even if he did, he could only discuss it with individuals whose clearances had been approved. The monolith had MMI on it, and some people thought it stood for Manned Martian Invasion. It really was hilarious. Do you want to see the photo from the newsletter?" he asked, handing his phone to Gabi.

"Well, it's not hilarious now," Percy huffed. "Have you looked at Twitter lately? Social media is going nuts claiming that Alek is working with aliens to use LENR to power UFOs. On top of that, Bradley's article reveals some classified technical info that shouldn't have been made public. The top guys in the Air Force are furious about getting dragged into this public nonsense. They're convinced this will hurt their appropriations. The Secretary of the Air Force just called and suggested I fire you, Alek."

Alek's mouth dropped open in disbelief.

"Not so funny anymore, is it?" asked Percy. "Several senators on the Senate Select Committee on Intelligence have decided to call a meeting with us about our collusion with aliens, so you'd better dust off your good suit and freshen up your UFO know-how because we are meeting in Senator Plumkin's conference room in the Hart Office Building tomorrow at 9 a.m."

* * *

Once again, Alek and Percy found themselves in the Senate Hart Office Building. Senator Larry Plumkin from Mississippi and Senator J.D. Braxton from Texas were present, along with *The New York Times* reporter, Bob Bradley, who wore a smug smile as if he had gotten the world's biggest scoop and was on his way to winning a Pulitzer Prize.

Alek rubbed his sweaty palms on the pants legs of his navy suit. It was too hot to wear a suit and tie during the summer in D.C., but Percy looked cool and composed in gray pinstripes. They sat together across from the senators. Senator Braxton began the discussion with an admonition that they tell everything they know and answer every question completely and truthfully.

Percy leaned over and whispered to Alek. "Don't worry. You know I've testified before Congress many times. I call it 'exposing your testimonials.' The legal staff at Los Alamos says never to lie to Congress, but they also say not to tell the truth about subjects that might lead to further problematic testimony. That doesn't leave much, so just stay quiet and let me do the talking."

Facing them from across the polished table, Senator Braxton removed his hat, but his western shirt, bolo tie, and accent left no doubt about his Texan heritage. "Gentlemen, my constituents are demanding a full explanation and the esteemed Mr. Bradley has kindly agreed to help me elicit the truth."

Was this guy for real? wondered Alek. Living in New Mexico, he had encountered his share of annoying Texans, especially on the ski slopes, but Braxton seemed to be taking the act to a new level of redneck power play.

"Dr. Spray, I am certainly hopeful that we can get to the bottom of this God-awful mess. Mr. Bradley, please ask the questions we discussed."

Alek squirmed in his seat. *Wasn't Percy supposed to be doing the talking?* Percy looked at Alek and raised an eyebrow. Even with all his experience dealing with Congress, he appeared to find this situation unusual.

Bradley flipped open his notebook and began peppering Alek with questions about the science of LENR. Glancing repeatedly at Percy to verify that it was okay to answer, Alek addressed each question clearly and completely. He tried to follow all the tips Percy had given him, using complex technical language to deflect any questions that could discredit his work.

But as Alek spoke, Senator Braxton began to fidget, rifling through his notes and tugging on his bolo tie impatiently. Suddenly, he gestured to the reporter that he had something to say. "Mr. Bradley, if I may interrupt, I have some questions of my own for Dr. Spray."

Bradley nodded as Alek swallowed nervously, wondering what would happen next. Braxton leaned forward. "Dr. Spray, you conducted research on alien space propulsion while you were a grad student at MIT?"

Alek struggled not to laugh. "No, sir, I didn't."

"So, you deny that your MIT research used your knowledge of alien space propulsion as the technical basis for your work?"

"Umm no. I mean, I'm not sure I understand the question."

"So, you don't deny this?"

"I mean, that... that isn't true... it isn't even remotely logical."

"Do you deny that you and your colleagues have access to an actual alien spacecraft?" Braxton shouted.

Alek turned to Percy who was sitting beside him looking dumfounded. "Uh... I don't know what you are talking about, sir," Alek replied nervously.

Leaping to his feet, Braxton pounded the table. "Dr. Spray, do you deny that you are reverse engineering alien technology so you can build a new space weapon?"

Alek stared, transfixed by the beads of sweat on the

cowboy-turned-politician's upper lip. Simultaneously wanting to both laugh and cry, Alek struggled to come up with a response. Before he could get a word out, a deafening alarm filled the conference room. Several staffers rushed in, ushering first the senators and then Alek, Percy, and Bradley out of the room with shouts of "decontamination alert." They herded the group down the stairs to the basement. With the alarm still wailing, staffers instructed them to disrobe, spray themselves with decontaminant, and replace their clothing with sterile white coveralls. Alek turned his back and hoped no one was watching him changing. How many people could say they had undressed in front of two senators? *Never mind, I don't want to know*, Alek thought to himself.

"What in God's name is going on?" shouted Braxton.

"We believe it's a bioweapons attack," answered one of the aides who had escorted them into the basement. "An intern was opening a senator's mail and found a white powder," the aide explained. "We are afraid it may have entered the ventilation system. You will all have to begin daily treatment with Cipro as soon as possible. It will save your life, but it will probably turn your tongue temporarily black."

"Black tongue? Nope, I don't think so," Braxton exclaimed.

"Sir, inhaling even minute amounts of anthrax could result in certain death if treatment isn't administered immediately," said Alek. "A temporarily black tongue seems like a small price to pay for your life."

Alek felt grateful for the treatment, but he was even more grateful that the uproar had put an end to the ridiculous meeting. No one seemed to be interested in returning to the meeting room or continuing the insane line of questioning. Still dressed in their white jumpsuits, Alek and Percy left the Hart Building and headed back to the Pentagon, while Bradley dashed to his office to break the story of this latest Capitol Hill intrigue.

Chapter 19
Revelations and Breakthroughs

LATER THAT NIGHT, GABI TEXTED Alek. "You don't have to take the Cipro," read the text.

Alek replied with, "?"

He received the response, "Meet me at the bar in the River Inn."

Alek couldn't believe that, like Percy, the FBI was springing for rooms at the River Inn. Was he the only government employee who cared about saving taxpayer money? Unwilling to deal with the system of buses and the metro required to get to Georgetown where the inn was located, he ordered an Uber.

The bar at the River Inn was pleasantly dark with lots of polished wood, flickering candles, and low-hanging pendant lights. Gabi was seated in a booth in the back corner of the room, wearing a simple black dress that skimmed her curves. She had pulled her blonde curls into a careless topknot that somehow managed to look elegant and effortless at the same time. Percy sat across from her.

As Alek slid into the booth next to Percy, Gabi leaned forward. Alek struggled not to notice the way the new hairstyle and black dress drew attention to Gabi's exposed collar bones and the curve of her neck. He also struggled to ignore that Percy seemed to be noticing too.

"So, here's the deal," Gabi said. "The white powder wasn't anthrax at all. It was cocaine."

"Excuse me?" Percy said.

"Apparently Senator Maxwell from Arizona had a

long-standing arrangement with the Cincoleta Cartel that involved a weekly delivery. Unfortunately, an overeager intern decided to help out by opening his mail and immediately jumped to the conclusion that it could be anthrax. After the 2001 anthrax attacks on Capitol Hill, the feds put in strict bioweapons protocols and once that alarm was sounded, they had to follow through."

"Remember the attack?" Gabi asked Alek. "Five people died, and 17 others were infected. It was a big deal."

Percy snorted. "Well, this will only be a big deal for Tom Maxwell, because tomorrow his cartel connections will be on CNN and in the paper. My guess is that no one will even remember you've been consorting with aliens."

"But I wasn't," Alek spluttered. "Bradley made that whole thing up."

"He's got a bigger story now in any case," said Gabi. "So, stop taking the Cipro before your tongue turns black."

"Thanks for the update, Gabi," Percy said. "I'm going to call it a night and head up to my room. I promised my wife I'd phone her tonight."

Alek and Gabi were left sitting across from each other in awkward silence. "Uh, I'm going to grab a drink," he mumbled. "Want anything?"

"Sure, I'll have a Dos Equis."

Alek returned with their drinks. "I always forget Percy is married," he said.

"Yeah, so does he."

"Were you guys... uh... did you go out tonight?"

Gabi laughed. "No. God no. I was seeing an old friend. It was nothing. I just felt like dressing up. I didn't want you guys to risk the black tongues though, so I got in touch as soon as I could."

"So, the cartel's controlling U.S. senators *and* the Chinese?"

"It certainly seems that way," Gabi answered. "Our surveillance has found that the Chinese lab in Mexico was disguised as a drug lab, protected by the cartel and the Mexican police. We have confirmed that Juan Velásquez, the notorious drug lord known as El Verdugo, visited the facility frequently. He also appears to have ongoing communication with a retired Chinese general named Wu."

"Hmph, retired Chinese general, huh?" said Alek. "From what I hear, Chinese generals never retire—they just move beneath the radar to carry out their government's dirty work."

"Speaking of dirty work, we verified the connection between the Ramos brothers and El Verdugo. It seems that Will and Joe Ramos had worked for Velásquez years ago. I guess they never really stopped collaborating. Heck, they even might have been working for the cartel at the same time they were at Los Alamos conducting experiments," she said. "Plus, we also found surveillance showing Will Ramos had contacted Professor Roberto Rodriguez several times."

"That makes sense," Alek said eagerly. "The Ramoses knew Sunli had studied the LENR with Professor Rodriguez, so they probably figured they could coerce him into revealing the secret of the trigger. That didn't work out quite the way they planned it."

The two fell silent, lost in their thoughts. Suddenly, Alek stifled a laugh.

"What?" asked Gabi. "What are you laughing at?"

"It's just you—in that elegant dress, drinking a beer and talking about drug cartels. You're a contradiction."

"What? I can class it up when I need to."

Alek continued to giggle. "It's just that... when I first met you at the Friggin Bar, you seemed, no offense, kind of dumb and trashy. Then you show up in jeans and sneakers and I find out you're bad ass, and now... now you've got this whole sophisticated money look going on."

"I'm an FBI agent. I can be a chameleon."

"So, which is the real Gabi?" Alek asked.

"Hmmm. I guess all of us... but mostly the one in jeans and sneakers. What about the real Alek?"

"This is it," he replied. "What you see is what you get. A nerdy scientist who can't figure out how to make the experiment of a lifetime work."

"You don't give yourself enough credit," said Gabi. "You guys are close to figuring out the trigger. You'll make it work."

Alek looked down at the table, shaking his head. "I hope so," he said. "It really matters to me because..." Alek choked up, unable to continue. "It just... really matters," he said.

The two sat in silence for a moment and then Alek said, "So this whole fancy get up—if it wasn't for Percy's benefit, who were you dressing up for?"

"An old boyfriend," replied Gabi. "We met at the Cosmos Club. He's... a little wealthy."

"A little? That's one of the most prestigious and exclusive clubs in the nation."

"Okay. He's a billionaire. Nice guy, good connection, but not the one for me."

Alek debated asking Gabi what kind of guy she was looking for and then awkwardly changed the subject. "Did you find out anything about Sunli's father?" he asked.

"You were right," said Gabi. "Esteban Hidalgo passed away about six years ago in Monterrey. He never lived in Beijing. He never even left Mexico."

"So, Sunli was telling the truth in Mexico when we talked about her family. But Chang said, 'Dr. Hidalgo's father sends his regards.'"

"Like we discussed, I think Sunli was trying to find a way to send you a message. To let you know things just aren't right."

Alek rubbed his eyes. Here he was sitting in a bar with a beautiful woman and his thoughts were on another woman—equally beautiful and yet distant in more ways than one. He couldn't shake the sense that he needed to find a way to help Sunli and he had to do it quickly, but how?

* * *

Will Ramos and General Wu escorted Peter Chang into

the laboratory. Sunli was sitting in front of her computer staring at a scale diagram of the high current accelerator the CPC was constructing in the tunnel adjacent to the laboratory. Wu called the device the Dragon's CLAW. The acronym CLAW stood for collective laser accelerator weapon. All that was missing was the elusive trigger mechanism and time was running out.

Sunli was grateful that Chang's superiors at the PLA were willing to lend him to the CPC to share his expertise in computer simulations. She felt certain his help would allow them to visualize the changes needed to complete their work. For the past two weeks, she and Chang had collaborated on the project, always under the watchful eye of the Ramos brothers. They hadn't had the opportunity to discuss anything beyond their work, but Sunli still felt comforted to have an ally. She hoped Chang could sense that her presence in the lab was not voluntary, even though she pretended it was.

"Dr. Chang," said Will, "could you show General Wu the work you've done so far in simulating the geometry of the dense plasma focus?"

Wu approached the scientists. "I'm delighted to see your work," he said. "So far it has been quite a disappointment to bring these brilliant minds together, yet still see no results."

Sunli could tell that Wu's condescending attitude didn't please the other two scientists and he appeared to be deliberately antagonizing them.

Wu gazed coldly at the three of them, shaking his head. "Dr. Ramos, when we met, you assured me that you were capable of building this device, but here we are still floundering. Dr. Chang, your work was so highly recommended that I certainly expected a faster turnaround. I'm still waiting to see which of you two is the superior scientist. Perhaps neither..."

Wu leaned forward and gently caressed Sunli's cheek. She pulled away slightly, keeping her eyes fixed on him. "And you, Dr. Hidalgo," Wu said softly. "I had certainly hoped you would be sufficiently motivated to find an expedient solution to our needs. Do I need to increase that motivation? I can certainly instruct my guards to be less... uh... gentle, if you follow what I mean."

"We're close to the answer, I promise," Sunli exclaimed. "We're working round the clock."

Wu nodded, continuing to gaze intently at Sunli, he appeared to be transfixed by the brilliant, beautiful scientist, who squirmed uncomfortably under his gaze.

Trying to break the tension, Chang pulled up the computer simulation on his laptop. "Look at this 3-D model I made. It shows that the vital last stage of the plasma collapse is when the focus splits."

Will Ramos rolled his eyes. "So what?" he said. "We already knew that much. Hell, I figured that out when I was working at Los Alamos. The information Joe and I stole from their lab already got us that far. Of course the plasma has to be swept into the end of the chamber, but then what? You obviously don't know how to design a damn thing."

Chang stood up, pushing away from the desk angrily. "You brought me here to insult my work? You have no grasp of the reality of simulations. We can only solve this problem by tailoring the geometric parameters to match Dr. Hidalgo's theories. You're just a technician. You can't understand the details of my work."

Wu watched the exchange with a wry smile. He seemed to be enjoying the conflict between the two men. Sunli, on the other hand, was growing increasingly uncomfortable.

Ramos turned away, muttering under his breath in Spanish.

"Look," shouted Chang, grabbing Ramos by the arm and dragging him back to the computer. "Take a look at this computer simulation model I created. You can see how the model reveals that the geometry changes everything. You see the last stage of the focus and how it suddenly splits into a vacuum gap in the plasma? If we use the concave multi-electrode conductor feeding the pulse into the chamber, this will work."

Ramos looked confused, while Sunli, forgetting her earlier discomfort grabbed Chang's arm in excitement.

"Multi electrodes," she exclaimed. "We can change the rate of final collapse of the pinch by delaying the convergence of the multiple filaments."

"Yes! By changing the number of filaments, we can get ever increasing compression and particle acceleration," Chang said.

Chang and Sunli seemed to have forgotten anything beyond the thrill of the breakthrough.

Wu calmly approached the scientists. "Dr. Ramos, do you understand what Dr. Chang is proposing?"

"Well, off course," Ramos replied, visibly struggling to regain his composure. "Multi electrodes. I knew that. It's really very simple."

"It isn't simple," Chang said. "But it does build on Ron Digali's theories. In literally a billionth of a second, the instantly changing magnetic energy is transformed into an enormous electric field, and the energy grabs the electrons and ions surrounding the gap."

Ramos bent over the computer, eager to see the simulation. Sunli joined the men, transfixed. They had resolved the key barrier that had been preventing them from building a functional trigger. This was the breakthrough they had sought for so long. "The electrons and ions in the tiny vacuum gap are accelerated to relativistic speeds in the enormous electric field," she gasped.

The three contemplated the computer screen in silence, then Sunli stepped back suddenly. Chang glanced up. "What is it?" he asked.

"I just feel we need to consult with someone who has more technical expertise constructing this type of mechanism. Before we use the 3-D printer, we need to make sure the schematic is just right."

Chang nodded. "I see exactly what you need. We could certainly use the assistance."

"What about one of our former colleagues from the national labs?" asked Ramos. "Ron Digali was known throughout the scientific community as an expert in dense plasma focus technology. Such a pity about his death. If only we had access to his notes and calculations, it could speed up the process considerably."

Suddenly, Wu smiled. Sunli wondered about the calculated gleam in his eyes.

"This is simple," Wu said. "I will arrange to bring some of your U.S. colleagues to Beijing for an exchange on accelerator technology. I am certain they will be eager to compare notes and inspect our laboratories, and we can find a way to gain their assistance." He turned and shot a pointed look at Sunli. "I can be very persuasive, as you know."

"I recommend you invite Dr. Alek Spray and Dr. Candale Gregory," said Sunli.

The general nodded. "Consider it done."

Wu turned to Ramos with a cold stare. "Dr. Ramos, I'm not impressed by your bluster. I need you to thank Dr. Chang for providing the breakthrough you desperately needed, but failed to achieve. In the future, I hope you will work harder to prove your usefulness to this operation."

Wu stood and addressed the scientists, issuing orders. "We need exact dimensions and, Ramos, you get the shops working now so we can try it out. We need a real demonstration of this weapon. The last thing we need is to get stopped by some kind of foolish arms agreement. We have to find a way to prove that we can get a real weapons output."

Ramos nodded. "We need to find a way to get a high gain reaction by creating a propagating ignition. You know, like a chain reaction, but I don't think we know enough to safely do that."

Wu did not try to hide his look of disgust. "Well, maybe Alek Spray and Candale Gregory will know," he sneered. "I want it done this week."

Chapter 20
The Dragon's C.L.A.W.

ALEK WAS GLAD TO SEE Peter Chang's friendly smile after the nearly 14-hour flight from Dulles International Airport to Beijing, China. Candale, in a sleep-deprived daze, followed Alek and Chang through the airport.

When Chang had first suggested they travel to China for a small conference on accelerator technology, Alek felt skeptical. But the more he considered it, the more convinced he became that the answers he needed were waiting in Beijing.

Alek hoped he could gain insight into Sunli's disappearance, and he looked forward to discussing his pet project with his former classmate. Sure enough, Chang didn't waste a moment to bring up the technology that they both were working on.

"Our researchers refer to the collective laser accelerator weapon as 'the CLAW,' and the trigger mechanism as 'the dragon,' which makes the whole device 'The Dragon's CLAW,'" Chang explained, grabbing Candale's suitcase from the bag carousel.

"There's mine," said Alek, spotting his own bag and elbowing his way through the crowd to get it. The Beijing Capital International Airport was living up to its reputation as the busiest airport in Asia. Now that he was here, Alek did not doubt the reports he had read claiming that more than 100 million passengers passed through this terminal each year.

Barely avoiding slamming into an elderly Chinese

woman, Alek wrestled his suitcase off the belt and returned to where Chang and Candale were waiting. The three waded through the crowd, shouting to be heard over a steady stream of Mandarin.

"So, the Dragon's CLAW uses the LENR as an energy source, right?" asked Alek. "No actual weapons applications for the LENR, it just powers the CLAW and plays a significant role in energy research?"

"That's correct," Chang replied as they finally left the airport terminal and began walking through the vast parking garage. "It would not be wise to mention weapons development. While we are building an accelerator that can clearly power a beam weapon, the PLA recognizes the volatile nature of the arms talks going on between our two countries, so we are focused on fundamental accelerator physics and energy research."

Alek nodded. Chang seemed to be trying to convey something important without actually saying it aloud.

"So that's why Sunli moved here," exclaimed Candale. "So, she could take care of her dad and continue her energy research."

"Yes, that's correct," Chang replied pointedly, loading their bags into his Volkswagen Tiguan. Chang and Alek's eyes met momentarily before Candale interrupted.

"You drive a German car? In China?" he asked.

"Volkswagen is a very popular brand here in Beijing," Chang said. "But people who want a Chinese-built vehicle buy a *Wuling Hongguang*. It's our version of the minivan."

After stopping at the parking lot exit booth to pay the fee, Chang maneuvered the Tiguan onto a busy highway. "I've made reservations for the two of you at the *Qiu Guo* Hotel near *Tsinghua* University. Tomorrow morning we'll meet on campus for a briefing and then after lunch we'll tour the Advanced Energy Lab."

"That sounds good," said Alek. He could feel the exhaustion of the trip creeping up on him. Candale was already snoring lightly in the back seat. Alek glanced back at his sleeping colleague.

"Peter," said Alek quietly. "I'm worried about Sunli. Something about this doesn't seem right."

"I think it's wise to be worried," Chang replied. "The PLA is working closely with the Chinese People's Consortium. I suggest you avoid any confrontation with anyone in the CPC. Their leaders are determined to control China's weapons development funding. Between you and me, it is not an organization that I trust."

Alek wondered who he could trust. Could he trust Sunli? Peter? Percy? Some days he wasn't even sure if he trusted himself.

Chang pulled up in front of the hotel and two bellmen rushed over to help with the bags.

"You're each registered under your own names and the rooms are taken care of," Chang said. "Try to get some rest. Tomorrow will be a long day."

* * *

Tsinghua University was located on a sprawling campus on the site of the former imperial gardens of the *Qing* Dynasty. The Institute of Nuclear and New Energy Technology, or INNET, had two locations: one on the main campus and a larger site about 10 minutes north, where large buildings housing nuclear reactors nestled in the shade of the *Hutou* Mountain. Just under 1,000 faculty members, researchers and graduate students spent their days at the INNET campus, studying everything from nuclear technology to new energy formats such as hydrogen, solar energy, fuel cells, and biomass.

As Chang pulled the Tiguan into the parking lot in front of a multistory granite building, Alek noted the numerous students biking and walking across pathways covered with golden leaves. Exquisite landscaping marked by fall foliage, fountains, and flowers offered a serene background for the bustle of the researchers hurrying from place to place.

General Wu was waiting to greet the visitors at the door.

"Gentlemen, so pleased you could join us," Wu said, extending his hand and ushering the three into the building. "I am General Wu Liu of the CPC and I'll be serving as your host during this visit. We have planned an amazing lunch of Peking duck and all our local specialties, but first, I'd like you to share some of your work on collective accelerators with our young scientists here at the university."

Alek was surprised. They hadn't prepared to give a talk and were not armed with the PowerPoint presentations and handouts that he normally brought to a speaking engagement. But Wu didn't strike Alek as being someone who would take no for an answer. As Wu ushered them into the elevator, Alek glanced over at Candale and noticed his colleague looked a little green.

Candale was always nervous about public speaking. He also tended to ramble and get off track easily. He rarely volunteered for presentations and required lots of help and coaching when he did agree to present. "I'm not prepared," Candale whispered to Alek.

"Me neither," Alek replied in a hushed tone. "We'll just be really general and quick and then we can eat lunch and tour the lab." Soothed at the thought of lunch, Candale sighed in resignation and plodded after the general. Alek noticed that Chang was also looking ill at ease. *What have we gotten ourselves into?* Alek thought.

Wu escorted the men into a large, tiered classroom. Students armed with laptops and notepads filled the desks ringing the room. A whiteboard, projector screen, and podium in the front of the room defined the speaking area. Speaking in Chinese, Wu introduced them to the crowd and stepped back as the audience responded with polite applause.

Looking around the lecture hall, Alek realized the audience was not composed of typical students. They were all men in their thirties, wearing glasses, black suits, white shirts, and black ties, hovering over their laptops. Alek wondered if they worked for Wu in the CPC's secret weapons program. The listeners had a look of anticipation on their faces that did not seem consistent with students awaiting a scientific talk.

Alek began awkwardly, pausing as the interpreter translated. "Collective accelerator technology could become part of the solution to our global energy crisis. At Los Alamos and Sandia National Laboratories in New Mexico, we are experimenting with finding new ways to apply the discipline of accelerator physics as we study the manipulation of relativistic charged particle beams and their interaction with an accelerator structure by electromagnetic fields."

The audience members quietly scribbled in their notepads or typed on their laptops.

Candale stepped forward, jumping in where Alek left off. "At Los Alamos National Laboratory, we've uh, we've had some luck with these experiments. We're, uh, learning a lot about two beam impedance and different types of particle interference... modulation instability in plasma acceleration... well... uh... that's pretty cool."

Alek wondered if he should stop his socially-awkward colleague, or at least try to find a way to modulate Candale's instability. Meanwhile Candale was beginning to enjoy his moment in the spotlight.

"Here's, uh, the thing," Candale continued. "We found out the, uh, high power laser does a great job bunching an electron beam but..."

Alek quickly interrupted. "But we can't really go into that because it's classified." He gave Candale a pointed look. "Are there any questions we can answer?" Alek asked.

"I have some questions," Wu said. "Could you address methods for achieving a high gain reaction... perhaps by creating a propagating ignition? What are the ways you have found to increase the overall energy output?"

Alek was taken aback by the question. Wu's question hinted at seeking highly classified information. Precisely what was this Chinese general trying to learn?

"Well, no, since our goal is strictly energy research, we haven't focused on a high gain reaction," Alek said.

"There was this one, uh, thing that happened with a denotation causing an EMP," Candale blurted out.

Alek smoothly interrupted, saying, "But that has nothing to do with this particular question. I'm sorry that we can't assist you there."

"Gentleman, we certainly appreciate your sharing what you know. Such global cooperation is essential for circumventing the coming energy crisis and we applaud your willingness to engage with us in the spirit of reciprocity," Wu concluded, repeating his remarks in Chinese for the audience.

Although Wu's words were polite, his eyes blazed with anger. Alek could tell that the goals the general had set for the morning had not been achieved.

Chapter 21
Sitting Duck

WITH A HISTORY STRETCHING BACK 600 years, *Bianyifang* was the oldest establishment in Beijing that served Peking duck. The restaurant belonged to the Chinese government and featured photos on the walls of foreign leaders who had dined there. The chefs at *Bianyifang* used a closed oven to slow cook the duck, making the skin crispier and the meat more succulent. Both tourists and locals agreed that the restaurant did not disappoint.

Wu had reserved a table in a private dining room at the back of the restaurant, which featured traditional Chinese décor including a red, black, and gold color scheme, with lanterns, inlaid tables, and dragon figurines throughout the large room. It was like plunging into the ultimate Chinese restaurant cliché.

"I have taken the liberty of ordering some of the restaurant's specialties," Wu explained. "As you may know, *Bianyifang* was founded in 1416 during the *Ming* Dynasty. In addition to Peking duck, they specialize in *Shandong* cuisine, which features a wide variety of seafood and authentic entrees such as braised colon in brown sauce and lungs in milk soup."

Candale wrinkled his nose at these options. "I think I'll stick to the seafood," he said.

Alek found himself seated between two Chinese scientists, neither of whom appeared to speak much English. On the other end of the table, Chang and one of the students from the presentation audience were immersed in a heated conversation in Mandarin. Meanwhile, Wu was educating Candale on the process of preparing Peking duck.

"The authentic Peking duck is slow roasted so that the oil drips away, leaving a thin, crisp skin," Wu said.

"What about the seafood?" Candale asked. "I love seafood. Living in New Mexico, we rarely get super fresh seafood."

"Oh yes, we will have all sorts of delicacies," Wu said, seeming to relish his role as the charming host.

Alek raised his voice so he could talk to Wu from the other end of the table. "So, we'll tour the lab after lunch? I'm really looking forward to seeing your work."

"Yes, of course," Wu replied. "And I'm still looking forward to learning about your research as well. Pity you couldn't share any more this morning."

Just then a team of waiters clothed in chef's whites arrived bearing brimming trays of food containing everything from the shiny roast duck to a tureen swimming with a wide variety of unidentifiable sea creatures. As one of the waiters sliced the duck tableside and demonstrated how to wrap the duck meat in a steamed soft pancake and dip it in hoisin sauce, Candale helped himself to a large serving from the seafood dish.

"Some of these guys don't seem quite dead," he remarked, poking at what looked like a tentacle with one of his chopsticks.

"Eat up, they are delicious. There aren't very many places you can enjoy the black-banded sea krait," Wu replied.

Candale took a large, wiggly bite and began chewing with intense concentration. Finally, he swallowed, saying, "Mmph, delicious," with his mouth still somewhat full. "What exactly is a black-banded sea krait?" he asked.

Wu laughed. "It's a type of sea snake. They must be prepared very carefully because of the venom," he said.

Alek thought Candale looked a little paler after learning he had just eaten a venomous sea snake. Then again, Candale was always fairly pale. Candale kept determinedly chewing the rubbery mouthful.

Wu patted the American scientist on the back and addressed Alek again. "Dr. Spray, what can you share about other potential applications for your collective accelerator research? Also, I'd love to learn more about the EMP your colleague mentioned. I realize that neither your country nor mine are focused on the weapons potential, but surely the possibilities have crossed your mind."

Alek looked at the crispy slices of duck on his plate. He was losing his appetite. Candale might be eating a snake, but it appeared that they were dining with a snake as well.

"We really aren't exploring the weapons applications, sir," Alek replied, nervously twisting his napkin in his lap.

"Naturally not. Particularly as our countries explore the idea of creating a treaty to prohibit the development and deployment of space weapons. Nevertheless, the potential to use this technology to create an entirely new weapon... it is intriguing, don't you think?"

As Wu spoke, Alek considered the role of deception in Chinese culture. The country was noted for its reverence of the work of philosopher Sun Tzu, who described deception as a vital aspect of security from threats. Alek thought about how back in 2020, the Chinese tendency toward deception was revealed to the world when the Chinese government had withheld evidence from everyone, including their own citizens, about the pandemic outbreak in the City of Wuhan. While he trusted Peter Chang explicitly, Alek did not feel at all comfortable discussing weapons technology with General Wu.

As Alek struggled to find a way to change the subject, Candale suddenly pitched forward in his chair, clutching his throat. Alek sprang up from his chair and rushed over to him.

"What's happening? What can I do?" Alek cried out.

Candale's face was flushed, and he was sweating and

coughing. His bulging eyes revealed his rising panic.

Wu grabbed his cellphone and began giving orders in rapid Mandarin. Satisfied that the situation was under control, he turned to Alek. "Something he ate must have disagreed with him. I doubt it's serious, but I've arranged for transport to the hospital just in case."

Then Wu addressed Candale, smoothly and calmly. "Relax, Dr. Gregory. Help is on the way, but I am certain you will be fine."

A team of EMTs arrived quickly and loaded the still-conscious Candale onto a stretcher.

"I'm going with him," Alek exclaimed.

Wu spoke in Chinese with the emergency personnel who were busily fitting Candale with an oxygen mask. "There isn't room in the ambulance," Wu replied. "You and Dr. Chang take your vehicle and meet us at the hospital." With that, Wu followed the EMTs and Candale out of the room.

* * *

Chang and Alek raced to the Tiguan, but it soon was clear they wouldn't be able to keep up with the ambulance, which was traveling fast with lights and sirens running.

"Text Wu and find out what hospital they're headed to," Chang said. "There are lots of hospitals in Beijing."

Alek tapped out the message on his iPhone and quickly relayed the answer. "Beijing Hospital. Do you need me to map it?"

"No," said Chang, "I know where it is. It's not very far."

As Chang weaved through traffic, Alek realized why people called Beijing 'Shoudo'—capital of traffic jams. He also noticed that despite the congested roads, the Chinese drivers seemed polite and patient. There were no signs of the road rage that was common in larger cities in the U.S. Alek, on the other hand, wasn't able to be patient since his worry about Candale was continuing to build.

"He's just the nicest guy, wouldn't hurt a mouse, and

such a hard worker," Alek told Chang. "I just feel responsible for him. You know, he makes me feel like I need to look after him. Like it's my responsibility to take care of him and I failed."

"Don't be silly. He will be fine. It's just an allergic reaction," said Chang. "Here we are. I'll pull up in front and you run in. I have your phone number. I'll find you after I park."

Chang watched as Alek raced through the doors of the emergency room and then turned the Tiguan around to search for a parking spot. He had just shut off the engine when he received a text from Alek.

"We're in the wrong place. They went to a different hospital," the text said. "Meet me in front of the ER."

Alek jumped in the car, out of breath. "He's not here, he's at Beijing Ditan Hospital. I guess I misunderstood."

"Beijing Ditan," exclaimed Chang. "That's nearly an hour away during rush hour. Damn it. We'll take the toll road."

"I tried to call Percy, but it just went to voice mail," said Alek. "We never should have come here."

"We have excellent medical care here. It will be just fine."

After about 45 minutes of tense driving through rush hour traffic, Chang and Alek pulled up in front of Beijing Ditan Hospital. Once again, Alek sprang out of the Tiguan, leaving Chang to park.

The hospital lobby was busy, and it took Alek a few minutes to get the attention of the woman running the front desk. When Chang returned from parking the car, he found Alek screaming "Candale Gregory" in the woman's face.

Chang grabbed Alek by the arm and took control of the situation. Following a brief conversation in Mandarin, the two were directed to the elevator.

"Room 552," said Chang. "Please, Alek, try to calm down. It's going to be okay."

But it wasn't okay.

The first person Chang and Alek saw when they exited the elevator was Wu screaming at a nurse.

"*Jìliàng cuòwù. Bù yìng gāi fāshēng,*" Wu bellowed, while the nurse cowered before the general.

"*Duìbùqǐ xiānshēng nà shì yīgè cuòwù,*" the nurse replied.

"What was that about?" Alek asked Chang under his breath.

"I'm not sure. She said it was a mistake," Chang replied.

Wu noticed Alek and Chang standing at the end of the hallway and strode toward them, holding his hand out to Alek.

"I'm so very sorry. Apparently, Dr. Gregory had a heart condition. The doctors did everything they could do. They couldn't save your friend."

"What? No!" Alek ran down the hall to room 552, Chang chasing after him.

Candale lay on the hospital bed, no longer breathing. Medical equipment strewn haphazardly around the room suggested an unexpected struggle to save his life. Alek sobbed and ran to his friend's side, while Chang stood back awkwardly.

"I just... I can't... I don't..." Alek couldn't even form a sentence. Embarrassed, Chang began picking up discarded medicine vials from the floor. He looked around for a trashcan but not finding one, slipped the empty vials in his pocket.

Finally, Chang walked over and put his hand on Alek's shoulder. "Come on, man. We need to call his family," he said softly. "Let's go."

Chang led Alek from the room. There was paperwork to be completed. Arrangements to be made. Absentmindedly, he stuck his hand in his pocket, running his hand over the discarded vials he had collected. He pulled one from his pocket and looked at the label: sodium thiopental.

Chapter 22
Going Underground

WILL AND JOE RAMOS LISTENED patiently as General Wu unloaded his anger upon them.

"You were supposed to get Dr. Gregory to talk, not kill him," Wu shouted. "The goal was just to give him enough truth serum to get him to spill the information on how to achieve the high gain reaction. The sodium thiopental should have worked."

"It, uh, turns out he had a heart problem," explained Will. "Plus, I'm not even sure he actually knew anything."

"Well one of those men knew something. Now, thanks to you, Gregory is dead, and Spray has left the country. Plus, Velásquez will be here tomorrow to check on the project and you two will have to explain why we have nothing to show."

"Sir, there are some issues," Will explained hesitantly. "We aren't at all ready to run tests in the underground tunnel. It is possible we could try an open air, ground-based LENR experiment at a remote location to see if the trigger will work. I'm fairly confident it will work, but I'm not so sure that the energy source will be adequately contained."

"This is because you couldn't get Gregory or Spray to reveal the science behind the high gain concept," Wu scoffed. "We have to figure out how to channel the output of the device from the initial small region to spread to adjacent fuel. That's the only way we can achieve the power we need to create a sufficiently deadly weapon. You figured out the target and the trigger, now you need to take the next step, which is achieving a high gain."

Wu paced angrily around the lab while the Ramos brothers waited for instructions. They knew the general well enough to keep their mouths shut until he issued orders.

"Get going on the ground-based experiment and get ready to deal with Velásquez," Wu barked. "We have to keep Velásquez happy since the cartel is supplying most of the funding for our weapons research. Make sure to give him a tour of the underground facility and try to impress him with the work we've done. And listen to Chang and Sunli—those two strike me as the only scientists of any value right now."

As Wu stomped out of the room, Will turned back to his computer. He didn't enjoy hearing Chang and Sunli praised, but he knew better than to talk back to the Chinese general. How had he and his brother ended up caught between a Mexican drug lord and a corrupt leader of a rogue branch of the Chinese military/industrial complex? Who would have thought he'd look back fondly at those long, boring days spent working in the Los Alamos lab?

The next day, Juan Velásquez heaped a steady stream of Spanish curses upon the brothers. They were accustomed to Velásquez's anger and anxious to stay on the good side of the man known throughout Mexico's drug syndicate as The Executioner. The fact that Velásquez had come to Beijing to check on their work did not reflect his confidence in their ability to get the job done.

"*¿Me estás escuchando, pendejo?*" Velásquez asked.

"*Si, lo siento,*" Will responded. "I'm very sorry—I was just thinking about our research. How would you like to see the underground accelerator facility we are constructing? I think you will be impressed."

"I've invested millions," Velásquez bellowed. "Do you think this is a game of show and tell? I want results. Are you trying to trick me? Okay, go ahead and show me what my millions have bought."

Will and Joe escorted Velásquez to the elevator that connected the lab to the underground missile tunnel where the accelerator project was housed. The accelerator facility was built into a portion of the 3,000-mile long underground tunnel system nicknamed the Underground Great Wall of China. The Second Artillery Corps, a secretive branch of the Chinese military, had built this tunnel system over many decades to provide a hidden approach for their intercontinental ballistic missiles. This system allowed the PLA to transport missiles to their launchers at high speeds, much like an underground missile highway. The Chinese leaders were extremely proud of the strategic advantage the tunnels offered them.

The actual existence of the tunnels had never been kept secret. In 1995, the Chinese government even advertised the tunnel system on television, and, in 2009, they completed an upgrade and released videos of 18 wheelers speeding along the giant tunnels as if they were on a racetrack, which in many ways they were. The one thing the Chinese did not advertise was the exact location of the tunnels.

Will hoped that Velásquez would recognize that a visit to the tunnel represented a pivotal disclosure, signifying cooperation and trust.

Will, Joe, Velásquez, and the drug lord's ever-present entourage of bodyguards crowded into the industrial elevator and traveled 30 meters down. The elevator doors opened to reveal a cavernous tunnel with gray concrete walls illuminated by repeating white fluorescent light fixtures every few feet. The tunnel branched in three different directions. Rails built into the floor and ceiling of the facility curled along one of the corridors and out of sight.

Will led the group to two waiting golf carts, and he and Joe drove their guests down one of the corridors, the white lights streaking past as they made their eerie journey to the accelerator site. Uncomfortable with the silence, Will took over the role of tour guide, his voice echoing off the tunnel walls.

"In order to move the 100-meter-long electron-beam accelerator underground, we had to transport the machine in pieces. We are currently re-assembling it here—where we are guaranteed secrecy and can proceed without any fear of detection."

Will and Joe parked the carts in front of the gigantic shining silver tube that served as the heart of the accelerator. Chinese technicians in white coveralls moved around the machinery, tightening bolts, checking settings, and adjusting connections. They worked in silence, punctuated by the occasional exchange of curt orders in Mandarin.

Velásquez slapped the side of the machine with his hand as if it were a farm animal. "So, are you going to give me a demonstration? How does this damn thing even work?"

General Wu stepped out from behind the accelerator. "Señor Velásquez," he said, holding out his hand to greet his visitor, "I am so pleased you have come to see the results of our research. Together, we are creating an entirely new weapon, a new source of income, power, and control. We will be invincible. This is where it begins."

Chapter 23
Politics and Perception

ALEK MANEUVERED HIS ROLLING SUITCASE onto the escalator leading to the departure gates in the Albuquerque International Sunport. Calling an airport a 'sunport' might have made it seem like more of an exotic destination, but Alek's trip to New Mexico had been anything but a lighthearted getaway. He was returning to D.C. after attending Candale Gregory's funeral. Burying two colleagues, two friends, in less than a month was more than Alek could take.

Finding his gate, Alek settled into an uncomfortable Southwestern-style chair with stiff wooden arms and a leatherette seat that seemed to have been designed expressly to prevent people from sleeping in the airport. He pulled out his iPhone, debating whether to text Gabi. She was investigating a lead in Mexico and hadn't been able to make it to the funeral. Alek wasn't sure whether he wanted to contact her to check on the investigation or whether he simply wanted to talk to her. Before he could get overly introspective about his true motives and feelings, his phone rang. It was Percy, who had also skipped the funeral to remain in D.C. to brief the President and testify before Congress about their work.

"Alek, we're packing up our Pentagon office," Percy said without any preamble. "The study is over since the arms talks with China are about to get underway."

Alek took a minute to process this, trying hard to shake off the thoughts of Gabi and focus on Percy's words.

Percy took his silence as an invitation to continue. "The China/U.S. Advanced Nonproliferation Committee is scheduled to hold negotiations to ban the development of beam weapons and space-based energy sources. Our efforts to develop the technology behind the LENR weapon have been effective after all."

"Effective?" Alek asked in shock. "We're closer, but we still haven't figured out how to create the trigger. How can you call that effective and why would we give up now when we are finally getting close to creating the ultimate energy source, to realizing the goals of Project Z?"

"Oh Alek," Percy said in a patronizing tone. "Making it work was never the goal. Our efforts to create the trigger, the information leaked to the Chinese military, the threat of a new, invincible weapon... those were the government's goals. Don't you see, we were fighting a battle of psychology, not technology. It seems we have won."

Alek shifted in the uncomfortable chair, feeling confused and frustrated. "Our goal was never to make it work?" he asked in disbelief.

"Our study forced the Chinese to agree to negotiate an agreement to put an end to all LENR research and all space-based weapons and energy sources. We are actually winning by failing," Percy said. "The Senate Select Committee feels that putting an immediate halt to our research will show the Chinese how cooperative we are, which could help them come to the table with a viable agreement. Shutting down our office sends the signal that the U.S. is all in on making the talks work. It's a demonstration of good faith."

Alek shook his head. "I don't understand. What about the energy applications? We may hold the key to the ultimate clean energy source, and we are just walking away?"

"Ideally the negotiations will maximize cooperative energy research between the U.S. and China while banning all weapons applications. So, we may be able to resume our research eventually. But even if that doesn't happen, our work has scared the Chinese government enough that they are willing to consider an agreement. And on top of that, I have scored close to $100 million in guaranteed funding for Los Alamos, so the time in D.C. has definitely been worth the effort."

Alek stood up. Oblivious to the travelers hurrying past him at the airport, he was no longer able to contain his anger. "Ron and Candale are dead and it's because of this project. How can we stop now knowing our friends gave up their lives for this goal that apparently you knew all along we were never supposed to attain?"

"Oh, Alek, I do love your idealism," said Percy.

"If Ron and Candale's lives don't matter, at least think about the consequences of this decision. What makes you think Wu will obey his government's directives? And what about Velásquez? Last I checked, drug lords don't care about nonproliferation treaties. What will keep this technology from falling into terrorists' hands?"

"Look, the Chinese government will take care of Wu and we will leave Velásquez to the FBI and DEA. It's not our problem. Now, I suggest you cancel your flight to D.C. and just stay in New Mexico. I've got to run. I need to pack."

* * *

"Look, bilateral negotiations to ban weapons of mass destruction have kept bureaucrats busy for decades," Percy told Lowe as he carelessly threw files into a cardboard box in what soon would no longer be the Percy Study team's Pentagon office.

"In the 80s, Ronald Reagan held arms control negotiations with the Soviet Union. Now we're doing the exact same thing with China to eliminate weapons applications of the LENR."

Lowe sighed. "It's just that we were finally making some progress on this research. Over the years, many countries and their leaders have tried unsuccessfully to ban nuclear weapons, but it's a hopeless attempt to stuff the genie back in the bottle. It won't work."

Percy handed Lowe the file box and held the door open for him, then the two began their long walk to the parking lot.

"Of course, it won't work. It doesn't matter," Percy said. "Sure, both the Chinese and the U.S. share the fear that if the LENR ever becomes a terrorist device, a backpack gadget could easily be carried into public spaces and kill thousands... maybe millions. At the same time, a joint energy program could possibly achieve the goal of the ultimate clean energy source for the world." Percy loaded the last box of files into the trunk of his rented Cadillac.

"So why are we packing up?" Lowe asked, looking back at the Pentagon where he had spent the last month focused on LENR research. "This technology not only could provide a new source of carbon-free energy, but it could also burn up tons of nuclear waste already stored in drums all over the world. We finally have the ability to eliminate the threat of global warming, but instead we are packing up and heading home?"

Percy shut the trunk of the Cadillac. "It's like I told Alek," he said. "This wasn't really about making the technology work, it was about scaring the Chinese enough so they would be willing to come to the table to negotiate. Plus, of course, the real goal—getting funding for our labs."

The two men walked back to their temporary office to make sure they hadn't left anything behind. "The problem is that reaching an agreement could end the hope of a major source of income for both the U.S. and Chinese military industrial complexes," Lowe said.

"Certainly," Percy agreed. "My friends in the aerospace industry are waving the flag of U.S. national security because they don't want to see politicians jump to any agreements that could cut into future business," he said. "But let's be serious here, even if they sign an agreement, neither side is likely to abide by it. Reagan coined the phrase that he mispronounced in Russian, '*Doveryai, no proveryai*,' which means 'Trust but verify.' The Chinese, however, tend to be opposed to on-site inspections and verification of agreements. Both the U.S. and Chinese economies are so dependent on advanced technology that they are reluctant to make a deal. That's why we need to make sure our lab keeps getting funding. We have to be ready to ramp back up to speed when the powers-that-be discover the Chinese have been cheating on their agreement. Not that it should come as a surprise."

"Plus, there are other countries with nuclear capabilities. How will we defend ourselves against that threat?" Lowe asked as they entered their old office.

"It's certainly a serious concern. For now, though, it's time to shelf this project. Our current goals have been met."

"So, what do you think will happen?" Lowe asked. "Did we just waste an entire month on this research?"

"I told you—it wasn't a waste even if it doesn't stand a chance of turning out the way you and Alek hoped it would. This isn't really about technology. It's all about politics and perception," Percy said, taking a last look at the empty office and turning out the light.

Lowe shook his head. "What about creating the ultimate clean energy source? Is it even possible?"

"Oh, it's possible," Percy answered. "As to whether it will actually happen though... I wouldn't bet on that."

Chapter 24
A Leap of Faith

ALTHOUGH THE PERCY STUDY HAD ended because of the ongoing arms talks between the U.S. and China, nothing had changed in the secret underground research facility next to the Advanced Energy Lab in Beijing. Sunli wasn't sure whether it was day or night. She had been working nonstop in the windowless lab for at least a week, the passage of days only broken by visits from Wu and Velásquez and the occasional meal. Chang, Will, and Joe had worked along with her, perfecting the trigger and running simulations. Although they hadn't managed to figure out a high gain concept, which would allow them to harness the initial electromagnetic output to create a greater burst of power, they were getting close to being able to carry out a field test of the LENR ignition. The key would be translating the technology that worked in the giant accelerator to a compact and portable device.

The Ramoses had gone to their quarters to get some sleep and Sunli was going over the results of the latest simulation, when Chang walked into the lab.

"Dr. Hidalgo... Sunli, maybe it's time to take a break," said the Chinese physicist. "Honestly, you're working on this like your life depends on it."

"Not my life, but a life," mumbled Sunli under her breath.

Chang sat down beside Sunli, gently removing the printouts from her hands and laying them on the desk beside the computer keyboard. "What do you mean? Why do you act like you are a prisoner here? Why is Alek so worried about your safety?" he asked.

Instead of answering, Sunli turned away and began to sob silently, her head buried in her hands. Chang hesitated as if uncertain whether to acknowledge her outburst. He looked around awkwardly for a box of tissues. Not seeing one, he pulled a paper napkin left over from lunch from his pocket and handed it to Sunli, who wiped her eyes and sniffled. "Thanks."

"Sunli, this isn't like you. In fact, I've never seen you... well... like this, you know, emotional. What's going on?" Chang pulled out a chair and sat down next to her. "Really, you can talk to me. I'm only working here because the director of the Advanced Energy Lab recommended me to General Wu and Alek asked me to check on you." Chang paused, unsure what to say next. Then he took Sunli's hands in his own. "Alek is really worried... and I am too."

Sunli turned to Chang, still openly crying.

"What is it?" Chang asked. "What is it that Wu has hanging over you?" He reached up and brushed a strand of Sunli's hair away from her face. The small gesture of tenderness unraveled her emotions more.

"Wu is... he's holding my mother prisoner. He's blackmailing me to complete the project and he says..." Sunli choked back a sob, "he says he'll kill her if we fail."

Chang stared at Sunli as the pieces fell into place and he finally sensed the gravity of the situation. "They're holding you here against your will and threatening to hurt your mother?" He grabbed Sunli by the shoulders. "Look at me," he said. She raised her swollen eyes to his.

"Wu and Velásquez think they have the upper hand, but only you and I understand the technology. We are the only people who can make this work. We won't fail. We will build Wu's weapon... the Dragon's CLAW... and we will rescue your mother. Have faith, Sunli. We will do this. You have my word on it."

Sunli drew a ragged breath and nodded, realizing that the help she needed had finally arrived. Chang would help her build the weapon, save her mother, and achieve her ultimate goal. Suddenly struck by how much power she had over her colleague, Sunli struggled not to smile. She covered her face with her hands to disguise her true emotions and stifled another sob. Chang was the answer. He was exactly what she needed to succeed.

"Thank you," she managed to say weakly, grabbing his hands in hers. "I felt so lost... so alone." With tears hanging heavy on her long, dark eyelashes, Sunli met Chang's gaze. "Thank you for giving me back my faith that everything will be alright."

"Of course it will. I'm here to help you," Chang said. "Now, let's get back to work."

* * *

Alek sat up on the lumpy beige couch in his Los Alamos apartment, trying to identify the sound that had disturbed his sleep. Someone was knocking on the front door, steadily, insistently. He waited a few minutes, but the knocking didn't stop.

Stepping over the half empty pizza box on the floor, Alek dragged himself to the door and unlocked it without looking through the peephole to see who was bothering him after 10 p.m. Not waiting for an invitation, Gabi strode through the open door.

"What's going on here, Spray?" she asked, grabbing a trashcan and thrusting it into his hands. Alek stood there dumbfounded as she gestured to the empty beer bottles and discarded trash lying on the coffee table. "How old is this pizza?" She sniffed it and shook her head. "You haven't replied to my texts or answered my calls and now I find you holed up in your apartment with this pathetic excuse for a pizza. What the hell is going on?"

Alek stared at the whirlwind that had overtaken his apartment and then mechanically started to pick up the trash. He rubbed the sleep out of his eyes and realized it had been a few days since he had shaved... or changed clothes.

"What are you doing here?" he asked.

"Well, I have news about El Verdugo, and I wanted to see how you were doing since Congress shut down the project. Since I couldn't get a hold of you, I told my boss I needed to follow up on some cartel connections in New Mexico. So, here I am."

Alek shook his head, wondering if he was imagining Gabi sweeping through his apartment. In just a matter of minutes, she had waded past the mess in his living room to the kitchen where she groaned at the dirty dishes piled in the sink.

Gabi was dressed in jeans, hair pulled into a ponytail. She rummaged in the kitchen drawer for a dish towel and then handed it to him as she filled the sink with hot water and soap.

"I'll wash. You dry."

"Um... hi, Gabi," said Alek. "You look great."

"Well, that's not true. You must be losing it," replied Gabi. "Let's get this place cleaned up and then you can jump in the shower and get yourself cleaned up. Then, we'll go to that Friggin Bar and get some real food and you can tell me what's going on."

* * *

Seated in the red, cracked Naugahyde booth in the Friggin Bar, Alek and Gabi devoured their green chile cheeseburgers. Alek couldn't help noticing that, although the table was still slightly sticky, the service was much better than when Gabi worked there undercover. For the first time ever, the burger he ordered with no onions had actually arrived without onions. Alek found himself lifting the bun up repeatedly, as if onions might suddenly materialize. For some reason, he missed the act of picking off the offensive onions and the small talk that came with complaining about it.

"So, what exactly happened to the Percy Study?" Gabi asked, taking a drink of her Dos Equis.

"Apparently our work was done. The China/U.S.

Advanced Nonproliferation Committee is meeting to discuss banning the development of beam weapons and space-based energy sources. Scaring the Chinese enough that they would agree to negotiate was apparently the goal of our work." Alek shook his head sadly.

"And all this success led you to hide in your apartment and abandon showering, shaving, and answering my text messages?" asked Gabi.

Alek rubbed the stubble on his chin self-consciously.

"Actually, I kind of like it," said Gabi. "You should grow a beard."

Alek hoped the bar was dark enough that she wouldn't notice he was blushing. It had been a long time since anyone had noticed any aspect of his appearance. How did he end up sitting in a bar with an attractive, intelligent, funny woman who for some inexplicable reason seemed to be interested in his well-being? Alek felt like he should pinch himself. Clearly this was a dream and any minute he would wake up.

"It's just that we were so close to figuring out the trigger," Alek said, deciding that if he was dreaming, he might as well enjoy it. "Finding this solution, creating an endless source of clean energy... that's been my life's work."

Alek rubbed his stubbly chin again. "I just hate having it all ripped out from under me when we were so close. Plus, I owe it to Ron and Candale. No matter what anyone says, they gave up their lives for this project." Alek fell silent, thinking about the other life this project had taken. He could not bring himself to tell Gabi about his past.

Seeing his solemn face, Gabi reached across the table and took Alek's hand. "You don't have to give up, regardless of what Percy says. It's a leap of faith, but sometimes faith is all we have."

Alek held her gaze for a minute and then, embarrassed, began peeling the label off his beer bottle. His mind drifted back to his past again.

"I've... I've made so many mistakes in my life. I've let people down in so many ways. I can't even tell you. I just wanted to do something worthwhile for once."

"You are doing something worthwhile," replied Gabi. "And, like I said, there is absolutely no reason for you to give up."

Alek couldn't wrap his head around how supportive Gabi was being. He had never felt this feeling of being around someone so warm and caring, someone who was in his corner no matter what. At the same time, she was a smart, sarcastic workaholic—just like him. They were kindred spirits. When he looked into her blue eyes, he felt at home, like they had always known each other somehow.

"What did you learn about El Verdugo and the cartel?" Alek asked, awkwardly changing the subject.

"We are 100 percent sure that Velásquez is funding the CPC research," said Gabi. "I'm fairly certain he intends to use the LENR weapon as a bargaining chip to maintain control of U.S. law enforcement. He has been spending a lot of time in Beijing lately. On top of that, both Peter Chang and Sunli Hidalgo appear to be contributing to the CPC research too."

"Yes, I talked to Chang when I was there, but he acted strange when I mentioned Sunli. And I still can't figure out why Sunli emailed Percy and said she was going to Beijing to take care of her father. Her father died years ago, and he never even lived in China."

Gabi leaned forward, lowering her voice. "Here's the thing. About two months ago, Sunli's mother, Lian Chen Hidalgo, went missing. None of her neighbors know where she is. One old lady told our agents that Mrs. Hidalgo must have gone to New Mexico to stay with her daughter, Sunli. And we know that's not true."

Alek sighed. "All along I've had a terrible feeling that Sunli is in trouble. She may not be the friendliest person I've ever met, but she is brilliant and if anyone can figure out how to make the LENR work, it's her. Plus, I just have to do something to help her. She's part of my team."

"Do you think Velásquez could be behind Sunli's

mother's disappearance? Maybe he and the CPC were using that as leverage to get Sunli to cooperate with them?"

Alek put his head in his hands. "I... I just don't know... but if people are getting hurt, it's my fault. I've failed at everything."

"Look, just because the Percy Study is over, it doesn't mean you have to give up. You have to keep moving forward. Sunli needs your help." Gabi rose and slid into the booth next to Alek. She slipped her arm around his shoulders, pulling him close. "Project Z will be a reality. The world needs you to continue your search for a source of clean energy... and you know what, I need you too."

Alek met Gabi's eyes. The two sat inches apart, motionless. Finally, Alek spoke. "A leap of faith, huh? I think I'm ready. It's time to get to work."

Chapter 25
Mischief and Mayhem

"WE HAVE AN ANNOUNCEMENT TO make. Señor Velásquez, please take a seat." General Wu ushered the drug lord into the lab, gesturing to a comfortable chair that had been moved into the room in anticipation of the meeting. Wu had gathered his staff and summoned his benefactor to explain his plans to test the Dragon's CLAW.

"Dr. Chang will brief us on the technological progress that he and Dr. Hidalgo have achieved," the general announced with a pointed look at Will and Joe Ramos.

Will cleared his throat. "And Joe and I will discuss the invaluable assistance we provided in developing the weapon," Will said, his voice quivering slightly.

"Yeah, that's right," Joe muttered. "We helped."

Sunli controlled her desire to roll her eyes. The Ramoses were buffoons. They had been nothing but an impediment to the research. Sure, they were responsible for the initial breakthrough in Los Alamos. They had stumbled upon the idea of using nickel, but that was just dumb luck. Without her and Peter, there would be no progress—there would be no Dragon's CLAW.

Peter Chang stood, addressing Velásquez. "Dr. Hidalgo and I have constructed an inertial confinement generator that uses a Low Energy Nuclear Reaction driven by a dense plasma focus to create an explosive energy pulse."

"That's right," Sunli added, jumping up quickly to stand beside Chang. "After many weeks of research, we have developed the triggering mechanism that will maximize the output of the beam. The result will be a sizeable detonation that will prove beyond a doubt that we have achieved the goals of the Dragon's CLAW."

"*Bueno, bueno*," exclaimed Velásquez, rising from his chair and turning to the general. "When do we test it? How soon can I see the power of this gadget you have built?"

"Quite soon," Wu replied. "Next week in fact. We'll test the... uh... the gadget... on one of China's artificial islands in the southern part of the South China Sea. The region stands as a testament to China's military power." Wu paused dramatically as if waiting for the others to acknowledge China's greatness. Velásquez simply nodded, gesturing for the general to go on.

"The area is defined by the nine-dash line stretching hundreds of miles south and east from the province of Hainan," Wu continued. "It contains islands built using dredging and land reclamation. The location is uninhabited and strategically positioned to house anti-ship and anti-air missiles. It offers the perfect place to test the LENR trigger since neither U.S. aircraft carriers nor other ships from the nearby countries of Vietnam, Malaysia, or the Philippines can approach the islands without violating Chinese sovereignty agreements over the waterway." Wu smiled as he concluded the explanation. "I also find the island's location amusing. It's called Mischief Reef."

"There definitely will be some mischief taking place," Velásquez chuckled. "So how will we get the gadget to this island?" he asked.

"We will transport the device in a shipping crate on a small boat," Wu explained. "We will trigger the detonation remotely from a heavily reinforced underground bunker. Drones will be deployed to monitor and record the resulting explosion. You and I," he said with a gesture toward Velásquez, "will watch the relayed video and energy output in real time from the reinforced facility."

"The amount of fuel we will use can fit inside a one-pint container," Chang added, "but it should provide a sizeable energy release. I doubt the resulting explosion will be noticeable except to those of us monitoring key conditions such as EMP sensors and temperature changes. I do have some concerns about the energy source containment system…"

"Nonsense, the containment system is perfectly adequate," Wu said sharply. "There is no reason for concern."

Velásquez rose to his feet, rubbing his palms together. "I look forward to this most exciting demonstration. With this gadget—the ultimate weapon—no one can stand in my way."

* * *

Sunli sat at the dressing table in her lovely furnished room—her windowless prison—and slowly brushed her hair. Staring into the mirror, she contemplated her pale skin, clearly the result of weeks indoors without sunshine. Her once lustrous, shiny black hair had turned dull and lifeless, and her blouse hung loosely from her shoulders. Despite the gourmet meals served in the nearby cafeteria, she had little appetite. Sighing, she rose, about to head to bed for another restless night of tossing and turning, when she heard a soft knock at the door. Before she could open it, the knob turned and in walked Chang.

"I told the guards we needed to discuss our work," he said softly. "We'll speak in English so even if they're listening, they won't understand."

"Yes?" Sunli said breathlessly. "Have you finally found a way to get me and my mother out of here?"

"The security is very tight. There's video surveillance, automated security systems, and guards in every hallway. But I think I may have a plan to get your mother away safely."

Stifling her disappointment that Chang hadn't mentioned her own rescue, Sunli nodded. "Tell me your plan."

"As a member of the PLA, I have the freedom to wander around the facility. So for the past few days, I've been exploring—trying to narrow down where your mother is being kept. I've watched the guards as they move up and down the halls and noticed where and when they deliver meal trays and return to the kitchen with empty dishes. I feel fairly certain I've identified your mother's locked and guarded quarters. Now the issue is figuring out how to get her out."

Sunli sat down on the couch, gesturing to Chang to sit beside her. "What are you thinking? How will it work?"

Chang outlined his plan and, while it was highly risky, Sunli agreed that it was just bold and outrageous enough to work. They decided to act on it as soon as Wu and Velásquez departed for the weapons test. Surely, they would also take many of the guards and other lab officials with them to the South China Sea. So, until then, all they could do is perfect their plan and wait for the right moment to execute it.

"I'll come back again tomorrow night so we can make sure we have everything in place for the rescue," Chang said.

"I'll eagerly await tomorrow night, then," replied Sunli with a smile. "Thank you, Peter, for giving me something to look forward to."

* * *

"*No es justo*," Joe Ramos said, petulantly slamming a fist into the lab table.

"No, it's not fair," Will agreed. "But what can we do?"

The brothers had just received the news that they were not invited to attend the Dragon's CLAW test in the South China Sea. Instead, Wu had announced that he expected them to stay at the lab and keep watch over the equipment, not to mention Sunli and her mother. The biggest shock to Will was learning that Sunli actually had a mother. She struck him more as the product of a test-tube in a lab.

"They don't need us to play guard to that old Chinese woman," Joe whined. "And they certainly don't need to hold her captive to make Sunli do the work."

Will agreed. Sunli had always been more interested in her research than anything else. He would bet that she cared far more about the Dragon's CLAW than she cared about her mother. Back when he worked with her at Los Alamos, she was entirely focused on her work at all times.

"*Es verdad*," Will sighed. "You and I have contributed more than anyone to the success of this project. We should be guests of honor at the CPC watch party with Wu and Velásquez—not sitting here at the lab waiting for the general to put down his glass of champagne and get around to texting us a report on the outcome of the experiment."

"*Sí*," agreed Joe. "We are the ones who made the big breakthrough. They couldn't have done anything without us."

* * *

Chang knocked quietly on Sunli's door and slipped in before the guard patrolling the hall had rounded the corner. His pulse quickened with the thought of spending another evening exchanging urgent whispers with her. For the past three days, the two had worked on their plan—although much of that plan simply involved watching and waiting. Chang realized that he didn't mind the waiting, however, because it gave him more time to get to know Sunli. Late into the night, they talked in guarded whispers about everything from the LENR research to their childhoods. Chang discovered that he and the impeccably dressed, intimidatingly beautiful scientist had more in common than he ever would have guessed.

"When I was a kid, I never really felt like I fit in anywhere," Sunli said with a sigh. "Once we visited relatives in China and the other kids teased me about my Mexican father. They made fun of me whenever I mispronounced a Chinese word or misused a Chinese saying. In Mexico, they bullied me for being half Chinese."

"They were probably just jealous of your looks," Chang laughed. "But I do understand. As a kid, I always felt like I was a disappointment to my father. Never smart enough, athletic enough, popular enough. I guess I never truly felt at home within my own skin."

Chang leaned back on the couch beside Sunli. "The only place I ever feel like I truly belong is in the lab— learning and discovering."

"Me too. Science was my salvation. My escape from myself."

"Plus, science gives us a way to help the world," Chang added. "Ever since I found out about the efforts to create a clean and affordable energy source that could revolutionize life in Third World countries... well, I've been obsessed."

"Oh, me too," agreed Sunli. "The LENR is so powerful. It offers such possibilities. For the past few years, all I've thought about is how to make it work."

The two spent the next hour exchanging stories about their experiments, laughing about mistakes, and sharing the excitement of close calls.

Sunli dissolved into giggles as she told Chang about the day she tried to explain the difference between continuous fusion and pulsed fusion to Joe Ramos. Then Chang laughingly explained how he spent two days troubleshooting a failed experiment just to discover that a cable was unplugged.

"I've never felt this... this connected to anyone before," Chang murmured.

Sunli took his hand. "Together we are a force. No one can stop us. I trust you, Peter, to rescue my mother and then rescue me."

Chang sighed, looking at his watch. "It's getting late. I should be going before the guards get suspicious about my whereabouts. Tomorrow is the day we'll carry out our plan."

* * *

When the sun rose the next day, the Chinese general and the drug lord stood together on the deck of a boat in the South China Sea.

"I must admit, this is the first time I have ever traveled by commercial fishing boat," Velásquez said, raising an eyebrow. "*Es muy interesante, pero* I am honored to get to take part in the first test of the Dragon's CLAW."

The nondescript and somewhat dilapidated fishing trawler chugged its way across the water, blending in with the many other similar boats that crossed the region every day. In the distance, the manmade islands of Mischief Reef were visible, rising from the water like rocky, grey growths. The artificial islands varied in size, some heavily militarized and others flat and abandoned. Some of the larger islands housed airstrips, military facilities, weapons, and other equipment. As they passed one of the islands, they were close enough to see the runway dividing the reef in two. The boat continued on toward one of the smaller outcroppings—an uneven, rocky island that featured tall cliffs of sand and dredged up rock and coral on all sides. In the center of this island lay an explosive test facility, well-shielded by the carefully constructed fake canyon walls around it. This was where they would conduct the weapons test.

The two men followed as the crew carried the crate holding the weapon onshore and over the hills to the firing point. Wu's men carefully removed the packing material and began to set up the device. The general wondered how much he should explain to the drug lord about the experiment. How much would... could... Velásquez understand?

"The Dragon's CLAW contains large, high energy density capacitors that provide the voltage for the detonation," Wu said. "This self-contained system means it does not need to be hooked up to the island's built in capacitor bank that has been used in the past to provide the charging current for explosive flux compression generator experiments."

Velásquez nodded, as if that made sense to him.

"See the cables they are hooking up to the device?

These will allow us to deploy the weapon and to monitor the detonation. From a reinforced underground bunker, we can watch displays showing the charging current, the output current and the output voltage from the dense plasma focus just as if we were watching it on TV. The monitoring technology uses high-speed optics and x-ray radiography along with seismic and infrared sensors. This test will provide a great deal of useful information we can use to perfect the weapon."

Velásquez nodded again, but Wu could tell his companion was losing interest. Any complex scientific explanation was wasted on the drug lord. Wu knew how to regain his attention. "So," he asked, "are you ready blow this thing up?"

Velásquez chuckled and rubbed his hands together. "*Sí*, I am ready to see *el dragón* breathe some fire."

With the cables connected and the initial tests run, the Dragon's CLAW was ready. "Let's go to the bunker," Wu said. "I'll even let you be the one who pushes the button for our very first test."

* * *

Meanwhile, back at the lab in Beijing, Peter Chang's day had not started on the deck of a fishing boat, but rather in a bedroom. *Sadly*, thought Peter Chang, *it wasn't he and Sunli waking up together in bed*. Instead, fluorescent lights revealed Sunli's mother, asleep in the room where she had been held captive for several weeks. Chang felt reluctant to wake up Lian Chen Hidalgo. He was about to discover his instincts were correct.

As Chang reached out to gently touch the old woman's arm, she bolted upright, eyes wide and blazing. "*Nǐ dàodǐ shì shéi? Nǐ zài wǒ fángjiān lǐ zuò shénme?*" screamed Lian Chen, leaping from the bed.

"I'm a friend. I'm here to help," cried Chang, and then added, "I'm a friend of your daughter's."

"Sunli?" Lian Chen asked, and then spit derisively. "*Méiyǒu shé me hǎo shīwàng de.* She should be rescuing me." Chang hadn't anticipated this reaction. The old woman was small—barely five feet tall—and elderly. Sunli had described her mother as being in fragile health, but she appeared to be wiry and fairly strong. Her fury amplified that strength.

"You shouldn't call your daughter a no-good disappointment," Chang protested. "She's a highly esteemed scientist. And she is rescuing you. She sent me to help."

Lian Chen narrowed her eyes suspiciously. "Everywhere there are guards. Everywhere there are cameras. This is your plan? We just walk out? Pah! You must be another brilliant scientist like my daughter. All school but no smart."

"No, no, I do have a plan. I'm going to hide you to get you out of here. I brought a... um... container."

"You plan to sneak me out the door in a box?" she scoffed. "Yeah, no one will look inside."

"I don't think they will," Chang said, going to the other side of the room to collect the secret to his plan.

He wheeled the large container across the floor toward the small, angry woman who resembled a cross between his own grandmother and, well, a Tasmanian Devil.

"Here's the thing," he told her sheepishly, "you have to get in this."

In front of the old woman sat a large radioactive waste storage drum.

* * *

Wu and Velásquez hiked to the bunker, just a kilometer away from the detonation point. The giant concrete bunker was a relic from World War II.

"*¿Estás seguro de que es seguro?*" Velásquez asked.

"Yes, I'm sure we will be safe here. It isn't even necessary for our little test, but this bunker is dug into the ground and built with a steel rebar reinforced concrete cover layered with cast iron armor. The concrete walls are several feet wide. Plus, did you see the blast deflection wall and berm in front of the bunker? If nuclear war broke out right now, we'd be perfectly safe."

Velásquez shrugged, unconvinced, as one of Wu's assistants swung open the giant steel blast doors. The general gestured to his companion. "After you."

Velásquez hesitated, reluctant to step into the darkness. Wu pushed past him. "Come on. We cannot waste time."

The men proceeded down a dimly lit hall to a large room lined with screens and monitors. Several technicians bustled around, flipping switches, pushing buttons, and checking readouts.

"This is where we will deploy the test. We can watch all of the measurements and outputs and see what's happening outside on that display," Wu said, pointing to the largest screen.

"*Por qué* all these people?" Velásquez asked.

"My team will track all of the results and data," Wu answered. "We will use the information we gather today to perfect the device."

The drug lord gazed into space, almost trancelike. "And then I will possess the world's most powerful weapon."

Suddenly focused, he turned to Wu. "So, where is the button? It's time to get this gadget working. Soon nothing will stand in my way."

* * *

Chang sat on the old woman's bed, his head in his hands. He had tried everything he could think of. Lian Chen refused to hide in the radioactive waste storage drum.

"Look, I don't know how to make this any clearer," he said in Chinese. "The radiation suit will protect you from any danger. All you have to do is put it on over your clothes." He held up the yellow Tyvek coverall. "This will protect you from any ionizing radiation left in the drum."

"If it's so safe, *nǐ jìnqù*," hissed Lian Chen.

"How would it help us for me to get in there?" Chang replied with exasperation. It felt as though he had been arguing with Sunli's mother for hours. Somehow, he had to convince her that he was trying to save her life.

"Just try it on. There's a hood and a face mask. I even brought gloves."

Lian Chen turned her back on him, muttering under her breath in Chinese.

"What did you say?" Chang asked.

"I said, 'Is it radioactive?'"

"Well, maybe a little. You know, just residual radiation, only slightly contaminated from low level radioactive waste."

The old lady raised an eyebrow.

"We can leave the lid of the container cracked like this, so you can get some oxygen, and do you see this?" asked Chang, holding up a small instrument that looked like a calculator. "It's a dosimeter. It measures the radiation in the storage drum. As long as the readout stays under 5,000, you'll be perfectly safe."

"What if it goes over 5,000 and I'm trapped in that thing?" Lian Chen snapped. "I'll die and never know my grandchildren. Not that Sunli will ever give me grandchildren. She waited too long chasing science instead of finding a good man."

Chang suddenly realized how he could convince the old woman to go along with his plan. He also realized, shockingly enough, that what he was about to say was 100 percent true.

Chang touched Lian Chen on the shoulder. As she turned around, he took her hands. "Mrs. Hidalgo, I have fallen in love with your daughter. I plan to ask her to marry me. Please put on the radiation suit. I promise I will do everything within my power to make you a grandmother soon."

Sunli's mother smiled. Without any more hesitation, she walked over and picked up the coveralls and put them on.

* * *

Inside the bunker on the South China Sea Island, the countdown had begun.

"Five, four, three, two, one."

With a grin, Velásquez hit the button. Every screen in the bunker flashed a blinding white and then the room plunged into complete darkness.

"Ai! *¿Qué chingados?*" Velásquez screamed, as the scientists milled around the pitch-black room in confusion.

"Stay calm, everyone," Wu commanded, reaching for his cellphone to engage the flashlight. The phone was completely dead. "Does anyone have a charged phone?" he asked. "We need some light."

Everyone in the bunker checked their phones. Not one of the phones would turn on.

"It was fully charged when we came down here," one of the men muttered, slapping his phone as if that would mysteriously bring it back to life.

"Why don't we have any flashlights or emergency lights?" Wu exclaimed.

Velásquez pulled a lighter out of his pocket and flicked it on. "The benefit of being a smoker," the drug lord said with an air of superiority.

In the dim glow cast by the lighter, Wu's team inspected their equipment. Everything was completely dead.

"There's nothing we can do here," Wu said. "We'll have to leave the bunker." He grabbed the lighter and headed for the hall, followed by the rest of the team.

Velásquez stood in the main room of the bunker, watching the others about to leave. "What if there's radioactivity out there from the detonation?" he asked Wu's retreating back. "Maybe we're safer staying in here."

"Nonsense," Wu said over his shoulder. "There is no danger." He strode down the hallway and swung open the steel blast door.

What he saw shocked him.

The berm and blast wall in front of the bunker were gone, reduced to a small pile of rubble. The small scrubby bushes that had struggled out of the rocky ground surrounding the bunker were now flattened. Overhead the sky glowed with unnatural brightness as if the heavens had been set on fire. At the edges of the blindingly white portion of the sky, small rainbows of light flared.

"*Tiān nǎ,*" Wu said in a hushed tone as Velásquez finally emerged from the bunker.

"*Santa mierda,*" Velásquez agreed.

* * *

Oblivious to what was happening in the South China Sea, Chang tried to look businesslike and unobtrusive as he pushed the large radioactive storage waste container down the hall. Fortunately, the old woman was small and not particularly heavy. *She probably weighs a lot less than a full container of nuclear waste*, Chang thought to himself.

He just had to get the drum out of the living quarters of the lab and into the research facility, where he could then take it to the loading dock. Chang's cousins would pick up the old woman and take her to his apartment where she could hide for a while. The next goal would be to get her out of China to the United States where she would be safe.

As Chang rolled the drum through the hall into the research area, a guard stopped him. "Where are you taking that?" the guard barked.

"To the disposal facility," Chang replied quickly. "We don't want to store radioactive materials here on site."

The guard looked skeptical. He placed his hand on the waste container and started to inspect it. Chang felt a bead of sweat sliding down his forehead.

"Uh, I wouldn't touch that if I were you. Residual radiation, you know."

The guard jumped back. "It's dangerous?"

"Of course. Why do you think we're getting it out of here. I hate having to be the guy to transport it." Chang had a flash of inspiration. He pointed to his crotch. "You don't want to get zapped if you want to have kids."

The guard jerked his hand away and stepped back. "I've heard that radiation can lower your sperm count. I don't need exposure to that. My wife is ready to start a family."

"Yeah," Chang agreed, hoping Lian Chen couldn't hear them from inside the waste drum. "It's really dangerous. I'd definitely stay away if you want to be a dad."

The guard left quickly, ordering the other members of the security force to clear the way for hazardous materials. Soon Lian Chen Hidalgo was on her way to safety.

Now Peter had to find a way to free Sunli.

* * *

The results of the first trial of the Dragon's CLAW had exceeded all of the researchers' expectations, but not in a good way. The energy output was 10 times higher than anticipated, and it had created a giant electromagnetic pulse. That pulse was responsible for knocking out all the power to the instrumentation in the bunker and rendering all electronic devices useless. The sky glowed white with rainbow auroras as charged particles from the blast collided with molecules in Earth's atmosphere. After 15 minutes, the glow faded and electronic devices resumed working, but it was too late. Wu's secret experiment was no longer a secret.

Several countries' satellites picked up the energy signature... all the way out to geosynchronous orbit. The electromagnetic pulse was detected as far away as Japan. Intelligence agencies throughout the world began investigating—realizing that the EMP revealed the existence of a new, tremendously energetic, and very dangerous device. This type of technology could destroy any nation's electrical grid infrastructure and all space-based communication, along with GPS—both of which were crucial to practically all aspects of the global economy.

The test had garnered the attention of the entire world.

As soon as his phone regained power, Velásquez called Will Ramos. "This is unacceptable," the drug lord screamed, using swear words in both English and Spanish to emphasize his point.

Wu also found the result of the test unacceptable, but his first priority wasn't scolding his team. Instead, his focus was international relations. Like Velasquez, Wu reached for his phone as soon as the EMP effect faded. He made a call to an old friend, someone he had collaborated with clandestinely off and on for decades. Wu had fostered this mutually beneficial relationship because it helped both him and his friend achieve their goals—particularly those related to obtaining government funding.

The general called Harold Percy.

"Can you believe that a rogue terrorist group would do such a thing," Wu exclaimed. "Deplorable. We should start hammering out a proposal to take to our respective leaders. We can work together to ensure this will never happen again."

"Indeed, we must work together on this," replied Percy smoothly, eliminating any hint of suspicion from his voice. "This unexpected detonation requires immediate action from both our countries. If you and I can shape the narrative, both our labs will receive an influx of cash. Here's what U.S. officials know: a Navy ship in the area has identified the boat that delivered the weapon to the island, and based on this information, state officials theorize that the device was small, portable, and extremely powerful. Based on the worst-case scenario analysis, I anticipate that President Thornton will call for an immediate meeting between our two countries."

"I look forward to our meeting," lied Wu, shaking his head sadly but disguising his true feelings with the bright tone in his voice. "Together our countries will ensure world peace."

Chapter 26
This Changes Everything

AS WU AND VELASQUEZ WERE setting out for the artificial island and Chang was arguing with Lian Chen about putting on the radiation protection suit, Gabi and Alek decided to go hiking.

Gabi said, "Why don't we take an afternoon off from worrying about everything and just enjoy the beauty of New Mexico."

"The Land of Entrapment?" replied Alek with a shrug.

"Not entrapment, enchantment. You've lived in this state for almost a decade. Have you ever taken time to appreciate it?"

"New Mexico is beautiful, but I spend most of my time working," admitted Alek. "Though I do enjoy jogging, I'm pretty focused on my thoughts when I run."

"Well, it's a gorgeous day and your project got canceled so you have some free time. Let's go hiking. It's about time you learn to appreciate New Mexico."

Alek thought about it for a moment. Gabi was right, and he did want to spend more time with her. "Sure. Let's go."

After stopping by the grocery store to pick up sunscreen, sandwiches, beer, and water—or as Alek joked, "the essentials"—they filled their backpacks. They added a picnic blanket and a couple of cookies, and Alek declared them "fully prepared."

Taking Alek's Ford Focus, they headed to White Rock Canyon, just nine miles southeast of Los Alamos. Carved by the Rio Grande, a river that stretches from the mountains of Colorado to the Gulf of Mexico, the canyon offered a sense of escape and solitude. After only hiking a few minutes, Alek and Gabi felt they had left their real lives miles away.

The river wound its way through ancient lava flows from volcanic eruptions, creating a rugged terrain with spectacular vistas that immediately soothed Alek's anxiety. He walked behind Gabi on the rocky trail beside the river, admiring the cascades of golden smoke blossoms and shocking pink verbena. He lost himself in the sounds of the gurgling river and the canyon wrens trilling in the nearby shrubs.

After hiking for a while, Gabi stopped and spread the blue and green checked blanket on a patch of fairly level grass along the riverbank and laid out their picnic. Using his Swiss Army knife, Alek popped open their beer bottles and leaned back, closing his eyes and soaking in the New Mexico sun. His bones felt loose and languid as the last of his remaining stress melted away.

"Why don't I ever do this?" Alek mused.

"Why don't you?" Gabi replied.

"I guess I'm too busy working. Too much to do." Alek flipped over onto his stomach, looking up at Gabi. Her blonde curls had worked their way free from her ponytail and framed her face in sparkling tendrils. Alek reached forward and gently brushed a strand of hair back from Gabi's face.

"Well, from now on, let's make time to do this on a regular basis," she said.

Alek raised his beer in a toast. "I'll definitely drink to that."

The two lay side by side in comfortable silence for a moment and then Alek sat up and turned away.

"Alek, what's wrong? It's going to be okay. This is just a setback. I'm sure they'll reinstate your funding and then you can resume work on Project Z," Gabi said, placing a hand on his shoulder.

Alek wrenched out of her grasp. "It's not okay. I don't deserve to be happy. I shouldn't be here with you."

"Help me understand," Gabi said quietly. "What's going on?"

Alek stood up and looked out across the river. "If I tell you..." Alek's voice broke. He stifled a sob, removing his glasses and grinding the heel of his hand into his eyes. "If I tell you, it will change the way you think of me." Alek sank to the ground, his back against a tree.

Gabi came over and sat beside him cross legged. She grabbed his hands. "Alek, you can tell me. I won't judge you. Whatever it is."

Alek looked away at the horizon. In the distance, the birds continued to chirp. "It was six years ago, back when I was married and living in Albuquerque. I was at my desk in my home office. My wife, Julie, well, now she's my ex-wife, anyhow, Julie was at work." Alek trembled as his unfocused eyes watched scenes from the past.

In a halting voice, he continued. "Julie and I had a daughter. Maggie. She was two and a half. She had curly brown hair and green eyes and I would lie on my back and balance her on my knees and pretend she was flying. She would laugh and laugh..."

Alek broke off, unable to continue. Gabi placed a hand on his shoulder and murmured, "Go on. You can tell me."

"That day," said Alek. "That day I was supposed to be watching Maggie while Julie was at work. Maggie was a quiet little girl who could play well by herself and so I left her in the living room with her toys. I was distracted, working on a new idea—the first prototype of the LENR. I had sketched out my ideas and started making calculations. I didn't hear Maggie slip out the door into the backyard."

Alek put his head in his hands, unable to face Gabi or the reality of what had happened. He would never be free of the guilt.

Finally, he continued in an unsteady voice. "When I went to check on Maggie, she was gone."

Alek raised his head and stared off into the distance, seeing memories from the past. "I called for her. I searched the house and then I realized the back door was unlocked. It was too late. I found her in the swimming pool."

Reliving the moment he first saw his daughter's lifeless body floating in the pool, Alek began crying softly. That image had been burned into his brain. The moment he lifted her from the water, the call to 911, the look of horror and accusation on Julie's face when she arrived at the hospital...

Gabi slipped her arm around him. Alek's sobs seemed out of place on the bright, sunny day.

"It was an accident. It wasn't your fault."

"It was. It was my fault. Our beautiful baby girl... If I just hadn't been so careless, so preoccupied with work... so irresponsible. It's no wonder Julie could never forgive me. I can't forgive myself."

Alek took a ragged breath, trying to pull himself together. "That's why I don't deserve to be happy. It's also why the LENR became so important to me," he explained. "Something good just has to come from this research. There has to be a reason. It just has to work."

"Alek, it will work," said Gabi. "Remember, we're taking a leap of faith... together."

Gabi gently brushed the tears from Alek's cheek as he buried his hands in her blonde curls. Their eyes met... and then Gabi's phone buzzed, shattering the moment. She glanced down.

"Good God," Gabi exclaimed at the barrage of notifications.

A steady stream of social media posts and news articles about the detonation in the China South Sea and the resulting electromagnetic pulse were blowing up the internet.

The headlines alone were terrifying: "Secret Chinese test creates dangerous electromagnetic pulse." "Sensors detect explosion on Chinese island." "Chinese test suggests use of deadly beam weapon." "U.S. officials fear China testing new weapons tech."

"Wow," Gabi said finally. "This is... unexpected."

In complete shock, Alek scrolled through the news coverage on his iPhone. "It certainly looks as if Wu and Velásquez have made progress on their research," he said finally. "I must say that calling attention to their work is a strategic error I'm sure they'll regret."

"Calling attention to it?" Gabi laughed. "They practically hired a plane to fly over the White House dragging a banner that says, 'We have a new weapon.'"

"I wonder what role Sunli is playing in all this," Alek mused. "I mean, I find it hard to believe that she isn't somehow behind Wu's success."

"Success might be the wrong word to use here," said Gabi. "I wonder what this will do to the China/U.S. arms talks."

"My guess is this will have a dramatic impact on the talks. This is huge. Now it's no longer a secret that someone in China is developing weapons applications from the LENR research."

"True," Gabi agreed. "The Chinese may not have meant to, but they've accidentally thrown down the gauntlet. We'd better get back to civilization." Gabi began packing up their picnic supplies.

"Absolutely. This changes everything. I need to get in touch with Percy. This kind of a weapon could create worldwide chaos. I bet it will kick the arms talks into high gear."

As the two started hiking back to the car, Alek decided he should stay focused on how much had changed in the past week: the end of the Percy Study project, the South China Sea detonation, the way Gabi had encouraged him to take a leap of faith. Everything was changing, but, maybe, finally, he was ready for some change.

* * *

In little time, Alek's prediction regarding the arms

talks became a reality. Television news channels ran 24-hour coverage of pundits analyzing the danger and discussing the need to abolish nuclear weapons. Headlines in publications from *The New York Times* to the *Washington Post* to the *Beijing Times* called for immediate action. Government leaders in both the U.S. and China, feeling the pressure of public opinion, realized that they had to reach an arms agreement and called an emergency meeting. U.S. President Jack Thornton suggested they convene at Camp David to hammer out an accord.

Although the South China Sea test had shown the world the power of the LENR as an electromagnetic weapon, General Wu had carefully concealed his involvement in the test and traveled with China's negotiating team to Camp David to address the technical aspects of the agreement. On the U.S. side, Harold Percy joined the group to offer his technical expertise.

The meeting would be Percy's first visit to Camp David. The Presidential country retreat nestled in the Maryland countryside had been built by the Works Progress Administration in 1935 and expanded over the years. The compound consisted of the large Presidential cabin called Aspen Lodge and several smaller cabins. Percy felt humbled to be in a place where so many historic events had taken place, but then, to his disgust, he learned he was assigned to share a cabin with Dale Croft, the President's science adviser. At least they would each have their own bedroom.

After settling into the cabin, Percy and Croft stood on the porch watching the Chinese delegation arrive. "The mood seems oddly festive given the serious nature of the negotiations," Percy noted as the Chinese foreign minister and his entourage sauntered past. Next came a full escort of military personnel in dress uniform surrounding the President of the People's Republic of China, Huang Ho, who also served as the general secretary of the Chinese Communist Party.

"Not only is Ho the president and the general secretary, he's also the chairman of China's Central Military Commission," Croft said.

"Heck, he's an entire negotiation delegation all by himself," Percy quipped, trying to hide the fact that he was rather intimidated by China's show of force.

Croft handed him the agenda for the two-day meeting. "The support teams for each country—basically the underlings like me and you—will meet first and hammer out a basic agreement, then brief our presidents who will make changes and then the leaders will meet. If all goes well, that's when there will be handshakes and photo ops and, of course, a pledge for world peace."

"Peace is rarely good for my business," murmured Percy. "Our laboratory's goal is national security, and we must ensure our country is protected against any possible threat."

Croft's eyebrow twitched and he sniffed loudly. "Harold, you are here for your scientific expertise and understanding of the Low Energy Nuclear Reaction technology. For once can you just go 10 minutes without trying to secure more money for your lab?"

Percy chuckled. "Where's the fun in that, Croft? After all, peace can be expensive. Especially when the country we're forging this treaty with is fairly likely to be less than truthful about its plans and actions. I'd think by now Thornton has learned to be cautious with his trust."

Croft shrugged and ducked back into the cabin, mumbling something about making a phone call. Percy sighed. Peace could be problematic. He knew that from experience.

The "underling" negotiations, as Croft described them, began the next morning in the conference room of the Laurel Lodge. Percy joked that he didn't mind being the B-team, the JV squad, or the warmup band, though he felt slightly miffed that he would be doing all the hard work of the negotiations while Thornton would take full credit. Plus, Percy would have to deal directly with General Wu. Despite the retired Chinese general's hidden connection to Chinese extremists, President Huang Ho often turned to Wu to assist with military strategy. Wu was leading his countries' negotiating team.

Percy had collaborated with Wu in the past, but he knew the general couldn't be trusted. While the two shared a desire to work together to influence their respective countries' funding decisions, Wu never revealed all of his cards. Percy felt certain that, based on the information he had gathered, and the story Alek shared, Wu was most likely the one behind the South China Sea detonation—something the Chinese would never admit. Wu was always hiding something and he always had his own interests foremost in mind.

Despite these misgivings, Percy planned to draw on what he called 'the peacenik arguments' that Alek had made over the years to help draft an agreement to end all space weapons development and cooperate with energy research. Preserving funding for LENR energy research remained crucial, but Percy had no faith that Wu would uphold any agreements they might make.

True to Percy's expectation, Wu began the conversation with denial. "I believe the people who carried out this experiment were part of a rogue group called the Chinese People's Consortium or CPC," Wu told the committee members gathered around the long conference table at Laurel Lodge. "The Chinese government is taking immediate steps to eliminate this faction and destroy this group's ability to harm the goal of lasting peace between our two nations."

"Indeed," said Percy nodding. "Lasting peace is the goal of these negotiations. It is fitting that we are meeting where the historic Camp David Peace Accords between Israel and Egypt were forged."

"Let us hope the peace we broker today is longer lasting than that agreement," Wu replied with a touch of sarcasm.

Percy took the bait. "The history of military technology has taught us that the development of weapons is always followed by the development of counter weapons. We can learn from the history of the army's battlefields that the infantry changes, from the machine gun to barbed wire and trenches, to tanks, to anti-tank weapons, to hardened armor, to defensive shields... and on and on. Space weapons will be no different and will be dominated by sensors and anti-sensor weapons, be they blinding lasers or command and control hackers and hyper-sonic missiles. The game will go on and on."

"So, what is the answer then?" asked Wu. "If we ban one type of weapon, another will emerge. Do we engage in an endless arms race?"

Everyone in the room had their eyes on Percy. He stood and walked to the other side of the table, speaking slowly and deliberately. "This detonation has served as a catalyst to enhance the power of fear of weapons proliferation over the military's natural desire to own the ultimate weapon. This is the ideal moment to admit that competition over space weapons would ultimately be mutually destructive for both countries. A cooperative global program is an imperative step. Should we invest both of our nations' limited resources in something that could benefit mankind? Something such as energy research? Today is our chance to lay the groundwork for lasting peace between our countries. We must draft an agreement to end all space weapons development and cooperate with energy research. The future of humanity depends on us."

Percy's passionate speech laid the groundwork for the meetings that miraculously ended with an agreement between the U.S. and China. The treaty specified the halt of any testing of the LENR weapons concept for at least 10 years and the end to any accelerator development in either country. Both countries agreed to destroy any equipment and technology connected to weapons de-velopment and authorized good faith inspection visits of each other's labs. But as the flashbulbs popped and the digital camera shutters clicked over the Chinese and

American presidents' handshake, Percy turned to Croft and muttered, "It's all bullshit."

"How can you say that?" the science adviser spluttered. "It's historic."

"Historic bullshit. It will never work. There will always be a rogue group that will continue with weapons development in spite of the ban. There will always be right wing activists who believe in the need to have nukes and the power of mutually assured destruction. Peace is a great idea but... it just won't work."

"Well, keep your thoughts to yourself if you want your lab to hang on to its funding," Croft spat out and walked away.

With the paperwork signed, a special session of the United Nations championed the agreement to ban further LENR testing. The U.S. media heralded the accord as a giant step forward toward world peace. Publicly, both Wu and Percy applauded the agreement, but privately both were busy trying to find a strategy that would secretly continue their weapons research and would leverage the largest amount of funding for each of their labs.

The two were pleased with one outcome of the negotiations. The agreement preserved some funding for non-weapons based LENR energy research. The question was, would the funding be sufficient? Percy had his doubts. He would have to convince President Thornton that the development of the ultimate energy source could essentially establish the owner of that technology as the dominant global economic power. Furthermore, preserving the energy research would keep the door open on weapons technology—technology that would be needed when a rogue group with a weapon decided to take control. Even as the ink was still drying on the proposed U.S./China nonproliferation arms agreement, Percy was planning.

As General Wu packed his bags to leave Camp David for a well-earned vacation, similar thoughts about the future swirled in his brain.

* * *

With the agreement signed, Alek found himself without a project to work on. He had spent nearly a week sitting at his desk aimlessly composing and deleting texts to send to Gabi when a surprise phone call from the lab director upended his day.

"I need you to go to China." Percy didn't bother with any sort of greeting.

Alek had become accustomed to the lab director's phone etiquette, or lack thereof.

"We're organizing a joint Chinese/American special forces team to inspect the Advanced Energy Lab in Beijing. The Chinese claim that they've ended all weapons development, but we need assurance that the accelerator facility there has been disabled. Like Ronald Reagan said, 'Trust but verify.' I need you to help verify that the Chinese are holding up their end of the deal."

"Uh, okay," Alek replied. "When exactly is this happening?"

"Next week. Gabi Stebbens will be going too, representing the FBI. Their intelligence suggests the accelerator is located in an underground tunnel located next to the lab, part of the Underground Great Wall of China."

Alek tried not to focus on being able to see Gabi again. "Well, surely they haven't had time to dismantle the accelerator," he said. "What exactly will we be checking for?"

"You need to ensure that it is no longer operating," Percy explained. "Plus, I want you to evaluate their set up. It's possible there are technological advances that we can borrow... you know, for our, um, energy research, of course."

"So, you want me to... keep an eye out?" asked Alek.

"Exactly. Keep an eye out, maybe take some photos. You know more than anyone about the hardware. Look for anything that can speed up our work. We need to figure out the small, multi-electrode plasma device used to trigger the electromagnetic pulse in the South China Sea.

Plus, see if you can get in touch with Peter Chang and Sunli Hidalgo. I guess Sunli has been working with the PLA on this research. It's a shame. I used to trust her," Percy said.

"The inspection visit should be pretty straightforward," Percy continued. "Just come back with some info. Congress may have ended our LENR study, but I have a feeling that if we play this thing right, we can make it very lucrative for our lab. I'm counting on you, Alek." Then, just as abruptly as the phone call had started, Percy hung up.

Alek texted Gabi, who had recently heard from her FBI supervisor about the inspection plan.

"Do you think they will allow us to see everything?" she texted back. "Will we be free to explore the complex and come to our own conclusions?"

Alek's response was swift and bitter. "Of course not," he texted. "This is a game, and we don't have the upper hand... at least not yet."

Chapter 27
Slaying the Dragon

WHEN WU LEFT FOR CAMP David with plans to take a few weeks of vacation after the treaty negotiations, he had put the Ramos brothers in charge of the accelerator facility. Since the general had ordered a halt to all testing in an effort to create the appearance they were actually abiding by the new arms agreement, the brothers didn't have much to do.

So, instead of working, Will and Joe spent their time drinking tequila and complaining to each other and anyone else who would listen. Both felt it was unfair for the retired general to blame them for the EMP incident. After all, technically, the experiment worked, it just worked a little too well. Angry with Wu, neither of the Ramoses were checking email or text messages, so they didn't know that the general had reluctantly agreed to allow a bilateral team to inspect the accelerator facility. Had they known, Will and Joe probably wouldn't have done anything to prepare for the inspection; however, they could have at least informed Velásquez, who, along with several armed bodyguards, was still residing in the living quarters attached to the Advanced Energy Lab. Despite Wu's recent ban on testing, Velásquez had continued to spend several hours a day in the underground tunnel strutting around and pretending to be the boss.

With Wu away from the lab and the Ramos brothers rarely leaving their quarters, some of the CPC guards also decided to take advantage of their boss' absence to visit their families. Meanwhile, Velásquez kept Sunli busy conducting experiments with the giant accelerator in the underground tunnel in hopes of perfecting the Dragon's CLAW.

Every morning, Velásquez dragged Sunli down into the tunnel where she humored him by pretending to continue the research. Velásquez, along with his armed bodyguards, spent his days monitoring Sunli's work in the accelerator control room, as she carried on a façade of analyzing data and calibrating equipment. Occasionally, she even fired the powerful laser in the LENR weapon to satisfy the drug lord.

Sunli was grateful that Velásquez's scientific knowledge was limited. Chang had once joked that El Verdugo couldn't tell a legitimate experiment from a kilo of cocaine, but Sunli hadn't spoken privately with Chang since her mother's rescue. He said he couldn't risk anyone connecting him to Lian Chen's disappearance. Sunli was starting to wonder if Chang actually planned to follow through with his promise to rescue her.

Today was no different as Velásquez and his men followed Sunli to the accelerator tunnel. None of them had any idea that today was the day an inspection team for the new treaty would arrive.

Sunli wanted Velásquez to think she was really trying to perfect the LENR technology, but she was tired of stalling the drug lord and the longer she went without contact from Chang, the more doubts she had. Did Chang successfully take her mother to safety? Had he gotten her mother out of China? When would Chang return to rescue her? The longer she waited, the more frustration Sunli felt about Velásquez, Wu, Chang, and the whole situation.

Plus, pretending to conduct experiments didn't satisfy her. She was desperate for news about the Dragon's CLAW test, the Camp David agreements, and the future of the LENR testing. She was ready to get back to work and resume her research. But instead, she was play-acting, pretending to conduct tests just to keep the idiot amused.

Fortunately, thought Sunli, *I am an excellent actress.* She could fool anyone, and though Velásquez didn't offer much of a challenge, she still threw herself into the part.

Handing him his safety protection goggles, she carefully explained in Spanish that they would fire up the accelerator and make another test of the laser beam.

"*Bueno,*" he exclaimed and clapped his hands together. "I'm ready to see some sparks."

* * *

As Sunli bustled around the accelerator control room in the underground tunnel, above them the bilateral inspection team was arriving at the Advanced Energy Lab. The team included Alek, Gabi, two other armed FBI officers, a PLA general, and two armed PLA officers. When they arrived at the AEL, they found nobody to meet them and the elevator unguarded. Surprised by the lack of a welcoming committee, the PLA general made an excuse and ordered one of his aides to call General Wu while they rode the elevator to the tunnel below.

When the elevator doors opened, Alek was shocked by the size of the cavernous tunnel. He stared at the gray concrete walls illuminated by repeating white fluorescent light fixtures. The tunnel branched in three different directions, but the PLA general knew the way to the accelerator site.

"Where are the golf carts?" said the general, sniffing in irritation at the inconvenience. "We'll have to walk. It's not far, although I have heard some Americans aren't physically fit," he added with a sneer.

They walked for about a quarter kilometer to where the tunnel dead-ended into a larger enclosure approximately five meters wide. The enclosure was dominated by a high current accelerator that looked similar to ones Alek had seen at other national labs. The machine stretched 100 meters long and consisted of 50 separate chambers. Alek quickly grabbed his iPhone and took some photos, trying to capture the details for Percy. He noticed that the entire facility was very clean, the spotless floor made of glossy polished concrete. Walkways led down each side of the accelerator with a target at the very end. Each chamber held a shiny stainless-steel container with cables and pipes leading from fittings upward to a second tunnel running overhead. Overhead cables leading to all of the high voltage equipment and vacuum pumping equipment snaked across the ceiling.

Alek was surprised to see a powerful pulsed laser device, complete with beam splitters and amplifiers, located above the accelerator. A beam pipe marked with a yellow warning triangle indicating laser radiation led to the accelerator's low voltage injector. Alek took some more photos. This was new to him, technology he had never seen before. He surmised that the pipe was there to protect the beam as it traveled to its destination—the target area at the end of the chamber. It would be filled with inert gas to prevent the laser beam from distorting due to moisture, dust, or air pressure. The construction was unlike anything the Los Alamos scientists had used.

Alek wanted to get closer to make further observations, but the PLA general barked, "Who is that in the control room?"

Alek lowered his phone and turned to look. Squinting and cursing the nearsightedness that his glasses couldn't fully correct, he spotted a handful of people inside the control room. *Was that... ? Yes, it was!* He grabbed Gabi by the arm and pointed to the glassed-in area. "It's Sunli."

Next to Sunli stood a heavy-set, Hispanic man with a mustache. Beside him were two large men who looked like bodyguards, armed with automatic weapons. All four of them were gathered around a bank of computer monitors.

"That's Velásquez!" Gabi yelled, pulling her gun.

Startled, the PLA general called out a question in Chinese, and the group in the glassed-in control room noticed they had visitors. Sunli's jaw dropped, and Velásquez's bodyguards reached for their weapons. *Uh oh,* thought Alek. *This doesn't look good.*

As Alek debated what to do next, Gabi acted on instinct and ran toward the control room. "Gabi, wait," Alek shouted, but it was too late to stop her. One of Velásquez's bodyguards lifted his AK-47 and began firing, as the FBI agents and PLA officers grabbed their own weapons.

"*¡Deténganlos!*" Velásquez commanded. "Stop them! Shoot to kill."

Alek froze, unsure of what to do, as echoing yells and the sharp crack of gunshots bombarded his senses. A bullet struck one of the FBI agents, who fell to the ground, blood spreading across the shiny concrete floor. Bullets ricocheted off the steel sides of the accelerator, sending showers of sparks through the air. Gunfire hit the high voltage cables running across the ceiling of the tunnel raining molten metal down onto Alek. Acrid smoke filled the tunnel. Panicked shouts in Chinese, English, and Spanish rang out.

Out of the corner of his eye, Alek caught a glimpse of one of Velásquez's men pulling a cellphone from his pocket. *Was he calling for reinforcements? Was the situation about to get worse?*

The deafening sounds overwhelmed Alek's senses. A bullet hit one of Velásquez's guards. Alek watched the man slump forward and collapse to the ground beside Sunli, who shrieked in pain as a bullet struck her leg. *I need to do something,* thought Alek. *But what?*

The PLA general surveyed the chaos and took off running away as fast as he could down the concrete corridor. Bullets struck the second FBI officer in the shoulder, causing him to drop his gun.

"*Alto al fuego.* Hold your fire," bellowed Velásquez. "*¡Deténgase!*" The shooting ceased as suddenly as it had started. The cathedral-like accelerator hall fell silent, though somewhere in the distance, Alek could hear someone crying in pain. His ears rang from the aftermath of the gunfire. He struggled to catch his breath, wondering, *what now?*

Velásquez emerged from the control room and Alek's stomach dropped. He realized with horror that the drug lord had one hand wrapped around Gabi's ponytail. With the other hand, Velásquez held a gun to her head. "Step back or I'll shoot her," Velásquez commanded. Alek and the remaining PLA officer both took a step back. The officer placed his weapon on the floor.

Gabi's eyes widened with pain as Velásquez dragged her across the chamber toward the exit. *Where was he taking her?* Alek winced seeing the fear and vulnerability in Gabi's eyes. *He couldn't stand by and let this happen. He had to act.*

Heart hammering, Alek ran toward the cartel leader, oblivious to his surroundings. Launching himself across the room, he slammed into the beam pipe hanging overhead. Alek fell to his knees, bleeding heavily from a gash across his forehead. He scrambled for his glasses, which had fallen to the floor, and wiped away the dripping blood. His head pounded from the impact. Unsteadily, he rose to his feet.

At the other end of the tunnel, the cartel leader tightened his hold on Gabi, practically drilling the barrel of his weapon into the side of her head.

Alek took a shaky step toward them. *"¡Ojo! ¡Quédense atrás!* Get back!" Velásquez shouted.

Alek stepped back several paces. He stood motionless, arms at his side. *His attempt to save Gabi had failed. He was a failure. Once again, he had managed to let down someone he loved.*

The two stood positioned at opposite ends of the chamber, Alek near the control room and Velásquez at the far end, still holding his weapon on Gabi's temple. *It's like a standoff in a terrible Western movie,* thought Alek. *One where everyone dies in the end.*

The Executioner faced Alek, glaring down the tunnel and speaking in a measured, condescending tone. "You think you can stop me?" he scoffed. "You think you can destroy my plans to control the ultimate weapon?"

Velásquez laughed derisively and spat on the floor. "I can't believe a scrawny scientist would attempt to challenge me. You have no idea how many lives I have taken, how much power I hold."

The drug lord pulled Gabi closer to him and kissed her cheek, causing her to wince and pull away. "*Puta*, do not defy me," Velásquez commanded sharply, yanking her back to him by her hair.

Alek shook his head. *He had to find a way to help Gabi.* Then, out of the corner of his eye, he spied Sunli dragging herself to the door of the control room. Blood flowed down one leg and she grimaced with pain, but she also seemed to be trying to get Alek's attention.

Alek briefly locked eyes with Sunli. "He's standing in the target area," she mouthed, pointing to Velásquez. Slowly, Sunli pulled herself over to where she could reach the computer control panel.

Alek glanced at where the drug lord was standing. Indeed, he was directly in the path of the laser beam, with Gabi right by his side. If Sunli fired the laser, it would easily hit Velásquez, but there was a risk it could hit Gabi too, or at the very least, blind her. *What should he do?*

Meanwhile, Velásquez kept taunting him.

"Clearly you don't realize who I am," he exclaimed. "You simply do not recognize the power I command. I have killed thousands and now, with the ultimate weapon, I will have even more power. You are nothing to me. *Yo soy El Verdugo*... and you... you cannot stand in the way of my plans."

Alek approached the drug lord slowly. A strange sense of calm had overtaken him. *This was it. His only chance.*

Alek faced El Verdugo. The drug lord raised his gun and pointed it at Alek.

"Clearly *you* don't realize who I am either," Alek said quietly and authoritatively, trying not to stare at the barrel of the gun. "You simply do not recognize the power I command."

Alek held up three fingers behind his back, hoping that Sunli was watching. Then, he made eye contact with Gabi. He spotted the faith in her clear blue eyes. Gabi gave Alek the slightest of smiles. *It was time.*

"You?" Velásquez laughed. "What power do you have?"

"I am Dr. Alek Spray..." he curled one finger, "the physicist..." he curled a second finger, "and I know how this thing works." He made a fist.

At that moment Gabi slammed her foot down on El Verdugo's ankle. He yelled and she slipped from his grip and dove to the floor. Alek flung himself away from the target area as Sunli flipped the switch on the control board. Lights flashed and the deafening firing klaxon sounded. The entire chamber erupted in blinding light.

* * *

Will Ramos was dozing in his room when his cellphone rang. "*Ven aquí imediatamente. En el túnel... Nosotros estamos bajo ataque.*"

Will struggled to clear the sleep from his head and understand the bodyguard's message, "We are under attack?"

Suddenly, his brother Joe slammed open the door. "I heard shots fired. I think it's coming from the tunnel. What should we do?"

Will could hear muffled sounds that might have been gunfire. It was hard to tell since the noises were coming from underground. Who was shooting at Velásquez? The only way to know was to go and check it out.

Will weighed their options. They could go down to the tunnel and try to help Velásquez, but that would risk getting shot. *There was*, he thought, *another option*. Now might be an ideal time to leave.

"*Empaca tus cosas,* but only pack the things you really need. We're leaving. Meet me in the back parking lot in 10 minutes. We need to get out of here."

Joe stared at his brother for a moment, wondering

what was happening.

"Velásquez is either under arrest or dead. Do you want to share his fate?"

Joe shook his head and ran back to grab his things. Will headed to the lab to get the laptop with all the research on it.

In 10 minutes they were in the back parking lot, climbing into a Didi, the Chinese version of an Uber, and headed to the nearby private airport where Velásquez stored his jet. Twice before, the brothers had ridden with Velásquez in his Dassault Falcon 7X, enjoying the plane's elaborate bar along with the company of the flight attendant, Sulema Sauceda, a would-be Mexican movie star who had traded her film career for a more lucrative job entertaining the drug lord. Will was certain that Sulema would assist them in convincing the pilots to fly them out of China. The question was, where should they go?

It took less convincing than he'd feared to get the pilot to prepare the plane. Will fretted and worried that Chinese soldiers would appear at any moment while they waited for takeoff. After what felt like hours, but was maybe twenty minutes after arriving at the hanger, the plane was moving. He had already decided on their destination and told the pilot.

As Sulema served him a glass of Dom Pérignon from the Falcon's elaborate and well-stocked bar, Joe said, "Where are we going? What will we do?"

Will sipped the champagne. "I told the pilot to fly us to the landing strip outside of the warehouse near Monterrey where we developed the LENR."

"Why there?"

"I have an idea that will land us big bucks."

PART THREE

Chapter 29
The Journey Home

THE FIRST THING ALEK SAW when he woke up was Gabi, her blonde curls in disarray as she hovered over him. He blinked a few times, trying to focus his eyes and figure out where he was. The light was dim, and he heard beeping sounds nearby. Alek tried to sit up, but Gabi put a hand on his chest.

"Alek, you're in the hospital. Just relax. Everything's okay," Gabi said quietly. Alek squinted, trying to see better. Gabi stepped back as a nurse entered to check his vital signs. Gabi greeted the nurse in Chinese.

"We're still in Beijing?" Alek asked weakly. Nothing seemed familiar. He struggled to remember what had happened in the tunnel and blinked his eyes, trying to see.

Gabi reached out to calm him. "Yes, we are in Beijing. An ambulance brought both of us right to the hospital. You've been unconscious for three days."

Alek grabbed Gabi's arm, pulling her closer so he could see her. He narrowed his eyes, trying to focus them. Her face seemed slightly bruised and scraped, but other than that, she did not appear to be injured. "You're not hurt? Are you sure you're okay?"

"I got out of the way just as Sunli fired the laser. The beam hit Velásquez right in the head and, Alek, you... you saved my life."

Alek rubbed his eyes with the heel of his hand. "Something's wrong with my eyes. I can't see very well. I mean, you look great, but... but everything is blurry."

"The doctor said both of us will have some trouble with our eyesight for a while since we didn't have protective safety goggles on when the laser fired. I think you got the worst of it, but the doctor says the vision problems won't last long. Plus, you may have noticed that you're missing something."

Alek touched his face and laughed. "Oh, my glasses!"

She handed his glasses to him, but he noticed a large crack in one of the lenses. "You are probably going to need a new pair. I guess yours got damaged somehow in all the excitement."

Alek ran his finger down a long scratch on the side of Gabi's cheek. "You're sure you aren't hurt... I couldn't bear it if..." His voice broke, choked with emotion.

"I'm fine," Gabi said, her face close to his. "Better than fine. I'm good. I'm great now that you are finally awake. The doctors say you hit your head on the concrete when you dove out of the beam's path. You took a pretty hard fall."

Alek sighed. "It's hard to remember what happened. What about Sunli?" he asked.

"You're worried about Sunli?" Gabi said with a sniff. "She was shot in the leg, but she's recovering. She's here in the hospital." Gabi stepped away from the bed, smoothing her shirt self-consciously. "I'll tell the nurse you're ready for visitors," she said.

Gabi walked into the hall and Alek could hear her speaking softly to the nurse in Chinese. While he waited, he carefully felt his arms and legs, checking for injuries. He was stiff, sore, but it seemed like nothing more serious than the blurry vision and the slight ache in his arm from the IV. How was it possible that he had survived this? He was okay... Gabi was okay... that was all that mattered.

Gabi reentered the room and returned to the spot beside the hospital bed. Alek grabbed her arm. "What about everyone else who was there? Is everyone alright?"

"One of my FBI agents didn't make it, and the other was injured," she replied, shaking her head. "One of the

PLA officers was shot too."

"I saw the PLA general running away," Alek remembered.

"He took off as soon as the shooting started. I've never seen anyone move so fast. Apparently, he said afterward that he was going for help, but I think he's just a coward. Fortunately, he did come back with a PLA strike team. One of Velásquez's bodyguards is dead and the other is in custody."

"What about Velásquez, is he...?"

"Oh, yeah, instantaneously. The laser hit him right in the head. It must have vaporized his brain."

"Oh," said Alek solemnly. "That's terrible." Then, despite himself, Alek giggled. "His brain? Pretty small target if you ask me."

Now Gabi was giggling too. "Yeah, that was some amazing aim. Not anyone could hit something that tiny." Their laughter built, bubbling out of them along with relief and sheer joy at being alive. Gabi gave a delicate snort, which made them both laugh harder. They convulsed in giggles in each other's arms.

"Hi, Alek, how are you?" a soft voice interrupted. Embarrassed, the two turned to see that Sunli and Chang had entered the room during their laughing fit. Both were in street clothes, but Sunli's pants were cut off at the knee and her leg was heavily bandaged. In one hand she held a pair of crutches. The other arm was wrapped tightly around Chang's waist. Behind the two stood Percy, in a neatly-pressed suit complete with cufflinks, looking more prepared to walk into a Senate hearing than a hospital room.

"Sunli, Peter, Percy," Alek said looking from guest to guest. "I feel like I just woke up in that scene from *The Wizard of Oz* at the end where everyone is standing around Dorothy's bed." He looked from Sunli to Chang to Gabi and said smiling, "And you were there and you were there and you were there." Alek pointed at Percy and chuckled. "You weren't there."

"True," replied Percy. "There's no place like home, but right now the Beijing Hilton will have to do."

Alek looked at Sunli. "You really went to China to take care of your... your mother?"

"General Wu had kidnapped my mother. He was holding her prisoner to motivate me to help him work on completing the LENR." Sunli turned to Chang. "Fortunately, he brought in Peter to help with the project. And Peter rescued us."

"You really were in China because of your mother? It wasn't a lie after all? But your message said it was your father." Alek rubbed his eyes. "I'm confused."

"You may need some medicine," Gabi said tenderly. "I'll fetch the nurse."

Chang wrapped his arm tightly, protectively around Sunli's shoulders. "She thought that by mentioning her father she could send a signal to you that she needed help. Wu was forcing Sunli to collaborate on the LENR research by threatening to torture or kill her mother if she didn't cooperate. Wu of course denies any involvement whatsoever and says Velásquez was to blame."

Alek squinted at Sunli. "Is your mother safe?"

"Peter rescued her," said Sunli, as the nurse entered the room and began bustling about checking vital signs and resetting monitors. "She's at Peter's apartment and we will all fly back to the states as soon as I'm able to travel."

"She may need a second surgery," Chang said protectively. "The doctors say it's possible that she will always walk with a slight limp."

The nurse laid her hand on Alek's arm and said in English, "I'm going to inject this medicine into your IV to help you relax a little. It may make you sleepy."

Ignoring the nurse, Alek pointed at Sunli. "So... you weren't working with the Chinese voluntarily? You're not a secret agent working for the Chinese Ministry of State Security?"

Gabi shook her head and grabbed Alek's hands. "No,

Alek. Sunli is still one of the good guys. She'll be working with you back at Los Alamos again before you know it."

Alek smiled and Gabi frowned slightly, straightening his blankets.

"Conveniently, Wu is still in the U.S.," Percy said. "He says he has no idea why a Mexican drug lord was working on weapons development in his lab."

"Oh, and get this," Gabi interrupted. "Our intelligence showed that Will and Joe Ramos were also working at the Advanced Energy Lab in Beijing with Wu and Velásquez, but no one can find them now. For the second time, the Ramos brothers have vanished into thin air."

Alek sighed. Just keeping his eyes open required a tremendous effort. "I'm glad you are okay, Gabi," he murmured as his eyelids fluttered. "You were right about taking that leap of faith."

$$* * *$$

A little less than a month after the incident in the Beijing tunnel, the sunset kissed the Jemez Mountains with flames of red and streaked the sky with pink and purple as Alek, Chang, Sunli, and Lowe met at the Friggin Bar in Los Alamos.

The team had continued their research and was making significant progress. Alek's dream of creating an inexhaustible source of clean, affordable energy appeared to be within his grasp thanks to the breakthroughs Sunli and Chang had made while developing the Chinese Dragon's CLAW weapon in Beijing.

Sunli's work had revealed the mathematical physics theory behind using a high current electron beam as the trigger. With the right beam parameters, she was certain they would be able to initiate a focused beam that would create collective-transmutation reactions in a controlled manner. This discovery was the crucial step that would allow them to create a predictable energy release.

Over the past two weeks, the group had incorporat-ed the trigger design that Chang and Sunli had perfected and had created complex simulations that showed the high gain concept in action. Chang had drawn on his simulations to design the trigger using both a compact plasma focus and a large high current accelerator. Alek had figured out how they could use the LENR to create an electromagnetic pulse from an ignited thimble of fuel flowing into a secondary fuel chamber. The result would be a limitless source of affordable power—an invention that could transform society. So far, the device only existed in theory, but Alek felt encouraged by how far they had come.

"Your simulations are great," Lowe told Chang, in between large bites of his green chile cheeseburger. "The big question now is how to test the theory."

Percy was lobbying Washington for the funding to build a new lab and hire hundreds of scientists to finish developing the device, but no one in the group at the bar that night saw Percy's plan as the solution for testing their energy application theories.

"A real energy program would require a large, heavily shielded facility in a very remote site," Alek said. He noticed that Sunli and Chang were sitting rather close together. In fact, she was eating the occasional French fry off his plate. *Sunli seems different ever since the incident in the tunnel*, thought Alek. She smiled more often and acted less tense. Although she still used a cane to support her injured leg, she somehow appeared healthier overall. She had cut her hair shorter and had moved her mother into her Santa Fe apartment with her, but she spent a lot of time after work and on the weekends in Los Alamos. Maybe because that's where Chang was living now.

"Alek, don't you agree?" Lowe asked.

"What?" Alek tuned back into the conversation. "Could you repeat that?" he asked.

"I said any substantial attempt to create a revolutionary energy source will be dominated more by politics and economics than by technology," Lowe explained. "Percy's right that we need to find some tremendous sources of funding, but funneling more money into Los Alamos isn't the answer. At this rate, the entire project could spend decades tied up in politics and red tape."

"It's true," Sunli agreed thoughtfully. "Although everyone supports the idea of clean energy, the political barriers, economic constraints, and social implications all stand in our way."

"If we really want to build this thing, we're going to have to out-Percy Percy and become experts at talking politicians out of money," said Alek. "When China and the U.S. signed the nonproliferation agreement, both countries agreed to commit to energy research. Now we just have to find a way to turn their commitment to cash."

"Why is funding always the issue?" Lowe asked. "I pursued a career as a physicist so I could create things and solve problems, not so I could worry about how to talk politicians into giving me the money for the projects that they insist I carry out. It's ironic. We should be worrying about science, but instead it's all about politics and money every time."

"I bet Gabi would have some ideas about how to get funding," mused Sunli. "Has anyone talked to her? I don't even know where she lives."

"Well, she has a place in Albuquerque and an apartment in D.C.," Alek replied, and then, noticing the inquisitive looks of his colleagues, quickly added, "At least that's what I think she said."

"Maybe you should get in touch with her," suggested Sunli. "It can't hurt to bring in someone who isn't a scientist to help us brainstorm. Gabi has a different way of looking at things."

"I mean, yeah... if you think so," said Alek, trying to ignore the way just talking about Gabi increased his heart rate. "If you guys really think I should, then, uh, I'll give her a call."

* * *

The New Mexico sun beat down on Harold Percy's

Mercedes S-class coupe as he pulled into the parking lot at the lab. He could feel the temperature rising. Though the mountains surrounding Los Alamos usually guaranteed cooler weather, the occasional warm day could quickly become oppressive since few homes and businesses had air conditioning. A handful of wispy clouds drifted across the deep blue sky stretching endlessly overhead.

Percy couldn't shake his growing sense of worry. The lab's personnel security manager had emailed late last night to say, "I need to talk to you about a matter of some concern." Percy knew that the tone of urgency underlying Amanda Berger Aragon's email indicated some sort of security breach. As head of the counterintelligence program at Los Alamos National Laboratory, Aragon spent her time investigating possible threats posed by foreign intelligence entities and following up on any suspicion of espionage, theft, or threat to national security. She took her job seriously. Almost too seriously, in Percy's opinion. Heading off bad publicity and keeping the politicians happy and the money flowing were the lab director's goals. Security problems only got in the way.

Percy walked quickly from the parking lot into the lab administration building where Aragon waited, pacing back and forth. She quickly ushered the lab director down the stairs to a tiny, secured room in the basement where they could talk without electronic surveillance concerns. Wasting no time with formalities, Aragon announced, "We have uncovered indications of espionage. Someone who worked for you had been sending intel to China. We believe that one of your former employees was a spy."

Percy leaned back in his chair, folding his arms across his chest. "And what exactly led to these suspicions?" he asked impatiently.

"The IT department was called in to troubleshoot some issues with your former administrative assistant's computer. Seems the computer was crashing a lot and IT suspected she had accidentally downloaded a virus or something. Instead, they uncovered a tiny, short-distance information transmitter embedded in the computer. It appeared to be designed to transmit large amounts of coded information in only seconds, thereby avoiding detection. In other words, an espionage device."

"Have you met my former assistant?" Percy scoffed. "I inherited her from the last director. She's been here since they built the lab. She barely knew how to use the computer, much less use it to transmit intelligence to the Chinese. I was so relieved when she retired last week."

"Well perhaps she decided to retire after receiving her pay off from the Chinese," Aragon replied.

"She's gone. Let's not dwell on her," said Percy.

Aragon's face grew red as she sputtered, "A spy in the lab director's office? That's a gross counter intelligence failure."

"We will discuss the device instead," Percy said dismissively. "What happened next?"

"Well, when we discovered the transmitter, we left it where we found it and started monitoring the signal. We found out it was being transmitted at the same time every month."

Percy rose from his chair in agitation. "Who was receiving the messages?"

"By tracking the dates and times of the transmissions, we correlated the signal with a monthly delivery of office supplies. We believe the delivery truck driver had a receiver tuned to pick up the burst of communication while parked next to the building. The messages were stored and then later transmitted to another location, allowing the extraction of sensitive information from a secure location. We've been monitoring the communications and we have reason to believe that information has been going from that delivery truck to China."

"What kind of information? Where is it going? Who is it going to?"

Aragon slid a photo across the table. Percy shook his head as he looked at the man in the photo. General Wu. He should have known.

Chapter 29
Put on the Money Suit

ALEK PICKED UP THE PHONE to call Gabi. He hadn't spoken to her since they'd returned from Beijing, and he felt shy and awkward. Did almost dying together in a secret underground tunnel in China count as a first date? What about their picnic by the Rio Grande or the kiss in the mountains in Mexico? Did she actually share his feelings or was she just grateful that he'd rescued her? Had he waited too long to reach out to her and... what would he say?

No, he couldn't call her... couldn't entertain the glimmer of a relationship—not after what had happened to his daughter. He couldn't even entertain the thought.

Instead, Alek called Percy to explain what they wanted to do. The next thing he knew, the two of them were on a plane headed to D.C.

Percy knew he had to figure out what kind of game Wu was playing, but he also understood Alek's urgent desire to raise funds. Wu could wait. Whatever the general was trying to accomplish, Percy felt he could beat his Chinese counterpart at this game. Meanwhile, with the prospect of receiving money for weapons development quickly evaporating, Percy knew they needed to focus on energy research. Plus, using the Dragon's CLAW technology for energy production would allow the weapons work to continue. Helping Alek was a win-win prospect for Percy.

While the lab director and his chief scientist often disagreed about how the lab's money should be allocated,

Percy's key talent was talking politicians into financing his scientific initiatives. He was notorious for his ability to explain scientific research in a way that leveraged funding. Somehow Percy had mastered the ability to tie special governmental favors to economic growth and voter approval. Alek knew he needed help from an expert, and no one could outdo Percy at the defense lobbying game.

The minute they deplaned in the Washington Dulles airport, Percy headed for the snack counter and ordered a corn dog. "I prefer food on a stick," he explained between mouthfuls. "Food on a stick is easy to eat while walking. Multitasking! You can get somewhere while refueling. It's the best of both worlds."

Alek looked dubiously at the snack counter. "Get yourself a corn dog," Percy commanded. "We have a dinner tonight with Dale Croft and Senator Plumkin, so you'll only want a snack to save room for later. We're going to Ruth's Chris Steak House. Plumkin's treat."

Alek shook his head and Percy shrugged and strode off down the concourse. Scrambling to keep up with his boss' brisk pace through the crowded airport, Alek marveled at how Percy could simultaneously maneuver a rolling suitcase, eat a corn dog, check his phone messages, and turn his head for a good look whenever an attractive woman walked by.

Alek knew that, for a man who liked food on a stick, Percy also had an appetite for the finer things. Especially when someone else was footing the bill. They bypassed the luggage carousel and headed out to the transportation kiosk to grab an Uber. After years of traveling with Percy, Alek knew better than to check his luggage. Never check your luggage was a conviction that Percy held the same way other people clung to religious beliefs.

"We're both staying at the River Inn this time," Percy said. "Plumkin offered to cover it. I hope you brought your good suit since we'll be doing a lot of wining and dining this week."

* * *

Percy cut into his rare filet and murmured approvingly as the juices pooled on his plate. Alek looked down at the white table linens. The dinner conversation was ruining his appetite.

Larry Plumkin, the Republican senator from Mississippi, had complained nonstop throughout the appetizer course and now he had a giant ribeye, a lobster tail, and a loaded baked potato left to consume. Alek took another bite of his steak. It looked delicious, but under these circumstances, tasted like sand.

"Now, I'll tell you my thoughts on energy," Plumkin said, while chewing. "Those damn green energy lobbyists are cutting into the crude oil market and hurting my state."

"Well, the LENR is an entirely new form of power," ventured Alek. "We call it Project Z and it really has the potential to change the world."

"So, would your new-fangled power plants use oil? That could help," said the politician, signaling to the server for more cabernet. "I could get behind that technology. You know, something that has the potential to help everyone out."

"Actually, Project Z is a kind of green energy," Alek started to explain, but Percy quickly interrupted.

"A kind of green energy that actually could be modified to take advantage of the oil production in certain states. With sufficient funding, we could explore this, if you know what I mean," Percy concluded with a wink. The senator chuckled.

Dale Croft, the President's science adviser, looked up from the salad he had ordered after explaining sadly that his wife insisted he follow a plant-based diet. Croft cleared his throat. "My concern is that it appears the LENR technology is best applied to weapons development, not energy. You don't see people using electricity from the atomic bomb, do you?"

Alek stifled a smile. Should he mention nuclear power reactors? Then again, nuclear power still faced issues of public approval and waste disposal. Probably better not to bring it up. Plus, he knew better than to call attention to Croft's ignorance. It just was so tempting. To avoid speaking, Alek took a big bite of his steak.

Two hours later, the evening ended without a funding commitment, but, on the bright side, Croft agreed to arrange for Percy and Alek to meet with President Thornton the next day.

The meeting was scheduled to take place in the Oval Office. Alek woke up early to print off some charts to share with the President. He dressed carefully, debating over which tie to wear and whether his shoes needed to be polished. As he was running a comb through his hair, he realized that there was a small hole in his suit pants. More specifically, the hole was in the rear end of his trousers—though he thought he could probably hide it by keeping his jacket on. Alek realized he shouldn't have put off going shopping. Buying clothes was never his favorite pastime, but who goes to talk to the leader of the free world about a billion-dollar project with a hole in his pants? Percy always dressed impeccably. He would be appalled if he noticed the hole. *Well, nothing can be done about it now*, thought Alek. He would have brought a second suit if it weren't for Percy's fervent opposition to checking luggage. Surely President Thornton wouldn't be looking at a lowly physicist's rear end?

Getting into the White House required a complex process of clearances, long delays, and Secret Service escorts. Finally, Percy and Alek arrived in the Oval Office with Croft hovering beside them, eager to find a way to take credit for their ideas and gain the President's approval. Alek welcomed the chance to sit down so he could stop worrying about the hole in his pants.

They began their pitch by explaining the concept and the breakthroughs they had made since beginning the study. Most importantly, they stressed the revolutionary payoff that building a cheap, clean power source could provide. Thornton murmured approvingly, nodding and smiling. "Extremely appealing concept," the President said. "Don't you think so, Croft?" The science adviser bobbed his head obsequiously, eager to align himself with the President's point of view.

"I'm confident that we understand the physics and can make this a reality," concluded Alek. "All we need now is a source of funding so we can put these proven ideas to work."

"I can provide additional information," Croft interrupted. "After all, I have supported this concept from the very beginning and have always had complete faith in this work."

Alek blinked in surprise. He couldn't believe Croft's dramatic change of heart. Not that long ago, the bow-tied science adviser had called the LENR research "a waste of time and money" and last night he argued that the technology was better suited for weapons applications. Now that it appeared the President favored the project, Croft had done an about-face.

"Here's what we are going to do," said Thornton. "I want you to meet with Derek McKensie, the head of the Pentagon's research directorate. You'll like Derek—he's a new breed of weapons specialist who thinks brains are more important than bullets. If anyone will be able to grasp the complexities surrounding this research, he's your guy."

Alek wondered if they were just being shuffled off to someone else, but he thanked the President. Tugging his jacket down, he awkwardly backed out of the Oval Office to avoid turning his back on Thornton and revealing the hole in his suit. Waiting for their car outside of the White House after the rather harrowing, but extremely brief, encounter with the leader of the free world, Percy gave Alek a friendly slap on the back.

"Good job, Spray. You did great in there—very clear and persuasive." Percy continued, "By the way, you have a hole in your pants."

Chapter 30
On the Prowl

MCKENSIE'S OFFICE WAS ON THE third floor in the E ring of the Pentagon. Security officers led Percy and Alek across the massive five-sided building. This was very different than the basement rooms they had occupied during the Percy Study. When they finally arrived, McKensie's assistant asked them to have a seat in the outer office. They waited in silence, staring through the window across the Potomac at the Washington Monument.

Finally, they were ushered into the inner office. Stationed behind a trendy treadmill desk, McKensie greeted the two scientists with a wave rather than a handshake.

"Feel free to have a seat," he said. "I'm just going to continue my workout while we chat. I find I can reach my target heart rate even faster during certain high-level meetings, if you know what I mean."

Alek looked around the large office. Floor to ceiling prints of brightly colored abstract art, reminiscent of a toddler's scribbles, decorated the walls. McKensie wore nylon exercise pants and gleaming white running shoes. Instead of looking cool and relaxed, he broadcast the image of a nearly 50-year-old man desperately trying to cling to his youth.

Percy sat on a plush, yellow velvet chair, while Alek, still awkwardly standing, launched into an explanation of the project.

McKensie listened intently, nodding and walking rapidly in place at the treadmill desk. Alek wrapped up his pitch and awaited the Pentagon official's reaction.

"Alex..."

"Uh, it's Alek," Alek corrected.

"Yes, of course. Alek, I have been encouraging the Department of Defense to focus on the people aspect in all large-scale international programs. The key is for leaders to hone in on perfecting decision making under the stress and confusion of complex programs undergoing periods of temporary success and inevitable failures. Using complex and contradictory information, this super leader can make wise decisions almost instantly and convince others to follow."

"Ummm, that's... interesting," Alek responded.

Percy rolled his eyes.

"I will email you some management articles that detail this vision," McKensie continued. "If you are really committed to take on the role of super leader in this global scale project, I will provide as much support as I can."

Alek smiled in relief, but Percy uncrossed his legs and leaned forward.

"Exactly how much support are you suggesting?" Percy asked.

"Well, honestly, I'm not sure." McKensie began walking faster on his treadmill.

Alek got the impression he was trying to run away from them. But of course, he wasn't actually going anywhere.

"The truth is, I don't personally know how to go from theory to reality," explained McKensie. "I really can't grasp the extent of this proposal or what resources it will require."

"Don't you have an engineering degree," Percy asked, raising an eyebrow.

"Yes, but I was schooled in the old-fashioned engineering approach of starting with the problem, taking the problem apart, solving the pieces, and putting it back together again," explained McKensie. "Plus, I haven't worked as an engineer or scientist in decades. I'm more of a policy guy."

Percy stood up. "We appreciate your time, sir."

"My pleasure." McKensie beamed at them from behind his treadmill desk. "I hope you don't mind showing yourselves out. I hate to interrupt my workout. Best of luck with your project, Alex."

"It's Alek," Alek muttered.

"What a bunch of bullshit," Percy grumbled as they headed for the door.

* * *

After a quick shopping trip to get Alek a new suit, at Percy's insistence, the two continued making the rounds in D.C.—visiting congressional offices, networking with political staffers, giving speeches at conferences. They even did some TV and newspaper interviews, but, despite the hard work, their efforts to raise funds were moving at a glacial pace.

Alek had begun to think of himself as more of a salesman than a scientist. He spent every day peddling the concept of developing a limitless source of clean energy. Perfecting the LENR energy application could change every aspect of the world, but, right now, the effort to get the funding was taking the last bit of personal energy that Alek had left.

One evening after a long day spent promoting his dream project that was quickly turning into a nightmare, Alek met Gabi at McNamara's Bar. She had recently returned to the D.C. area after spending the past few months working at the border on a case involving changing loyalties in the drug trade. Velásquez's death had caused shifting alliances and the FBI had taken down several big players in the cartel.

"You're my hero," Gabi said, slipping into the booth next to Alek, her blonde ponytail swinging. "With Velásquez gone, the *tenientes*, the lieutenants, in the cartel are all trying to take control, making it even easier to take them out."

"That's great, I guess," Alek replied. He hadn't seen Gabi since their return from Beijing and, while they had texted a few times, he wasn't sure how to handle the feelings that simply sitting beside her sparked in him.

"Yeah, I'm going to spend a month in court testifying against these guys. You didn't just take down Velásquez—you wiped out half the cartel."

"It ain't much, but it's honest work," laughed Alek. "Seriously, though, the credit for taking down Velásquez belongs more to Sunli than to me."

"Well, you're the one who kept him distracted so I could get away and she could push the button, so you get the credit." Gabi took a drink of the Dos Equis that Alek had ordered for her. She smiled. He smiled back and lifted his beer bottle in a mock toast.

"So, what's the latest in the unlimited energy business? Are you and Percy beating the bushes for bucks?"

"Yes, and I hate it," said Alek. "I never wanted to be a fundraiser or deal with politics and now I'm spending every waking moment doing both."

Alek noticed that Gabi's bare arms were tanned, suggesting her work at the border had involved lots of time outdoors. Her perfume smelled of vanilla mixed with a hint of something complex and spicy. Was it cinnamon? Maybe a little chocolate? In any case, it was a delicious scent.

Gabi put a hand on Alek's arm. "Don't get discouraged. I mean, this is really important."

"That's an understatement," replied Alek. "Honestly, this invention could change the world. We have the only large-scale, carbon-free energy solution ever created. Project Z produces no greenhouse gases. It is clean, it is safe, it is affordable. We can end climate change while meeting all sorts of energy demands—powering homes, recharging batteries, creating clean fuels, driving chemical processes, the list goes on and on. Imagine the difference this technology could make in third world countries. Inexhaustible, safe power can transform every aspect of life across the globe."

"I love your passion," said Gabi. "Your desire to help others... to change the world. I know this is hard, but you can't give up. You just have to take it one step at a time."

Alek dropped his eyes. "I'm... I'm not used to this."

"Used to what?"

"Someone supporting my ideas. Back when I would try to talk about my scientific ideas and plans with Julie, all she would do is tell me why nothing would work. She said I should stop jousting at windmills and accept reality. Go to work. Go home. Go to sleep. Rinse and repeat. That was Julie's idea of how a real grown-up should act."

"Well, I don't know if you noticed, but I'm not Julie," Gabi said, tucking a stray blonde curl behind her ear. "Go ahead and dream the impossible dream 'cause I think you can reach that unreachable star."

Alek laughed. "I always did like 'Man of La Mancha.'"

"I played Dulcinea in our spring high school musical," Gabi said. "But the kid who played Don Quixote was shorter than me and had bad skin. You're a lot cuter."

Blushing, Alek leaned closer. The stray curl had escaped again from Gabi's ponytail. He reached out and wrapped the strand around his finger, drawing her in. He was just about to say something completely cheesy along the lines of 'You are more beautiful than Dulcinea,' when Gabi's phone rang.

"Yes? Okay. Hang on." Gabi turned to Alek and whispered, "It's my supervisor." He nodded and looked away in an awkward attempt to give her privacy.

"Okay, what? A report released today about Chinese scientists stealing U.S. weapons secrets? No, I haven't been watching the news."

Alek gestured to the bartender. "Could you turn on CNN please?" He walked closer to the bar, reading the captions on the screen, as Gabi wrapped up her phone conversation with a series of 'yes, sir's and 'uh-huh's. She clicked off the call and headed over to Alek.

"A private company released a report today about how the Chinese are recruiting scientists from Los Alamos and other national labs. They're calling it a systematic effort to steal U.S. talent and weapons secrets."

"But the scientists they're recruiting—I mean, allegedly recruiting, are Chinese nationals. We have lots of foreign scientists visiting and working at the lab."

"Yeah, China is paying people big bucks to come home and bring their knowledge with them," said Gabi. "This isn't in the report, but the FBI has uncovered the Chinese leader in charge of this so-called talent acquisition program."

"Let me guess," replied Alek. "General Wu."

"Of course," she said, nodding. "It seems wherever there is something rotten going on, he can be found. Listen I have to get back to headquarters, but..." She grabbed Alek's hand and locked her blue eyes on his. "I meant what I said tonight. Keep dreaming the impossible dream."

* * *

Percy met Alek in the lobby of the River Inn the next morning. "Ready for another round of politics?"

Alek sighed. "Who's on the agenda today?"

"We'll start with Senator Tom Bianchi. He's funneled a lot of money into New Mexico over the years for national security projects, maybe he can throw us a little bit more."

Alek held open the hotel door for Percy and they walked to the waiting Uber. "Percy, uh... I'm not sure we have the right space to build this prototype in New Mexico. Ideally, we need a large underground facility—something heavily shielded and pretty remote, kinda like the Chinese had. By the way speaking of the Chinese..."

Percy waved his hand dismissively. "That report on the Chinese recruiting lab scientists? That's just more bullshit. Goddamn reporters think they have an exclusive.

This has gone on for decades. Undoubtedly some Chinese scientists leave Los Alamos and go back to work at labs in China. That's where they're from."

"But Gabi said Wu is behind this. How do we know he's not still running a secret weapons program in violation of the treaty using scientists that we trained?"

Percy threw his hand across this forehead in a mock display of horror and shock and exclaimed, "Oh heavens! A secret weapons program. Whatever shall we do?" Dropping the act, he turned to Alek. "Of course he's running a secret weapons program. Who isn't? Surely you didn't think peace was breaking out 'cause we signed a peace of paper and shook hands?"

Alek turned to look out the window as the Uber driver headed down Constitution Avenue past the Washington Monument. Percy shrugged and started checking email on his phone. The two rode in silence until the car pulled up in front of the Hart Senate Building.

"C'mon, let's get some money," said Percy. "Just promise the Senator that supporting this project will mean more jobs for New Mexico, and we'll have him eating out of our hand."

* * *

An hour later they were in another Uber. This time they were headed to the Department of Energy office to meet with Diana Dehoyos, the Secretary of Energy.

"Don't blow it this time," Percy hissed as they walked into the building. "Less honesty and more smiling and nodding. Just let me talk."

"Senator Bianchi flat out asked if we could build the accelerator in New Mexico. Did you want me to lie?"

"Don't lie, just fib a little. Spin it. Say something more like, 'That could be possible' instead of blurting out that you're considering DOE land in Nevada. Bianchi is a New Mexico senator—he wants to boost his state's economy. He wants projects that will bring his state jobs. Tom Bianchi doesn't give a damn about unlimited energy."

"Well, he should," Alek replied with a sniff. He was about to discover that Secretary of Energy Diana Dehoyos actually did give a damn about unlimited energy. She just wasn't interested in Project Z.

Sitting behind her desk, Dehoyos had a commanding presence that her navy suit and short grey hair only emphasized. As a Washington insider, the former California Attorney General's law degree and limited science background did not slow her down in her new position. Percy had forewarned Alek that Dehoyos was both intelligent and well-informed.

The Secretary nodded as Alek wrapped up his presentation and asked a few follow-up questions about LENR technology and Project Z. She smiled and Alek began feeling hopeful. Had he finally found a source that would fund the final development of his dream?

The answer was no.

"Gentlemen, this is a fascinating project, and it certainly has intriguing weapons applications, but I'm afraid our advanced energy development funding is tied up in the ITER agreement."

Alek sighed. He was familiar with the International Thermonuclear Experimental Reactor Program—a collaborative fusion megaproject that involved 35 countries working together to create the world's largest magnetic confinement plasma physics experiment and build the largest experimental nuclear fusion reactor. The goal was to conduct research that could lead to fusion-produced electricity, but ITER had started in the 80s and remained a work in progress. It had been described as the most expensive science experiment of all time.

As Dehoyos described the DOE's commitment to ITER, Alek felt his frustration building. Once again, politics was getting in his way. Percy shot Alek a glance. His message was clear—stay quiet, but Alek couldn't stop himself from speaking.

"The LENR technology is on track to produce results in less than a year. ITER has gone on for decades. If we can just build this prototype accelerator and refine our process, we can be establishing Project Z powerplants across the world in just a few years. This is the unlimited source of clean energy that we once thought traditional fusion applications would deliver. Project Z is different than ITER because Project Z will work."

Dehoyos stood. "I appreciate that, and I have enjoyed learning about your work, but the United States has signed an international agreement to support ITER. It would look bad for us to head in a completely new direction when we are finally getting close to success."

"Close to success?" Alek exclaimed. "ITER is decades away from producing energy. Why double down on a bad idea, when a global energy solution is standing right here?"

Percy cleared his throat. "What Alek meant is that at Los Alamos National Laboratory, we stand ready to assist the DOE with all of its efforts to find new forms of energy and we will do everything within our power to act collaboratively and in good faith."

Percy grabbed Alek's forearm. "I think we've probably taken enough of the Secretary's time today. We look forward to working with you in the future," he said over his shoulder as he hustled Alek out the door.

Chapter 31
Secrets and Solutions

"I NEED TO WALK," SAID Alek as he and Percy exited the James Forrestal Building, a brutalist concrete structure that housed the DOE.

Percy hurried down the sidewalk after his senior scientist. "Now, Alek..."

"It's okay. I understand. It's just politics. I just need some time alone. I'll see you back at the hotel."

Head down, he strode rapidly away from the Forrestal building, heading down Independence Avenue and then crossing into the wide grassy area of the National Mall. Alek's bleak mood seemed at odds with the sunny spring day. The cherry trees were just beginning to blossom and children flying kites ran past, taking advantage of the breeze.

Dodging a group of foreign tourists with an enthusiastic tour guide, Alek hustled along, barely taking in his surroundings. They had come so far. Project Z was so close. How could this be the end?

He noticed a woman in a hot pink sundress sitting alone on a park bench. The woman's blonde hair sparkled in the sun. Then she turned and smiled. It was Gabi.

"Hey!" shouted Alek, quickening his pace as he walked toward her.

"Hey," replied Gabi, standing up.

"You look, umm, spring-y," he said awkwardly.

"Well, I was kinda on a date."

Alek struggled to hide the way that sentence hit him

in the stomach. A date?

Oblivious, Gabi continued. "We were going to see the Yayoi Kusama exhibit and the sculpture garden at the Hirshhorn, but he got a business call and had to leave."

"That's too bad," said Alek, wondering what kind of guy would put work ahead of Gabi. A stupid guy for one thing. And for another thing... there was a guy?

"So, umm, your, uh, boyfriend?" he said awkwardly.

Gabi laughed. "My friend, who happens to be a boy. We've known each other for a long time. Where are you headed?"

Alek looked across the grass at the buildings bracketing the National Mall. He couldn't tell Gabi that he was pitching a fit by running off by himself because he didn't get the funds to build his project. "I was going to the Air and Space Museum," he said and added, truthfully, "I always like to visit it when I'm in D.C. Want to come along?"

"Don't mind if I do," said Gabi, slinging her crocheted bag over her shoulder. "Aren't the museums here amazing? You could stay all week and still not see everything." The two walked in pleasant silence past picnicking families, guidebook-toting tourists, and harried businesspeople until they reached their destination.

Inside the museum, they strolled through the soaring galleries, admiring the wide variety of aircraft on display. Suddenly Alek grabbed Gabi's hand and dragged her around the corner to the 1903 Wright Flyer display.

"This has always been my favorite," said Alek. "Ever since I first visited this museum on a special trip in middle school, I've been fascinated by the Wright brothers. Orville and Wilbur Wright were just two bicycle salesmen from Dayton, Ohio, but they built the first airplane. No government grants, no special funding, with only the money they earned selling bicycles, they built an airplane. They were the first people to fly."

"I take it today's meetings didn't go well?" asked Gabi.

Alek shook his head. "We're getting a fraction of the funding we could get for weapons development. It doesn't make sense. Why is our government more interested in weapons research than this opportunity to bring the world clean, affordable energy? People keep complaining about global warming and high energy costs, but when it comes right down to it, our government won't commit."

"So, they did agree to give you something?"

"Yeah, but not enough. Building a viable prototype of Project Z will be expensive. Once we get to that point, replicating it should cost less. Unfortunately, we can't just build it out of wood and fabric—like the Wright brothers used for their plane." Alek gestured to the exhibit. "If you think about it, this is so amazing. I... I've always wanted to follow in their footsteps and use my scientific knowledge to create something that changes the world."

"And you will," said Gabi. "What you need is private funding. Y'know, like the Wright brothers had."

Alek laughed. "I don't have a bicycle business."

"You just need to know someone with a bicycle business. Maybe someone like Elon Musk."

"He's into wind energy and solar. Project Z is competition for Musk."

"Good. Maybe he needs some competition." Gabi walked around the plane thoughtfully. "Have you thought about looking for private investors? Doing more of a public/private partnership? Look at this plane. It's a fabulous example of a private investment from two very creative people that completely changed the world. On top of that, if these Project Z powerplants are going to go up all around the country... it could definitely pay off for the right investor."

"True," said Alek. He gazed at the plane, imagining Orville and Wilbur setting off on their first flight. "I don't know any wealthy businesspeople. I'm a scientist. I don't even know how to play golf. I've never run with that crowd."

Gabi walked back to him, eyes alight with a new idea. "Yeah, but I do. I have an idea that will help with the fundraising. There's someone I know who I think would be happy to kick in a large sum of private money."

"Really?" said Alek, his excitement building. "Give me the person's name and I'll make the phone calls. Let's set up a meeting as soon as we can."

"Here's the thing," Gabi interrupted. "I need to be the one who contacts him first. You see, this person... he's kind of an old boyfriend."

Alek felt jealousy constrict his excitement. Much as he wanted to raise funds, the last thing he wanted was to send Gabi into the arms of a former lover.

"In fact, he's the guy I was planning to hang out with today." Alek looked at Gabi in the close-fitting, bright pink sundress that flared at the hem to reveal delicate low-heeled sandals. Suddenly everything made sense.

"Remember the night we met at the River Inn and I was all dressed up?" she asked. "He's the one I was out with earlier that night."

Alek hadn't forgotten how Gabi looked that night at the River Inn in her sleek black dress after she had apparently been out with this... this investor. Did he really want to encourage her to spend more time with this guy?

"I mean, I'd love to explore the idea of a public/private partnership with an investor. There's definitely the potential for that kind of an investment to pay off for both the individual contributing the money and for the entire world. The thing is..." Alek looked at Gabi and then glanced away. He didn't know how to say this.

"The thing is... I don't want you to have to... to entice your, uh, boyfriend to get me funding."

"He's not my boyfriend," she protested. "We were just going to spend the afternoon together since I was in town."

"And you got all dressed up to hang out with this old friend of yours?" asked Alek, hearing and disliking the petty tone in his own voice.

"His name is Sal Gutierrez and he's a billionaire—a self-made inventor."

"Hey, I've heard of him," Alek exclaimed, his excitement rising again as he considered the possibilities. "That's the guy from Albuquerque who developed the electrically-charged nanomask during that terrible virus outbreak a few years ago!"

"Yep. The key was in the zinc nano material and the use of a millivolt battery to kill viruses. The masks sold for $29 apiece, and in that one year, Sal's company manufactured and sold 100 million masks. He licensed that concept and now he's looking for new tech ventures to invest in. Project Z might be right up his alley."

Alek sighed. *Did he really want the woman he... did he really want Gabi to spend more time with this quasi-boyfriend just so he could get funding for his project?* He took a deep breath. "Look, honestly, Gabi, I know you and I aren't seeing each other but... somehow I can't stand thinking about you with anyone else."

Gabi laughed and grabbed Alek's hands. "I'm glad to hear that. Honestly, Alek, I know you and I aren't seeing each other but... I don't like to think about you with anyone else either. Somehow you and your crazy ideas about saving the world and your passion for science have wormed their way into my heart."

"Hmph, wormed their way? Actually sounds kinda disgusting," said Alek, sitting down heavily on a nearby bench.

"But," she continued, "you don't have to worry. This will be good for your project. I think he will be interested in a very appropriate way."

"Ummm, how can you be sure it will be uh... appropriate," asked Alek. "After all, you two used to date each other and apparently, you're still hanging out."

Gabi smiled. "Yes, we used to date each other, and, actually, we still go out sometimes, but you don't need to be jealous."

Alek cleared his throat. "Look, I know what you do is none of my business and I've never been all that good at talking about my feelings but..."

"Trust me," said Gabi, glancing down as her phone

buzzed. "Uh-oh, it's my boss. I'd better take this outside." Alek watched as she walked around the corner, the hem of her dress swishing around her legs. He looked back at the Wright brothers' plane, his mind spinning. Clearly, he was never going to understand women. *Heck*, he thought, *I can barely understand myself.*

* * *

As the limousine pulled up in front of the River Inn, Salvador Gutierrez reached out to stop his companion from exiting the car.

"What?" asked Gabi. "Alek is expecting us."

"I know," Salvador replied in his strong Spanish accent. "Tell me a little more about this guy you're so crazy about before we go in."

Gabi blushed. "I never said I had feelings for him, Sal. We've been working together."

"I've known you since high school, Gabi," he said with a laugh. "I can tell something's different. Plus, if he's that special to you, I want to make a good impression."

"Sal, are you nervous? You deal with high-powered business people all the time."

"Yes, but you're my best friend, and if you like this Alek so much, I want him to like me too."

Gabi smiled, thinking back. "Do you remember when we first met during freshman year in high school?"

"How could I forget? I spoke no English and every day I came to school terrified that someone would report me as undocumented and send me and my parents back to Mexico. I stuck to myself, completely alone till one day this *guera* came up and talked to me in perfect Spanish. I was shocked."

"Well, you weren't that shocked after I explained that my *abuelita* was from Mexico and I was born and raised right there in Española, *New* Mexico."

"Still, a blonde-haired and blue-eyed American who spoke Spanish—it took some getting used to," Sal said with a chuckle. "I was so shy back then. So scared."

"You weren't too scared to ask me to the homecoming dance," quipped Gabi.

"Well, it worked," he replied. "You said yes and turned into my good luck charm."

"It was more than good luck," Gabi teased. "Look at you now. A billionaire manipulating chairmen of the board from Fortune 500 companies."

"True. I've learned a lot about human nature over the years we've known each other. Plus, I've learned a lot about myself. But if you hadn't encouraged me to go to college after high school and helped me get that full-ride scholarship, I'd probably still be working at Allsups Convenience Store in Española." Sal adjusted the collar on his hand-tailored Ermenegildo Zegna suit jacket.

Gabi knew he had come a long way from Allsups. She was one of the very few people who actually understood how hard he'd had to fight to get to where he was today.

"Remember how angry your engineering prof at the University of New Mexico was when you wouldn't go to grad school somewhere prestigious like MIT or Stanford or at least take an entry-level job at one of the national labs?" asked Gabi.

Salvador shook his head. "I wasn't interested. I had ideas and I knew I could make money."

"That's an understatement. Your ability to charm investors, form partnerships, and forge agreements has become a legend in the high-tech business world."

Sal gestured to his phone. "Speaking of that, I got a call just before the limo arrived. I just received a billion-dollar settlement in that regulatory lawsuit. I have money I need to invest in a hurry, so I sure hope this Alek's energy plan is the real deal."

He turned to Gabi and took her hands in his. "*Mi querida*, this meeting tonight is about much more to me than money. I finally know how it feels to find that person I want to spend the rest of my life with. I want you to feel that way too."

Gabi pulled Salvador into a hug and then kissed him

on the cheek. *"Sabes cuanto te amo?"*
"I do," replied Salvador. "Let's go meet Alek."

* * *

Perched on a tall stool, Alek drummed his fingers nervously on the River Inn's polished bar. Three days had passed since his conversation with Gabi at the Air and Space Museum, and she had finally set up a meeting with her so-called friend.

Alek had done his research on Salvador Gutierrez, which wasn't difficult since information about him was all over the internet. Gabi had told him that she and Gutierrez had met in high school. That's where they struck up a friendship and started dating. But Gutierrez had left Española High long behind. Apparently, he was some sort of *wunderkind* who understood engineering and business and had a knack for inventing highly marketable products.

The New York Times had described Gutierrez as the next Elon Musk. Alek couldn't forget how the news article went on to describe Gutierrez as "far better looking than Musk with an air of suavity and mystery." Who writes that kind of garbage in a newspaper story? The reporter seemed half in love with the billionaire. Then again, who wouldn't fall for a guy like that? What was he thinking, encouraging Gabi to spend time with a gorgeous, rich guy that she used to date. Or maybe she still dated him? She had never really made that clear.

Alek knew he couldn't compete with someone like Gutierrez for Gabi's attention. Obnoxious, entitled rich person who thinks he has every solution and gets every girl. Alek raked his hands anxiously through his already messy hair. Why did he agree to this meeting? But Gabi had told him to trust her, and this looked like the only way he would ever be able to get the funding for Project Z. Did he even want the money if that meant losing Gabi? Alek reminded himself that he had sworn off romance, hell, he had sworn off happiness. He didn't deserve happiness. He had to focus on perfecting the LENR.

Alek removed his glasses and began cleaning them with the hem of his shirt. Project Z meant so much to him and yet... so did Gabi. He'd never met someone who made him feel like this. Alek had spent his whole life pursuing the dream of creating a technological solution that would provide the world with clean, unlimited energy. Now he was finally close to achieving it. Was that worth giving up Gabi? Why did he have to choose?

Alek rose from the table. He couldn't do this. Maybe he could write some grants, wait a few years, go back to the Department of Energy... Gabi was more important than the money, more important than the project, more important than he had realized until now.

Tucking a $10 bill under his empty beer glass, he headed for the front door of the bar—just as Gabi and Gutierrez walked in.

Salvador Gutierrez was taller and more athletic look-ing than Alek expected, with thick black hair and deep tan skin. He wore a dark, clearly expensive suit, and Alek im-mediately regretted his own choice of khakis and a polo shirt. Gabi was also dressed elegantly in a sleek pantsuit. The two of them made a striking couple as they entered the bar.

Gabi grabbed Gutierrez by the arm and whispered something in his ear. Alek winced. *Getting through this evening would be worse than he had even expected. If only he had left five minutes earlier.*

Gutierrez nodded and took a seat at a table by the bar's entrance, gesturing to the waitress for a drink. Gabi headed to Alek's side.

"Before you two talk about business, there's some-thing I need to tell you," she said.

"It's okay," said Alek, trying to hide the lump in his throat. "You don't have to tell me. I get it. You two clearly belong together."

"Alek, just shut up." Gabi sat down on the stool next to him and said, "Yes, Sal and I went out in high school and

a few times in college and a few times after that but..."
Gabi glanced across the room at Gutierrez, who smiled
and raised his glass. Gabi smiled back at him and Alek
coughed, wishing he could vanish instantaneously.

Gabi returned to her story. "Listen, it was never like
that between me and Sal. He's like my big brother. A few
years ago, Sal admitted something to me that finally verified my suspicions," said Gabi. "You really don't have to
worry. Here's the thing—Sal's gay."

Alek raised an eyebrow in disbelief as Gabi continued. "Seriously, I'm touched that you're jealous, but me
and Sal—we love each other like siblings—we have never
had romantic feelings for each other. In fact, Sal's engaged
to be married. I'm good friends with Miguel, his fiancé."

Alek coughed, choked a little, tried to swallow. He
felt a tremendous sense of relief flood through him as he
looked across the room at Gutierrez, then back at Gabi. He
coughed again. "Gabi, I'm a scientist," Alek finally managed
to say. "I'm trained to analyze data and reach documented
conclusions, to stay disciplined and objective and not to
be controlled by... umm... feelings."

Gabi laughed. "Alek, it's okay to have feelings. Just
remember, Sal isn't interested in me one bit—not in that
way—but he is interested in Project Z." Gabi gestured to
Gutierrez, who strode quickly across the room.

"I heard you were looking to fund an energy project,"
he said, holding out his hand.

Epilogue

WHILE ALEK HAD BEEN SPENDING his time searching for funding in Washington, Will and Joe Ramos had
been in Mexico making plans to acquire some money of
their own.

A little over a month earlier, the two had fled China in
the stolen cartel jet that came with attentive service from
Sulema Sauceda, the aspiring Mexican movie star who
made her living as Velásquez's personal flight attendant.

After refueling in Hawaii, the stolen Dassault Falcon
had touched down in the forest outside of Monterrey,
Mexico, on the well-hidden landing strip next to the
warehouse where the brothers once had conducted
their secret LENR research. Both the weapons lab and
the nearby fentanyl production facility had ceased
operations. Following the shoot-out at the warehouse
and the subsequent investigation, the FBI and PFM had
seized all of the equipment from the facility and left it
abandoned. Other than squirrels and insects, no living
creatures had been in the building in several months.

Sulema had walked through the dusty warehouse
disdainfully, anxious to get back in the $50 million private
jet with its gold trim and plush seats and return to China
to wait for Velásquez. Little did she know that the drug
lord would not be calling for her services or sharing his
wealth with her ever again.

Will had enjoyed one last passionate embrace and
said goodbye to Sulema. He needed to get to work on the
new plan.

* * *

Three weeks later, after what felt like nonstop work inside the warehouse, Will Ramos stepped back from the workbench. He had finally achieved his goal. *"Esta terminado,"* he declared triumphantly. He had constructed a device similar to the one Wu and Velásquez had detonated in the South China Sea.

"¿Cuál es tu plan?" Joe asked hesitantly, looking at the device. "Will, this is a dangerous weapon. What are we going to do with it?"

"Eres un idiota. Use your brain, Joe. With Velásquez gone, we will be able to take over the cartel. This," he said, gesturing to the device on the workbench, "this gadget is our leverage. "We now have a weapon of unprecedented power. We just need some cash to kick off our business and we will be the most famous brothers in the world."

Joe smiled. "Kinda like the Wright brothers. They were famous for making the first airplane."

"Yeah, that's nothing compared to what we're gonna do," Will scoffed. "Ever since Velásquez died, the cartel has been in total chaos. Now is the time for a new leader."

"Um, new *leaders*, right?" asked Joe, drawing out the 's' at the end of the word.

"Right, you and me, *hermanito*. We made the right decision to get the hell out of Beijing when we did. And it's lucky that Velásquez died in that lab in China. We are much better off with him out of the way."

"What about the general?" Joe asked.

Will began cleaning up his work area, stopping now and then to run a hand over his finished contraption, almost lovingly. "I haven't been able to reach Wu. We don't need him. I am sure he is trying to distance himself from the whole thing." Will put his arm around Joe's shoulders. *"No te preocupes, hermanito.* I have it all figured out."

Will's plan was simple. He intended to contact Harold Percy and inform him that, unless he and Joe received a transfer of $100 million into an offshore account, they would begin systematically deploying the Dragon's CLAW weapon across the U.S.

"I'm sure the threat will work. Percy knows we have mastered the LENR technology. He also knows that the gadget can create an electromagnetic pulse that will destroy all of the computers that control the power systems in all of the country." Will clapped his hands together gleefully. "*¿Puedes imaginártelo?* We can just threaten to shut everything down. Think about all of those freezers filled with rotting food, all of the water supplies cut off, and all of the transportation gone. We can threaten to stop everything unless he hands over the money."

Joe shook his head. "*No lo se,*" he murmured. "You want to blackmail the U.S. government?"

"Yes," Will exclaimed. "Percy will waste no time calling in the higher ups in Washington. U.S. leaders tend to do whatever they can to prevent terrorism and $100 million is a small price to pay to protect American lives. We can even text Percy a photo of the device to drive home the danger. The scarier and more possible the attack seems, the sooner we can get our hands on the government pay off."

So Will made the phone call and explained the situation to Percy, but instead of quivering in fear and agreeing to Will's demands, the lab director laughed. "You wouldn't do that," Percy scoffed. "You and Joe don't have the technology, the ability, or the *cojones* to detonate a device. Thanks for the laugh, Will," Percy concluded and hung up.

Will was furious. How could Percy doubt them? Didn't the lab director realize he was dealing with ruthless terrorists who had access to unprecedented weapons technology? Why would Percy disrespect their conviction and skills?

Will stomped out of the warehouse, fuming. He had a compact LENR device and the technology to trigger it. He would show Percy they meant business. All he had to do was get the American's attention. Then Percy would pay.

"Uh, Will," Joe said tentatively. "I have an idea that maybe could help convince Percy."

"What is it, Joe? I'm kinda busy right now trying to figure things out."

"So, you want to scare Percy, right? To convince him we have dangerous technology and he needs to do what we say."

"Yes, Joe," Will sneered. "I'm glad you were listening."

Ignoring his brother's sarcasm, Joe plunged ahead.

"So, I have an idea. Most of the nuclear power stations are still vulnerable to a short range EMP attack since their cooling water control and transmission systems are located outside. An attack on a nuclear power station would disrupt the operation and cause panic because everybody thinks about a melt down and then all hell would break loose."

"So?" asked Will.

"So, let's set off the device at a nuclear reactor. Show Percy and everyone else in the world what we can do."

Author's Note

As a child, I was captivated by science fiction. I remember attending the movies with my older brother. We would walk to the Shaker Theatre on Saturday afternoons. With a quarter from my mother, we could buy two 10-cent tickets and still have five cents left over for a box of Jujubes candy that glued your teeth together—making them nearly impossible to chew. I specifically recall seeing *The Day the Earth Stood Still* at age 13. The movie featured an alien who, accompanied by a death-ray shooting robot, comes to earth to save the planet from war. Naturally, the film ended with dire warnings of death and destruction, while prominently featuring beam weapons that wipe out everything in their path. Produced at the height of the Cold War, the science fiction classic also provides a powerful anti-war message. At the time, I wasn't thinking about the political implications of the movie, but now I can't help but wonder if somehow *The Day the Earth Stood Still* influenced my scientific career.

So, I grew up and became a scientist, devoting my career to the pursuit of scientific discovery, always eager to test the boundaries of my curiosity and explore what problems science can solve. Then one day I was reminded of my early love of science fiction, so I decided to write a novel. The first thing I discovered was, it's not as easy as it looks.

Several years earlier, I had collaborated with my daughter, Jill, on some scientific articles and a memoir of my time spent as the chief scientist of Reagan's Strategic Defense Initiative (also known as the Star Wars Program), which led to the publication of the book *Death Rays and Delusions*. I decided to ask her to collaborate again, this time on a work of fiction, but she looked at my notes and ideas and simply said, "No." Then the COVID-19 pandemic hit, and she finally agreed to help me. It is no exaggeration to say that having the novel to work on during the pandemic lockdown saved both of our lives.

Writing together has opened our eyes to each other's worlds and has stretched our imaginations. As we worked, the characters became real to both of us and the novel grew into a series. It reminded me of when my children were little and we played make-believe. I remember introducing Jill to Harold the Forest Ranger, sending her searching for the Lost Dutchman Mine (or was it Mind?), and taking her on pretend adventures without leaving the living room. Long before she had learned to read and write, she would tell me a story and I would write it down for her. Now, the only difference is that we've switched roles.

In closing, I just want to say that while the technical knowledge and expertise in this book, and some of Alek's experiences, are loosely based on my career, everything I have written is a product of my imagination—science, technology, and politics invented out of thin air. But the same could be said of H.G. Wells or all the other science fiction writers who inspired me over the years with their visions of the future. Who knows what will happen? We'll just have to wait and see.

Acknowledgements

First and foremost, I want to thank my family, especially my daughter, Jill Gibson, who turned my disorganized pile of notes into a readable, riveting novel. Huge gratitude also goes out to my wife, Jane, who had to suffer through several early drafts and innumerable conversations about what fictitious characters might actually do.

I also want to thank our publisher Geoff Habiger, for his patience, his amazing editorial contributions, his guidance, and his willingness to take a chance on an inexperienced author. Thanks also go out to Derek Weathersbee for the incredible cover and website design and his support of this project.

Additional thanks are due to Peter DeBarra, Jonathan Miller, Lisa McCoy, and to all our early readers and supporters, including Larry Logan, Edward Arthur, Greg Canavan, Katarina Stenstedt, Howard Yonas, Amanda Boers, Jay Sawyer, Terry Wilmot, Ken Prestwich, Pace VanDevender, and anyone else I managed to coerce into reading an early version of this book. Read it again. It's better now.

Finally, I want to thank all the real scientists who are hard at work at the real national laboratories striving to solve wicked problems and make the world a safer place. Keep building that knife.

About the Author

Dr. Gerold Yonas served as the acting deputy director and chief scientist during the implementation of the Strategic Defense Initiative, also known as Ronald Reagan's Star Wars Program. He has consulted for numerous national security organizations including the Defense Science Board, DARPA, the Air Force, the Army, the U.S. Department of Energy, and the Senate Select Committee on Intelligence. He is a Fellow of the American Physical Society and a Fellow of the American Institute of Aeronautics and Astronautics and has received many honors, including the U.S. Air Force Medal for Meritorious Civilian Service and the Secretary of Defense Medal for Outstanding Public Service.

Yonas has published extensively in the fields of intense particle beams, inertial confinement fusion, strategic defense technologies, technology transfer, and "wicked engineering." After his time leading the Strategic Defense Initiative, Yonas went to work for Titan Corporation in San Diego, where he managed a group of small research companies. Three years later, he returned to Sandia National Laboratories to lead the pulsed power fusion program and several weapons related programs in the role of vice president of Systems, Science and Technology.

At Sandia, Yonas went on to create the Advanced Concepts Group and explore new opportunities including brain research. Following his retirement from Sandia, he joined the Mind Research Network as the director of neurosystems engineering where he explored the link between neuroscience and systems engineering. He also developed a graduate course in this field and taught as an adjunct professor in the Department of Electrical and Computer Engineering at the University of New Mexico.

Yonas holds a Ph.D. in engineering science and physics from the California Institute of Technology and a bachelor's in engineering physics from Cornell University, where he also received a varsity lightweight crew letter. He is married to his high school sweetheart, Jane, and is the father of two daughters, Jill and Jodi, and the grandfather of five: Libby, Jenna, Jonathan, Emily, and Ben. Yonas makes his home in Albuquerque, New Mexico.